Aurora's Wilderness Love

Christmas Cruise Mistake

Harmony Noble

TrueLoveWriters

ISBN 978-1-963074-48-2 & ISBN 978-1-963074-51-2

Story creation, cover, and illustrations by Melody Noble & Harmony Curtis

Thank you for choosing this book.
We hope the story
brought you as much joy reading it
as we had in creating it!

We'd love to hear from you! Feel free to reach out via email at TrueLoveWriters@gmail.com, and follow us on Instagram, Facebook, TikTok at @truelovewriters for the latest updates and behind-the-scenes fun.

Get access to exclusive offers, bonus content, new release updates, and recommendations for more great reads.

Sign up for our e-newsletter at HarmonyNoble.com.

To my dear friend Adam—

Who once crashed our girls' cruise trip and turned it into the most romantic, chaotic, unforgettable proposal ever.

Your spontaneity is a reminder that love shows up boldly—without permission and without warning.

Thank you for the laughter, the lunches, the conversations, and for making my dearly departed friend so deeply happy. You set the proposal bar sky-high that day.

I couldn't be prouder to see you bravely chasing your happily-ever-after once again… even if it means trading Alaska's frost for Florida's heat.

With love,
The Twins

Aurora's

WILDERNESS LOVE

Christmas Cruise Mistake

Harmony Noble

TrueLoveWriters

Chapter 1

First-Impression Frostbite: A Holiday Princess Disaster at Sea

Day 1: Whittier, Alaska

My flip-flop sandals skid across the cold, slick pavement, but whatever—*I'm unstoppable.* Nothing, not even my questionable footwear choices in December, will keep me from my winter-escape, Caribbean vacation.

"Miss, that's not the gangway," a deckhand calls out.

I stop in my tracks. His patient smile tells me that I look like a clueless Lower 48'er leaving their Alaskan vacation for the sunny holiday cruise.

I swallow. *At least I'm fitting in.*

Salt wind lashes my face, carrying the sharp scent of a chilly ocean breeze. I blink my frozen eyelashes at him, squinting against the glare of the four pm December setting sun.

"You're telling me this ramp doesn't board this huge cruise ship?"

He gives me the look people reserve for small dogs in sweaters, and confused tourists.

"That's the *supply* ramp. Guests board through the main gangway."

I follow his gesture, and—of course—the entrance is *way* down the dock, more than fifty feet away, and up two flights of icy stairs, where a person with a clipboard is wishing "Merry Christmas" to each person.

Perfect!

I force a cheerful smile. "Right. I knew that. Testing you."

He blinks.

"Good job," I add, scurrying off before my dignity completely melts.

My Christmas scarf—a decorative sparkling red—flutters behind me as I grab the handle of my wobbly suitcase. The wheel emits a death rattle promising imminent betrayal. My sandals slide on the frosted dock, the chilly air biting my toes.

I chew my lip and shake my head. *Even though it's a Caribbean cruise, I should have planned for our Alaskan departure and wore my boots.*

The suitcase catches on an uneven board and jerks me forward. "Don't you dare quit on me," I mutter, giving it a tug that earns a dramatic *pop*.

Somewhere behind me, a laugh rolls through the cold—deep, low, amused. It slides under my skin, warm enough to melt the frost on my cheeks.

"Need a hand there? Holiday Princess?"

Excuse me!

I spin around, half-offended, half-trying not to slip on black ice. My scarf whips into my mouth, muffling my curses as I choke on it.

"Princess?" I grumble into the fabric, yanking it free from my sticky lip gloss. I tuck my loose curls that have managed to escape from my bun behind my ears.

The owner of the voice leans casually on the railing, framed by the glinting ship behind her. She's tall—no, *commanding*—broad-shouldered beneath a navy coat that fits perfectly. Espresso dark hair, cut short and precise. The military precision of her look says she doesn't have time for nonsense.

Expensive, mirrored sunglasses hide her eyes, but the curve of her smirk makes me instantly defensive.

She looks like she's enjoying my slow-motion humiliation far too much.

I narrow my eyes, trying to look confident instead of windblown and hypothermic.

"My name's *Aurora,* not *Holiday Princess.*"

"Aurora."

She lifts a brow, the corner of her mouth tugging upward. Her voice has this soft, lilting accent—something European? And exotic—and my name from her lips makes my stomach do an odd, hopeful flip.

My brain freezes for a full second. *Is she teasing me or flirting?*

Before I can decide, she gestures toward my misbehaving suitcase. "May I help?"

"No." My pride stands taller than I do. "I'm fine. Thank you. *Bye.*"

I tug the bag forward and turn, attempting a casual sashay away. My boot immediately skids on an invisible patch of treachery. I pinwheel for a terrifying second—arms out, dignity flapping in the wind.

She steps forward, hand half-raised like she's ready to catch me around the waist—but I right myself at the last second, regaining my balance.

Her hand drops. I *feel* the heat of her gaze—amused and hot.

I beam at the other tourists as I join the line, ignoring her with fake confidence that I absolutely do not own.

Totally fine. Totally normal. I'm totally fitting in.

I start trudging up the stairs, dragging my squealing suitcase behind me.

Halfway up, I pause—partly to breathe, partly to tighten my hold of the freezing metal railing while questioning my life choices.

"Totally fine," I mutter, my words coming out in fog puffs in the cold. "Totally normal. I am totally fitting in."

The suitcase gives a loud, rubbery squeal in protest.

I catch a glimpse of her still watching me.

Like she's memorizing the way I move. Or waiting for me to look back.

I shake my head. This trip is for rest. For clarity. For doing my job and documenting the cruise experience.

It is absolutely, unequivocally *not* for falling in love... Right?

I glance back, and, again, she is watching me.

Her almost-smile deepens, like she's enjoying the show.

The audacity! And calling me a Holiday Princess.

Marching toward the gangway line past the holiday-themed penguins, I resolve to not look back and to avoid any eye contact.

By the time I reach the boarding welcome lady with the clipboard, my pulse is still hammering.

"Miss Aurora Thompson! Deck 14, Cabin 5A, right? Welcome aboard the *Royal Caribbean Holiday Princess!* Your bags will be available in your room and your room will be available after the Welcome Aboard Party."

My mouth falls open.

Wait.

Holiday. Princess.

Oh.

I quickly close my lips as blood rushes to my cheeks. "Right! Yes. *Holiday Princess* is the ship's name."

The ship's "Royal Caribbean Holiday Princess" banner looms above me—huge, glossy, and basically smirking at me.

My tall, way-too-sexy tormentor strides past effortlessly, like she owns the ship.

Every deckhand snaps to greet her, spines stiffening in formality. Apparently, she's not just gorgeous. She's a respected crewmember.

That's perfect. *Wonderful.*

Exactly what I need on my attempt to board without drawing attention to myself. The sundress among all these winter jackets isn't helping that mission much either.

"Captain Rossi," the clipboard person says.

My stomach drops straight into my flip-flops.

Captain.

As in... the whole, *entire*, cruise ship's captain.

Of course, the stranger I thought was sexually harassing me—and I just vowed to ignore—is the ship's captain.

Why can't I just stay out of trouble?!

The captain's mouth curves again—making my pulse go haywire—as she pauses before me.

"Welcome aboard, Holiday Princess," she murmurs in her smooth accent.

The words send a shiver through me.

"Oh my God," I whisper, primarily to the ground. "I have to find Darius."

"Pardon?"

"Nothing!" I beam, too wide, too bright, to the clipboard person waving me into the plush carpeted atrium.

"Merry Christmas," she says, handing me the room key.

"Merry Christmas!"

Chapter 2

A Very Merry Mistake

Day 1: Whittier, Alaska

My dignity is clinging by a single frostbitten thread, marching toward the vessel's gleaming glass doors, following the arrows to the *Welcome Aboard Champagne Party.*

Two seconds later, I'm ready to find my friend as I'm snatching a tall flute of bubbly from a passing silver tray. The champagne fizzes in the crystal, catching the light like liquid gold.

Despite my nerves, the atrium is breathtaking in its golds, lush carpets, crystal chandeliers, a wide-open space with mirrors reflecting the dying sunlight, and white beyond the floor-to-ceiling windows. It's breathtaking.

One sip, and the entire atrium tilts.

Then, a scent hits me—salty, citrus-clean, and laced with expensive cologne, making me inhale. The fizz shoots up my nose.

"Achoo!" Mid sip, I'm a tiny champagne fountain.

"Hey, girl," a familiar voice—pure sunshine dipped in sass—says behind me. "Love the scarf. You are a sparkly vacation elf. Your champagne spraying isn't exactly high-class cruise passenger vibes."

I spin, and my best friend Darius is radiant as ever in a nautical-chic ensemble that could double as a luxury cruise advertisement. Of course, *he* looks like he just stepped off the cover of *Yacht Weekly.*

"Thanks," I say, wiping my nose and chin with as much dignity as I can salvage. "The scarf is part of my cruise signature look. *Frostbitten chic chaos.*"

Darius squints at me, amusement on his glossy lips. "Are you wearing a sundress? Maybe I should cut you off already?"

"I've just got here," I defend, straightening my scarf. "I'm ready for sun, sand, and tropical drinks in coconuts under palm trees. *The works.*"

Darius's laugh bursts through the atrium—loud, bright, completely unhelpful, drawing even more eyes to us.

I duck down a little and turn away from the looks.

"Sun, sand, and tropical drinks?" he repeats, still chuckling—until he notices I'm quiet.

"Girl," he says, leaning in with a dramatic flair, "it's December in Whittier, Alaska. There isn't a tiki bar or palm tree within a thousand miles."

I blink at him. Hard. "But... We're sailing to the Caribbean by tomorrow, right? This is a Royal Caribbean cruise on the Holiday Princess."

The name of the ship makes me blush and reminds me that I still need to tell him about my embarrassing encounter with the captain.

He places a hand on my arm and looks at me, the way people look at a wild animal that you shouldn't startle. "Aurora, it's an *Alaskan* cruise. Royal Caribbean is the brand name of the company, *not the destination*. We are doing an eight-day cruise around the interior of Alaska."

"What? No!" The words shoot out of me in a high-pitched whisper that only small dogs can hear. "We'll be in the Caribbean by tomorrow. Right? You're joking? How long does it take to sail there—a day? Two tops?"

He shakes his head. "It's not your fault," he says, patting my arm as he flags down a passing server. "I blame the public education curriculum." He hands me another flute of champagne.

I sip, trying to swallow around the knot forming in my throat. "But the confirmation email said *Caribbean.* And the brochure had palm trees all over it!"

"It's their logo. The Caribbean?" He lifts his drink and scans the atrium. "Aurora, do you *see* any palm trees?"

Now that he mentions it...

Everyone around us is dressed in puffer coats, parkas, and boots. A cute couple is taking selfies next to a sign, "*Romance at Sea! Welcome, Newlyweds, to Our Inaugural Alaskan Newlyweds Cruise!*"

A cluster of women passes by wearing matching "JUST MARRIED!" sashes... And is that a heart-shaped ice sculpture?

Meanwhile, I'm standing here on an Alaskan Newlyweds cruise in flip-flops and a pineapple sundress.

The overhead speaker crackles.

"Welcome aboard the Holiday Princess!" A tall, game-show-looking host announces in a game-show voice. "Your *romantic Alaskan newlywed adventure* begins now—where love is as majestic as our glaciers!"

Darius clinks his glass against mine. "Cheers to our romantic dream cruise. This vacation is even better than I thought."

"What? This can't be real," I whisper. "Who takes an Alaskan cruise in *December?*"

He grins. "We do. Hello, easy hookups and free champagne!"

"I'm sorry, what? No!" This situation cannot get any worse. "We should sneak off the boat and tell Dad–

"You mean our boss—" Darius chimes in.

"Tell him we missed the ship."

"Smile!" A guy snaps our pictures, not waiting for a smile or any consent. "Here," he hands us a card. "The prints are available in the ship's atrium every night or check online #HolidayPrincessNewlywedDreamCruise."

"That's an excessively long hashtag," I call after him.

Darius laughs, and he lifts his glass. "It's too late to run away. We are probably posted to their socials. They took video clips at the Welcome Aboard Newlyweds Champagne Party!"

"If there's only one bed in our room and heart-shaped chocolates on our pillow–"

Darius cuts me off. "Why would your dad ask us to review a Caribbean cruise when we work at Alaska Cruise and Tours? We are reviewing Royal

Caribbean's newest cruise. There's no way we could even get close to the equator in an eight-day cruise."

The color drains from my face.

"You brought more than summer dresses and bikinis, right?"

"Don't make me cry," I beg, staring down at my goose-bumped arms. "I thought the work trip gift was a sunny, relaxing Holiday Christmas miracle, not a snowy seasonal nightmare. We are surrounded by newlyweds when we both just got dumped."

"It's fine," he says, shifting into full cheerleader mode. "I mean, sure, you thought Alexis was your soul mate, but *I'm totally recovered.* And the best way to get over someone..."

Thinking of Alexis and seeing all these happy couples... I blink fast—too fast—but one traitor tear escapes.

Darius catches it immediately.

His whole face softens. "Oh, no. Don't cry. No crying on a Romance Cruise. We'll make this work, okay? Picture it... Champagne in a hot tub and jazz bars. I'm sure they have karaoke bars, too."

A pathetic laugh hiccups out of me.

"You're bringing sunny vibes to our cruise. I love it. Fashion forward."

My voice cracks. "Darius... I didn't pack anything warm. I have two pairs of panties and twelve bikinis because I thought I'd wear them instead of underwear."

Darius gently sets down his drink with the same caution people use before delivering bad news. "Okay, sweet disaster, breathe. It's fine. Honeymoon cruises have the *hottest* gay hookup scene—trust me. All those repressed husbands and heterosexual-pretending lesbian ready to let loose before they have to spend eternity in a loveless prison of matrimony." He leans in with a scandalous whisper, "It'll be epic. I promise. You'll put the *ho* in honeymoon, girl."

I blink at him, teetering somewhere between shock and despair. "I can't do this. I'm not ready to even *ho, ho, ho*. Let alone see all these happy couples."

"You'll totally forget your emotionally unavailable boss—"

"Ex-boss," I snap on reflex.

"—and heal by champagne distractions." He beams, far too pleased with himself. "Which is why I'm preparing. I already booked a couples waxing appointment for tomorrow morning."

My brain shorts circuits. "You what?"

He clinks his empty glass against mine with a wicked grin. "Smooth skin, smooth sailing."

I stare at him. Then, the snow flurries drifting past the atrium windows. Then, look down at my lemon-yellow sundress reflecting in the glass. My throat tightens.

The tears come again—this time I let them. They spill over as hiccupping little laughs escape me. "You don't understand, Darius. I needed this relaxing sunny trip. After finals, after Alexis, after my no contact with my toxic Mom—this was supposed to be my first grown-up vacation. A work trip I'm getting paid to enjoy. A real tropical, dream vacation." My voice cracks. "Not a floating iceberg ready to sink me."

He loops his arm through mine. "Come on. Let's find a heater before your toes get frostbite."

A gust of cold air sneaks through the entry doors, slicing straight through my sundress and making me squeak. I shiver, clutching my champagne like it's soup. Outside the atrium windows, steel-gray sky and swirling snowflakes mock me.

Then a man in a penguin costume waddles by, handing out more champagne.

Darius pats my shoulder. "Perspective, girl. You've never been on vacation. This ship is gorgeous. There are pools, buffets, and hot tubs full of beautiful people. We will have fun."

I force a smile.

"That's the spirit!" Darius toasts, raising his empty glass with gusto.

"I'm about to get my post-breakup ho phase on." He winks. "You should, too."

I follow his gaze to the blonde Cruise Director, wearing a festive name tag "Chase, Florida, Cruise Director."

Chase gives Darius a polite nod—the kind that says, *Oh, I see you.*

"Take this and try to have some fun!" Darius presses his almost-full champagne into my hand and sashays toward Chase with the confidence of someone born to flirt.

He's right. I *can* make the best of this. I've never been on a vacation before. Not a real one. And this ship is huge—maps advertising themed bars, hot tubs, a casino, a theatre, bingo, and even a bowling alley. Who needs sunshine when there's a variety of poor decisions waiting for me?

"I've got this," I tell myself, forcing a smile and finishing the champagne in one heroic gulp.

The string quartet shifts into a jazzy rendition of "Rudolph the Red-Nosed Reindeer." The crowd cheers, and for a second, my pulse settles.

Then I see her.

Tall. Confident. Now standing in a crisp white uniform, gleaming under the chandeliers.

Captain Rossi.

She looks even more striking indoors.

Our eyes meet across the atrium. Her gaze is steady. My eyes are wide and panicky. Even from here, I feel her intensity under the brim of her captain's hat, dark espresso hair tucked neatly beneath it. Her lips soften into that almost-smirk I'm already familiar with.

Our eyes remain locked, and she tips her chin upward as she starts toward me.

I frown—then look up to see a glittering sprig of mistletoe hanging above me, perched smugly from the golden archway.

Heat races into my face. My champagne glass trembles between my fingers. I go to take a step away from the weed.

The Captain is striding toward me—long, self-assured steps that part the crowd like she's the ocean and everyone else is a polite little wave.

My pulse kicks into a sprint. She stops too close. The air between us fills with salt, citrus, and something darker—amber and spice.

"How are you adjusting to the ship, *Cara mia*?" she asks, voice low and smooth, warm with Italian edges. Her gaze flicks over my sundress, my painted toes, then back to my face. "Your attire is... ambitious."

"Thanks," I manage, clutching my champagne.

Her gaze lifts to the mistletoe again.

My heart launches into my throat. "Oh no," I whisper. "We're not doing that. Absolutely not."

Her smile curves into something slow and devastating, lighting up every nerve in my body.

"You are already under it, Holiday Princess. It is a tradition, no?"

I open my mouth, but no words come out.

Her laugh is low—warm, rich, and dangerous in a way that makes my knees threaten mutiny.

The ship hums beneath us, engines vibrating through the floor as the Holiday Princess prepares to sail. The mistletoe swings gently overhead. Her eyes hold mine with unnerving calm.

And in that charged breath of space between us, I realize something with bone-deep certainty. This cruise is not going to be relaxing.

Not even a little.

Chapter 3

The Mistletoe Mix-Up

Day 1: Whittier, Alaska

Her voice drops an octave—warm, amused, laced with command. "Holiday Princess, it's bad luck to refuse a holiday tradition and an order from the captain."

My lungs forget how to function. "R-really."

The mistletoe overhead glimmers in the atrium lights. The shiny green leaves and bold red ribbon cannot be ignored. It's just a quick kiss.

And then—holy frosted gingerbread—her mouth is on mine.

It isn't some dry-lipped peck. It's worse. And better. Soft. Deliberate. A kiss from someone who knows exactly what she's doing.

I'm completely at her mercy, and honestly, I want her to kiss me. Her lips dance playfully against mine, a tantalizing mix of sweetness and strength that sends shivers down my spine. Her fiery tongue is teasing the edge of my lower lip, and it sparks, igniting wildfire inside me.

My heart is racing like a wild stallion, pounding with the warning. This alpha woman is my weakness — dangerously delicious, and oh-so-tempting.

My mind—attempting to be sensible despite the champagne fog and my treacherous heart—is waving a giant red flag screaming, No!

And I'm powerless against it. Her.

Older. Confident. Bossy.

Just like Alexis.

I want to put my arms around her and pull her closer. I want my lips to open and kiss her back—God, I want to—but I don't. I freeze. I'm not going to make another mistake. My brain is clear enough to know that this is a mistake.

My therapist's warning flashes. *Choose yourself first, Aurora. Set boundaries.*

Oopsies.

She chuckles against my mouth, entertained by my internal crisis and trembling lips. Pulling away from me, the heat of her lips lingers, and my ability to speak is gone.

The quick kiss is not just a quick kiss.

Someone gasps. A flash goes off. I jerk back.

"Happy holidays!" a photography staff member chirps, oblivious to the meltdown happening inside my chest.

"Captain!"

The captain smiles and gives a slight nod to the man.

I blink at her. My brain is static. Actually static.

Then, before I can form a single coherent thought, the captain's hand brushes mine, grounding me. A quick, confident touch that carries the promise of a slow burn beneath it. Electric. Another shiver dances on my spine.

I am going to faint. Or giggle. Or combust directly under the mistletoe. Honestly, any of the three would be a mercy.

"That's my girl!" Darius shouts, lifting a glass to break the trance I'm in.

The crowd around us laughs and hoots, fueled by too much champagne, the newlyweds' vibes, and seeing a passenger kiss the captain.

I let out a nervous giggle, a blush creeping across my cheeks and down my neck.

Champagne flutes rise like they're toasting a royal engagement. One woman presses a hand to her chest as if she's just witnessed the most romantic moment of her life. “That’s the spirit, Darling,” she says with a honeyed Southern drawl.

The captain winks, her amber eyes sparkling like dangerous holiday lights.

Did she feel the electricity in the air, in our kiss, too?

Then—oh no—the onlookers start clapping.

Actual, raucous clapping. This was so far off-script from my carefully crafted plan to melt into the background that my cheeks flamed hotter, and I could practically feel the floor swallowing me up.

“Happy holidays!” someone hollered from a lively second-floor balcony. “You go, girl!” another voice chimed in, way too enthusiastic.

At that moment, my soul detaches, drifting somewhere far above the chaos.

Captain Rossi stands there, a picture of cool composure, her lips still curled into her dangerously charming half-smile. The entire atrium buzzes in celebration for the upcoming festivities and my current internal crisis. Unruffled, Captain Rossi looks like she expected — and absolutely deserved — the spontaneous standing ovation.

And judging by the gleam in her mischievous eyes, she is savoring every second.

“Tradition, sì,” she whispers, her warm accent caressing each syllable, creating another wave of chills in me.

Across the atrium, Darius is saluting me, mouthing WOW.

“Oh—uh—y-yes. Tradition!” I squeak, staring at the nearest exit for an escape route. “I-I’m a big fan of... holiday traditions.”

A playful glimmer flickers in Rossi’s bright eyes, and I can’t help but get lost in their depths. Clad in her sharp uniform, she’s the epitome of confidence. She is a captivating force that could steer through the wildest Alaskan storms without breaking a sweat.

“I-I’m sorry,” I stumble over my words, my cheeks reddening. “Earlier, I thought you were calling me a Holiday Princess, and I — well, I might have been a bit rude.”

"Ah, si. The Holiday Princess. That's my ship! But it's a good name for you too, don't you think, Cara?"

Cara! The way she says it sends butterflies fluttering in my stomach. I can't help but grin, caught in the magic of this holiday moment and her charm.

Behind me, Darius makes a strangled noise—somewhere between laughter and unhinged celebration.

I open my mouth to say something witty or at least coherent—something that doesn't make me sound like the girl who fell for her boss and is apparently about to fall for a captain—but Captain Rossi steps even closer.

Too close.

Close enough that her scent—salt, cedar, a thread of jasmine—wraps around me and renders me speechless. Her mere presence is a spell I absolutely cannot break away from.

"Not so bad, sì?" she asks, voice low and velvety.

"Totally not bad," I croak. "Just... extremely normal tradition of kissing complete strangers under mistletoe during a champagne party behavior."

She chuckles—low, dangerous—and a shiver ripples down my spine. "You do not seem to mind, Cara mia."

I summon a polite smile, even as my nerves erupt into chaos—sirens, sparks, and adrenaline rushes making my whole body feel like it's dancing on a live wire.

And that's when the PA system crackles.

"LADIES AND GENTLEMEN!" Chase's voice blasts through the atrium with a force that makes a champagne glass explode near the penguin ice sculpture.

I jump. Several passengers jump. The penguin remains, somehow, unaffected.

"LET'S HEAR IT FOR OUR CAPTAIN ROSSI!"

The atrium erupts into applause, and Captain Rossi is still standing close enough that her uniform brushes my arm.

OMG!

She inclines her head gracefully, the picture of calm authority, while I shrink away.

"And may I have your attention for one more announcement, please—NEWLYWEDS!" Chase hollers, practically glowing with excitement.

Newlyweds.

Why is he calling *all* of us newlyweds? Surely the entire ship isn't full of newlyweds.

"Fun fact, y'all!" Chase chirps, a deranged holiday elf. "On our inaugural first-ever Alaskan newlyweds cruise, one lucky couple receives the ultimate prize—an upgraded cabin, complimentary shore excursions, and bragging rights as our Winning Newlyweds! I selected a very special pair of newlyweds... completely at random!"

The crowd buzzes with excitement.

The Captain hasn't moved away from me. Not an inch. Her presence radiates steady, cool authority, and she glances sideways at me with an unreadable flicker in her eyes—amusement? Pity? Interest?

I relax now that the spotlight has moved away from me. Chase draws out the announcement like it's the Academy Awards. My heart pounds an ominous drumroll.

I scan the room of cruise passengers, trying to guess which lucky couple will get picked.

"And this year's lucky, lucky lovebirds are...AURORA AND DARIUS!"

Oh no. Oh no no no no—

The atrium erupts in cheers.

I go completely still. Frozen. Petrified.

This cannot be happening. First, I kiss the captain—in front of literally everyone. Now, I'm apparently winning a newlywed competition... I never entered... because I am married to my gay best friend? The universe is laughing directly in my face.

Darius, of course, snaps his fingers. "I always get lucky! I told you this cruise was only getting better, Girl," he croons with a wink and sashays forward to the stage and spotlight.

Oh, I wish I could just vanish into thin air.

Why didn't I sneak off the ship earlier?

Captain Rossi steps back, giving me just enough breathing room, yet her presence remains — intense and unyielding. Her lips twitch—just barely—betraying the faintest hint of amusement. "Married to a man. You are full of surprises, Cara," she murmurs.

As Chase congratulates Darius with a hug, he bounces toward me and thrusts something soft and sparkly into my arms. "Aurora! Your official, limited-edition winning Bride bedazzled honeymoon hoodie! The Winning newlyweds get all the best cruise perks, including a photo package so we can assure your honeymoon and our first Alaskan newlywed cruise are captured. Great, right?"

"Great," I echo, as I shrug on the bride hoodie.

It is aggressively pink. Fur-lined. Bedazzled within an inch of its life. It is also the warmest item I've touched since setting foot on this not-tropical cruise. My traitorous body instantly decided to love the hoodie since I didn't pack a single warm item.

Chase hands Darius a matching oversized white hoodie that screams GROOM in silver studs. The crowd cheers for us.

"I—thanks," I whisper, tugging the hoodie around me to completely cover my yellow sundress. The warmth hits instantly, and honestly? I could cry for relief from the warmth.

Darius drapes an arm around me, beaming in the spotlight. He leans in, stage-whispering, "Ready for our trip, Wifey-Poo?"

"Congratulations," the captain murmurs, her voice dipping low enough to curl around my ribs. "You make a beautiful bride."

My cheeks heat instantly, and my heart starts thumping like it's trying to punch its way out of my chest.

Before I can respond, my eyes meet hers. And I swear—she likes this. She likes seeing me flustered.

I'm completely confused.

"Congratulations!" Chase interrupts my thoughts, patting my hoodie and letting his hand rest on Darius's shoulder. "Enjoy our VIP Winning Newlyweds Honeymoon Experience Package!"

"What does it include?" Darius asks.

"We are upgrading you to the honeymoon suite. And all expenses are covered in your upgraded package—private, exclusive excursions, couples spa treatments, and romantic dinners under the Northern Lights!"

Darius's eyes widen, then his smile blooms across his face. "Private. Spa. Oh, Wifey, we're about to be waxed on the house!"

I flinch at the thought of hot wax near... anywhere.

Captain Rossi's mouth stays in a half-smile, as if she's suppressing a laugh.

"Thank you, everyone! We're honored. Love wins!" He announces, posing for a picture between the Captain, Chase, and me. He jostles me against the captain.

"Darius," I hiss behind my forced smile, "I swear I'm going to shove that hoodie down your—"

"Smile, Wifey-Poo," he purrs.

Captain Rossi folds her arms, watching. "Well, Holiday Princess Bride," she says, "it appears you have quite the adventure ahead."

Her tone is teasing, but under it—something smoother. Sharper.

I straighten. "Guess I do, Captain."

But also no. I came here for a quiet, relaxing vacation. To forget Alexis, my ex-boss slash ex-girlfriend, and to relax after my heavy work and university schedule. Not to fake a marriage, flirt with a sultry Italian captain, and become the viral winning newlywed couple of the cruise.

Before I can argue, Chase appears. "Captain! Could you officially toast the winning newlyweds? For the promo reel?"

Captain Rossi looks like she wants to decline... but the attention clearly delights her. Then her gaze slides to me.

"Of course," she says smoothly, stepping forward with effortless authority. "It would be my pleasure."

A flute of champagne appears in her hand like magic. She raises it, commanding the room with a single look.

"To our winning couple," she says, her Italian lilt turning the words into velvet. "May their voyage be warm... even in icy Alaskan seas."

The crowd cheers again. I downed my entire glass in one go.

As people drift off, Darius leans in. "Told you this trip would be unforgettable."

The crowd disperses as waiters refill glasses and a soft jazz version of Jingle Bells trickles into the atrium.

Captain Rossi steps aside, granting me space, but not before her fingers brush my sleeve—light, intentional, enough to make my skin hum.

"Enjoy your cruise, Cara," she says softly. "We will see each other again soon."

Something in her voice curls around me—not quite comfort. Not quite a threat. More of a warm promise wrapped tightly in an Italian accent.

"Captain?" I say, lifting my chin. "I'm planning to spend this entire trip in my cabin. I doubt we'll... interact again."

She smiles—a slow, dangerous unfurling. "We'll see about that. The winning newlyweds won a place at the captain's table tonight. Ciao, Holiday Princess."

Darius chokes on his champagne. Actually chokes. "I can't—oh my God—Aurora, are you and... Did the captain just nickname you? As your friend and new husband, I'm totally into this."

I shake my head.

"You're blushing like Rudolph's nose, Wifey-Poo. And honestly? Even I'm a little turned on by her uniform."

I yank my hood over my head, mortified. "You're supposed to be my wingman, not my saboteur. You literally handed me a glass of champagne and left me alone under the mistletoe—what did you think was going to happen?"

He shrugs, unrepentant. "I don't know, babe. But I must admit you are a chaos magnet, so I should have guessed."

Ding.

"Attention passengers," Chase chirps overhead, sounding hopped up on holiday cheer. "Please wave goodbye to Whittier, Alaska, as we embark on your Royal Caribbean Newlywed Holiday Cruise!"

Through the atrium glass, snow swirls across the dark water. The port lights shimmer against looming mountain shadows. The air smells of sea salt, pine wreaths, and crisp winter snow.

Whittier shrinks as the ship eases out of the harbor, engines thrumming beneath us.

I press my hand to the cold glass, watching land fade. The ship's horn bellows—a deep, resonant sound that vibrates through my ribs.

My reflection stares back—half excited, half oh-god-what-have-I-done.

The ship's horn gives a low, resonant blast.

Darius squeezes my shoulder. "So," he says with a playful grin, "do we tank the honeymoon games early, or lean in?"

"Can we make a game plan that includes our actual work assignment of being regular passengers and checking out the cruise and its excursions?"

"Sure," he says, waving away my words. His grin widens, and he adds, "Maybe we win more prizes?"

"You're insane," I whisper.

"Insanely photogenic, maybe." He flicks his sunglasses up his nose. "Also—your dad is definitely giving us a Christmas bonus when he gets the lowdown on all the exclusive cruise perks we are going to do. This is so much better than expected."

Before I can respond, the captain returns and leans in, her voice cuts through the noise—low, close, right beside my ear. "I will see you at the captain's dinner."

The way she says it—slow, deliberate, laced with heat—sends a shiver down my spine that has nothing to do with the cold.

I turn, but she's already walking away, coat swinging, stride crisp and confident.

And just like that… I'm doomed.

Chapter 4

Rose Petals & Rough Seas: Newlywed Chaos Begins

Day 1: At Sea

By the time we make it to our Honeymoon Suite, I've cycled through all five stages of my lost relaxing-Caribbean-cruise-vacation grief. Denial, panic, sarcasm, panic again, and frost—because yes, there's actual ice forming on the windows… or portals? I'm not even sure I'm on a boat anymore because as I stare into the suite.

The cabin door opening reveals the full implications of our winning newlywed perks of the honeymoon suite, and the smell hits me first.

Roses.

Too many roses. Red rose petals stand stark against the light gold carpet and furnishings.

"Winners!" Darius singsongs behind me, shimmying in with the suitcase. "Move aside and get ready for our cruise bliss, Wifey-Poo. Daddy's home!"

"*Daddy* needs to stop calling himself Daddy," I say, groping for the lights in the romantically lit room.

The switch clicks, and our "honeymoon suite" explodes into warm lamplight and more red.

Red bed runner. Red satin throw pillows. Red petals sprinkled across an absurdly huge king bed. Rose petals are leading to the heart-shaped rose petals on the bench at the foot of the bed, a chilled bottle of champagne on a silver tray, and a red sign against the mahogany headboard announcing, "Congratulations, Newlyweds!"

"This room," Darius announces, sweeping his arms wide, "is divine."

"It's... enormous," I breathe, spinning in the enormous space. A velvet-upholstered full-sized sofa faces a flat-screen TV, a dining table with two upholstered chairs, an elaborate vanity with a lit mirror, and—*oh my God*—a bathroom with double sinks, a separate shower, and an oversized jetted tub. There's even a tray of heart-shaped chocolate truffles and a fruit-and-cheese platter arranged as if it's waiting to be Instagrammed.

I didn't even know cruise ships had rooms like this. I was expecting a tiny twin bed and a shower too tight to wash my hair in. This is breathtaking. It's... *too much.*

Darius dances in the middle of the room, arms in the air. "Look, we've got a private balcony with fjord views." He fans himself and adds, "That bed is so big we could fit six people in it without ever having to share a pillow. Girl, this is a dream."

"We cannot accept this," I mutter, collapsing into a ridiculous fur-lined chair by the glass door. The cushions swallow me like expensive quicksand. "A sparkly, embroidered, big honeymoon nightmare."

He flops onto the bed, sending a puff of rose petals into the air, and buries his face in a pillow. "Nope. You deserve this. And you're welcome."

"For what?" I demand.

"For saving you from trying to ruin our best cruise vacation." He rolls onto his back, grinning at the ceiling. "You wanted palm trees. I gave you bougie accommodations and free champagne."

"I wanted to get a tan and impress my dad by reviewing this new cruise. I'm totally not up for... whatever this is," I snap.

"This is our destiny. Picture it, singing karaoke every night, getting VIP treatment, and still getting paid."

"This is a mistake!"

He peeks over at me, still grinning. "Potato, potahto."

"Darius!"

He props himself up on his elbows, finally serious. "Okay, okay. Listen." He smooths the duvet, and I sit by him, shaking my head as I wonder how much it would all cost.

"You can't be mad about a free cruise upgrade. It was total luck. We might as well enjoy the..." He picks up the daily itinerary. "... midnight holiday chocolate buffet and singing karaoke. There are holiday pub crawls, socials, and holiday shows. Ohhh, at the captain's table it's all champagne and caviar, too. Girly, this really is a dream gig."

"There's also having to lie," I remind him. "And a shipful of people who think we're legally wed."

He waves a hand. "Semantics."

I grab a throw pillow and hurl it at his face. "We have to backtrack and tell them the truth. Besides, when you sing Celine Dion for karaoke–I think someone's gonna know."

"What would we say, *we aren't newlyweds* or even *regular paying passengers. We are here for work to review the cruise.* No way. We're supposed to be incognito and what better way then to act like newlyweds and enjoy all the perks. We'll totally blend in."

He snatches a piece of dark chocolate from the charcuterie board and pops it into his mouth. "Telling the truth would totally be messy."

Then he raises a brow. "Besides, I can tell you have sparks with the Captain."

"Yes. And I don't need a fling. I need a quiet holiday. Besides, now that I'm married, that goes out the window."

He waves off my words, "You'll love it, and you can have a secret affair. That's a cruise requirement and telling the truth now would be too much drama."

"Plus," he says, pointing the chocolate at me like a mic, "we already had a shared a room, we spend every waking minute together like some weird married duo... The only difference now is we get to do it in a free upgraded suite with all the perks." He snatches two plush bathrobes off the bed and wiggles them at me.

"How do you not have an ounce of shame?" I groan, rubbing my temples. "You're impossible."

He gives me his dazzling, wicked smile. "Impossibly amazing, you mean. And technically, we're in too deep, we might as well make it fun." He wiggles his brows. "Come on, fake wife—let's order room service, and destroy this charcuterie board. You can review the food service."

"You're enjoying this way too much," I say, weakly, already giving up on the fight as I unwrap a chocolate heart.

The chocolate truffle is stupidly good—rich, dark, melt-on-the-tongue amazing. Maybe because of the lie, it is the best chocolate I've ever had—and I eat a lot of chocolate.

"We both know you thrive on chaos," he says. "Also, did you see the Newlywed Winning complimentary spa menu? It includes 'couples seaweed wraps and hot Matanuska rock massages.' I refuse to allow us to miss that posh level of vacation fun. Your dad is going to be totally on board with this. He'll probably give us a bonus!"

I throw my hands up. "Fine. But no weird backstories. If anyone asks, stick as close to the truth as possible. I'm not going to let you tell people I'm a trans flamingo dancer. We are high school sweethearts who work together in Anchorage."

"I was hoping we could be influencers who run a doggie fashion design company in Colorado," he pouts.

"Seriously!"

He laughs. "Just kidding. The truth sounds fab! Maybe I can fake a poultry allergy to ensure they only serve us filet mignon and lobster," he says, thoughtfully.

I stare at him deadpan, my expression flat enough to be a warning.

He sighs, crossing his heart. "Fine, Girl. No more lies. Scout's honor."

Darius flops back onto the duvet again. "A romantic cruise vacation," he declares. "Kind of poetic that it's exactly what we need after our breakups, right?"

I chuckle and hold his hand. "Yep. But considering we're besties and gay, I'm thinking that's not happening."

He laughs and hands me another chocolate, "Definitely not, girl."

The ship hums beneath us, a low, steady vibration under my feet—part lullaby, part warning. Through the sliding glass door, Turnagain Arm stretches out in a wide silver ribbon, tidal currents etching lines across the water. The mountains shoulder up against the sky, capped in snow and dusk, looming over the ship.

I stare at the ridiculous towels folded into swans with their necks forming a heart, the rose petals, the balcony, the shimmering water outside.

And for just a second—beneath the dread and the fake newlywed lie—I feel it. Darius nudges me and then hops up to turn up Beyoncé while starting to unpack his bag. He's over-the-top and unashamedly himself.

I love him! This *could be* fun.

The ship intercom crackles faintly in the hallway outside our room, followed by a cheerful little greeting.

I tense and stand up, and Darius dances around me.

Please do not announce that the formal holiday dinner is about to start. Please... I'm not ready to perform in front of the entire ship and certainly not prepared to see Captain Rossi.

But it's just an announcement about the itinerary located in the rooms.

My phone buzzes. I flinch so hard I launch it into the jetted tub, then snatch it up reflexively, checking that the screen is intact.

The notification bar glows with three texts from Grant, *my dad*, one from Lisa, *my friend*, an ominous blank-white message thread from my mother— and...

Oh. *Oh no.*

Alexis.

My stomach lurches. I force my gaze away from her name as if it burns. Later I'll read it. I can emotionally unravel later. I need to prepare for my big dinner performance.

Darius watches me with a twinkle in his eyes. "Go on, cellphone addict. See what your dad—" then he tilts his head and smiles, "or your old ex is texting you."

I turn to ignore him and open Grant's thread first. My dad messaged me, "Enjoy the cruise, and a simple note on anything you like or dislike is fine. Thank you for taking on this assignment and reviewing the new Royal Caribbean cruise from the guest perspective. I can't wait to see how you like it. And I'm proud of you, kiddo, for finishing your first university semester and for the great work you're doing. I appreciate you."

Warmth unfurls in my chest at his words, *proud of you*, and *appreciate.* I bite my lip and savor having a parent who can say those words to me. I'm lucky to have found Grant.

I text back, "No problem. I'm taking notes. BTW, somehow we 'won' the newlywed suite with exclusive tours. I'm hoping we can remain undercover despite being the ship's winning newlyweds. The upside is that we get free spa services I can review. Also—THANK YOU. I'm proud to be your daughter. And I love you. Is that a thing we can say? I'm practicing."

Three dots appear. Vanish. Reappear.

"It's definitely a thing. Have fun. Learn a lot. Call me if you need anything."

I stare at the message, throat tightening. The empty place my mother carved out with neglect and her harsh judgments of finding me never enough doesn't feel as vast. The space inside me feels... fixable. Fillable. Like someone finally poured warmth into the space in my heart that has been cold for too long.

"Hey." Darius taps my ankle with one perfectly polished shoe. "Eyes up, Wifey-Poo. You're emotionally spiraling."

"I'm not spiraling."

I am absolutely spiraling.

"I'm preparing for a controlled descent in the crazy fraud we are about to commit at sea. Is this an international crime?"

He grins, delighted. "We are internationally wonderful and sensational. But also—look." He gestures dramatically toward the small table beside the bed. "Your fashion advisor—who is also your new husband—may have gotten you a cruise gift."

He opens a velvet jewelry box with a flourish worthy of Broadway.

I move my hand—carefully, dramatically, catching the vibe he's throwing — since he's singing "Pretty Woman" to me, as he pretends to close it with a laugh. Inside the box is a sparkly diamond-esque set of necklace, earrings, and a sparkle-heavy ring.

"They're costume pieces, but kismet, right? Wifey-Poo!"

Then he drops to one knee.

"Will you make me the happiest fake husband in the entire galaxy?" he purrs, pulling the glittery ring from the box.

I can't help it. I laugh. Then I extend my hand.

He slides the ring onto my finger, and the weight of it—fake stone or not—is heavy, and it fits perfectly.

He wiggles his brows. "Girl, wearing a ring makes you even more of a lesbian magnet. The captain is going to enjoy some romance à la carte tonight."

My face burns.

Buzzing, my phone saves me. Lisa, this time. "YOU DID IT! You're on a cruise!! VACATIONING!! Enjoy!!"

I snort. "Lisa is cheerleading from afar."

"Of course she is."

The ring glints on my finger. The roses. The humongous suite. The ridiculous romance vibe in this room—it's suddenly too much. Too sweet. Too fake. Too much.

I push the balcony door open and step into the cold. The blast of air knifes straight through the rose-perfume haze inside the suite, slicing it clean. Outside, the balcony is slick with ice, the leftover snowfall clinging stubbornly to the railings. I drag a long breath in—sharp, bracing. Below, the sea churns in dark steel swells, restless and wild. And beyond it all, the mountains rise like silent judges, carved in shadow and snow.

"It would be more fun, easier if..." I start, then stop, because the truth is ridiculous and will never happen.

Darius waits.

"If I were sharing this honeymoon suite with someone who actually... my lifetime partner."

Someone who didn't push me away.

Someone who didn't pick work over me.

Alexis's laugh echoes through a memory so sharp it hurts.

Darius doesn't flinch. He just reaches out and wraps his fingers around mine, the ring pressing into our hands uncomfortably.

"I know, girl," he says softly. "Breakups are hard. And I love you. I *love* you. This is gonna be fun, I promise."

Then—because he can't leave a moment un-theatrical—he starts singing.

"Never gonna give you up... never gonna let you down..."

"Ew," I groan, but a smile cracks through. "Never gonna run around and desert you."

He bumps my hip.

"You knew what you married into, Girl."

And against all odds—against the cold outside and the warmth inside and the confusion churning in my chest—I start giggling. Then sing along with him.

For a brief, ridiculous moment, this honeymoon suite is full of love and laughter.

The intercom in our room chirps again, and then Chase's voice, our Cruise Director, booms through the speakers. "FUN FACT, folks! Turnagain Arm is named because Captain Cook had to turn around *eighty times* to find Anchorage to stop for fuel! Ha! Trust me, we've all been there with

Siri's bad directions. Now, if y'all look to your left—port side—you'll see Portage Glacier! And to your right—you'll see Russia!"

I stare at the ceiling speaker. "Chase," I whisper, "you absolutely cannot see Russia, and that Captain Cook stuff is just wrong."

Darius cackles. "The cute ones are always so dumb. Be nice—he's trying his best."

I lift a brow.

Darius shrugs, "He told me the ship's Naturalist didn't show, so he's filling in. Give him a little slack. I mean, for a Florida guy, it's not terrible."

"He's lucky I can't correct him," I groan. "Publicly humiliating the Cruise Director-slash-Naturalist-slash-Himbo would totally make waves and blow our newlywed cover."

"Right," Darius says, nodding solemnly. "Our cover. I'm totally asking you to be nice because of 'our cover' and not his amazing Prince Charming thick hair and jawline."

"I.." My stress level rises. I don't even know how to respond to my way-too-flirty fake husband. I inhale deeply. "This is New Aurora. Glacier-calm, ready for fun."

"That's my wife-poo." He bumps me. "I promise. I'll behave. We do the kiss-on-cheek photo ops, melt into the crowd, sip free champagne, and we slay this cruise like the queens we are!"

"And you," I say, pointing a pen at him, "try not to flirt so loudly that the crew suspects us."

He slaps a hand over his chest. "How dare you. My flirting is subtle. Soft. Tasteful. To be enjoyed by all."

"You're going through your breakup ho-phase and your flirting is as loud as your high school marching band auditioning."

"Rude." He grins. "I was learning to play the drums." Then he waggles his brows. "Anyway... you're one to talk. *Cara* Princess. Kissing the Captain on day one."

"I didn't—we weren't even married yet when that happened," I mumble, cheeks heating.

Just thinking about Captain Rossi's low-lilted "See you soon" has me altogether nervous and excited. I want to hide, and shower, shave, exfoliate, and moisturize, all at the same time.

He bumps my knee. "You deserve a ho-phase too, girl. But most of all, you deserve actual happiness."

Something warm loosens in my chest. I twist the ring on my finger. Then give him a decisive nod.

The roses sprinkled everywhere fill the room with a ridiculous, over-the-top romance vibe, and somehow give me courage instead of nervous hives.

"Dinner?"

"Copy," I sigh, grabbing my hoodie to put over the sundress. It's the warmest thing I own, now. Plus, the sparkly *Bride* lettering completes the whole blissfully newlywed aesthetic.

"A little casual for a formal dinner," he declares.

"Alaskan chic," I deadpan, tugging the hemline of my sundress lower as if two extra inches of fabric might magically save my thighs from hypothermia. "And don't tease my wardrobe. We are going shopping at the first port. I'll get a dress and warm clothes. Clothes meant for—" I gesture at the snow swirling outside the balcony "—*this*."

He smiles. "I was planning on shopping anyway."

Chapter 5

Salmon Lies & Sequined Surprises

Day 1: At Sea

The neckline of my wrap dress is so low I can practically see my own heartbeat.

Did it shrink in my suitcase? Or—*more likely*—did I plan to have a bikini underneath this?

I tug at the dress for the hundredth time. No amount of fiddling can make the halter dress look even remotely black-tie appropriate. It's made for beaches and humidity—not glaciers, chandeliers, and people who eat caviar.

The rhinestone necklace Darius gifted me is cold against my collarbone. Cold. Itchy. Sparkly.

The ring matches.

Darius insisted I look like "an Alaskan bride who is fashion-adventurous."

Which would be flattering, if I wasn't one wrong inhale away from flashing the entire Captain's table, including the captain.

Heat creeps up my neck.

Not cozy warmth with the icy conditions outside—actual nervous sweating.

I mutter, "Breathe, Aurora. Just... breathe. It's only dinner. With the Captain. In front of strangers who think you're a glowing newlywed. No pressure."

Darius bumps my hip with his elbow, glittering like he personally invented tuxedos. He's always been the calm to my chaos—the friend who talked me down from crying in bathroom stalls during high school AP tests, and sat with me during every heartbreak at school dances. He's the friend who always shows up. Even now he's here, as I'm doubting that we can pull this newlywed's performance off.

"Wifey-Poo," he says, "you're fine. You're glowing."

"It's not glowing—it's panic sweat," I say under my breath while giving him a fake smile.

"No, girl," he sighs theatrically. "That's love and free champagne."

"Darius—"

"Also, the lighting here is criminally flattering. You should be thanking someone."

I grit my teeth. "I should have faked seasickness, I can't breathe in this dress."

"You don't need to breathe," he says. "You need to smile and enjoy being spoiled."

Before I can hiss a response at him, a woman in a sequined dress—who smells like bourbon and Christmas miracles—leans over with a sympathetic smile.

"Honey," she drawls, taking in my dress, "are y'all bringin' the tropics to this black-tie dinner?"

My dress suddenly feels loud and totally out of place.

It's waving a neon sign that reads, *I don't belong here!*

"I—I... I thought it was a cocktail fun attire?" I squeak.

Darius swoops in smoothly. "This is Aurora, and I'm Darius—the ship's winning newlyweds."

"Oh, we *know*. You two are *adorable.* Look at her glow, Baron!" Maggie Jo gushes.

"I see it, dear," he replies dryly. Then, gentler, to me, "Congratulations."

Sequins Lady beams. "I'm Maggie Jo, and this is my husband, Baron."

Baron gives me a tiny, polite nod.

"You look stunning," he says, adjusting his cufflinks. "We were just as overwhelmed on our first cruise. Couldn't decide what to wear or even tear ourselves away from the room."

Maggie Jo giggles at the memory and nudges him. "Let's let the newlyweds breathe and get in there before the crab legs vanish."

I actually laugh—soft and real. "Yes. We better go too. Newlyweds. That's... us."

Something in my chest loosens. Just a little.

Maybe... maybe I can relax.

"I think we are all sharing the Captain's table tonight with you, honey."

"Super!" I say, too enthusiastically.

Darius squeezes my shoulders like he knows exactly what's happening inside my head. "We're delighted to be sitting with you. And incredibly honored to get advice from seasoned cruisers."

"Bless your hearts," Maggie Jo says. "You two stick with us. We've cruised more times than I can count."

"Thank you," I say softly. And I mean it. They will be a great distraction, so maybe I won't have to talk too much.

The panic in my chest eases by a few degrees.

Darius shoots me a look—*See? We'll be fine*—and I find myself believing him.

He can handle the talking — he always does.

And with Maggie Jo and Baron flanking us like seasoned cruise parents, I suddenly don't feel like the lone tropical disaster at the Captain's holiday dinner.

The dining-room doors sweep open.

Warm golden light spills out, and I let myself exhale. We enter the large dining room with illuminating silverware, crisp linens, a gold crystal centerpiece so extravagant it looks like Martha Stewart ascended to godhood, and—oh—actual whales breaching beyond the panoramic windows.

"Alaska," I breathe, stunned at the majestic scene despite being an Alaskan.

Darius offers his arm. "Shall we, Wifey-Poo?"

"You sound silly calling me that."

"Too late. Your pet name is cute."

I take his arm because, *why not?* We step inside—and every head turns toward us.

Fantastic. Just fantastic.

And then I see her.

Captain Rossi.

A vision in navy and command, sitting at the head of the table at the center of the room. Her posture is straight, poised—effortlessly pulling the room's gravity toward her.

Presence. Power. And the kind of confident smile that says she knows exactly the effect she has.

Her gaze finds me instantly. She doesn't blink.

"Ah," she says, voice a soft velvet lilt. "The winning newlyweds."

Darius practically vibrates with joy. "That's us!"

We're guided to our seats—directly beside her.

Of course, since I'm the most unlucky person. *Fate hates me.*

Captain Rossi shifts slightly toward me, her voice pitched for my ears alone. "*Cara mia,*" she murmurs, amber eyes glinting under the rim of her hat, "you look... radiant."

My vocal cords immediately malfunction. "Oh," I squeak. "That's just humidity."

Her brow lifts.

A waiter fills my glass, and my fingers nearly slide right off the stem, making me almost drop the glass. *Sophistication?* I've never met her.

Captain Rossi stands to give a toast, and with Maggie Jo and Baron joining us, we all stand, obeying her silent signal. "To romance," she says, voice rich, warm, entirely too intimate, "and to breathtaking voyages together."

I freeze and want to slide under the table and hide as my blush blossoms. Darius, on the other hand, looks like he's about to climb *on* the table and launch into his own speech, but he wisely raises a glass and sips.

When everyone settles, Captain Rossi turns her attention back to us—*me.*

"So, newlyweds," she says, "how long have you known each other?"

I'm still frozen. Luckily, Darius absolutely is not.

"High school sweethearts," he says brightly, squeezing my hand. "We were in the drama club together."

I cough, nearly spilling my water. "Uh—yes. High school. Drama team. Love. Then we got married."

"Very young to marry," the Captain muses, her amber gaze lingering—*lingering too long*—on my mouth. "It must have been a very passionate first love."

"Passion," I blurt. "We're... full of it. Love. And hormones. Crazy stuff being young and in love. *So* in love. All of that."

Darius beams proudly. "I knew the moment I saw her dancing as an Oompa Loompa in Charlie and the Chocolate Factory."

I whip my head toward him. "Wha–"

He pinch-smiles. "Okay, it might have been the way you wore those little knee-high socks in The Little Orphan Annie performance."

Darius's talking is worse than my nervous rambling and being unable to talk.

Chase—now in a too-large gold bow tie that sparkles under the chandelier—appears and sits with us, practically vibrating. "So tell us," He begs, "*How did you propose?*"

Darius inhales, preparing to deliver a Tony Award–winning monologue.

He has the whole table's attention. I have a cold sweat forming in places I didn't know I could sweat.

"I took her," he says dramatically, "to the zoo. Our favorite spot." He gives me a glittering look. "Wifey-Poo, you tell the rest."

We *had* recently visited the zoo to see the famous Antarctic gay penguins, who chose each other as lifemates and took on a rock as their egg. The zookeepers replaced the rock with an abandoned penguin egg, and they have been fawning over it, while the whole world waits for it to hatch for the sweetest penguin dads.

"Right," I say, praying my voice doesn't crack. "We watched our favorite penguin couple, and then he went down on one knee—"

"Even though it was snowy and I was wearing suede shoes," Darius adds, winking at me.

"—and he was so romantic when he handed me a rock—"

"Wait, what?" Chase interrupts.

"You know," I stall, "like how penguins give each other stones?"

"They symbolize diamonds," Darius finishes triumphantly, gesturing to my very-much-rhinestone necklace and ring.

The table erupts into laughter.

Chase says, "Darius, you do have exquisite taste."

Maggie Jo fans herself dramatically. "Oh honey, a penguin proposal! That's so so *darling*."

Baron, deadpan beside her, adds, "Economical, too. I took Maggie Jo to Paris."

Captain Rossi's lips curve, and she glances at me sideways.

It's enough to rattle me, and rattle something hot and dangerous under my ribs.

Her eyes are sharp. Assessing. Like she's memorizing every detail for later use.

Oh no.

She knows. She can see right through this lie.

Servers glide forward like synchronized swans, lowering silver domes with a flourish.

"Miso-glazed King Salmon over black rice with sesame-ginger greens," one announces.

Before I can marvel at how fancy the plate looks, Chase's voice booms across the table—bright, proud, and absolutely unhinged.

"FUN FACT!" he declares. "Did you know salmon—pronounced *salll-mon*—are bottom feeders? Queen salmon are actually the largest of the four breeds of salmon in Alaska!"

I immediately choke on the water I was swallowing.

Four breeds? Bottom feeders? *Queen Salll-mon*?

Darius looks at me, and I look at him, and in one shared moment of telepathy we think of the other person we know who calls them sal-mon and how ridiculous everything he is saying is.

My Alaska-raised heart shrieks internally. *There are five species. King salmon are not bottom feeders. And nobody pronounces it "salll-mon" unless they want to be shunned by an entire state.*

But Chase continues on his version of Alaska education, blissfully unaware.

"They're basically big carp!" he chirps. "Solo hunters. Moody little guys. That's what gives the meat such a complex flavor, almost floral, depending on the season. Like perfume. But, you know... *fishier.*"

I open my mouth—*I must correct him*—but before I can speak, Darius squeezes my hand so hard my knuckles pop like bubble wrap.

"And!" Darius continues, sweeping up momentum, "how better to celebrate our *first night* aboard this magnificent ship than with more champagne for this royal carp meal? Let's toast to Chase and his astounding knowledge."

The next course arrives—silver domes, perfect plating, the whole nine yards. Between bites of halibut and scallops, Captain Rossi continues her interrogation.

"You're Alaskan," she says, head tilted. "Why choose an Alaskan honeymoon cruise?"

I walk a conversational tightrope in four-inch heels. Each answer is worse than the last, but it couldn't possibly be as bad as Darius's lies or Chase's supposed knowledge of Alaska as he explains Halibut as, "an invasive species from Australia."

The champagne does not help the situation.

By the time I'm describing our "romantic first kiss on the coastal trail after eating salmon fish sticks," Darius has committed to full method acting—fake crying into his napkin and asking the waiter for caviar.

Maggie Jo is fanning herself to not faint with the delight at our love story.

Baron just sips his wine. Unbothered. Unimpressed. And also requesting caviar for the table.

But Captain Rossi?

She's listening, the way predators watch prey.

Halfway through dessert, a plate arrives just for me.

Pineapple. Coconut cream. Shaved chocolate. A perfect tropical escape in miniature.

"I heard," the Captain says softly, leaning just enough to make my pulse trip, "that you prefer something tropical. Something sweet."

My fork pauses midair. "How did you—?"

She smiles. "Captain's privilege. I know *everything.*"

I want to evaporate. Instead, I nod awkwardly and stab the pineapple dessert, unable to talk, and unsure of what to do.

The head waiter announces that the welcome photos—from embarkation *and* tonight's dinner—are ready for viewing and purchase in the atrium.

Darius springs from his chair like someone just yelled, *free diamonds.*

"Oooh, I need to see my good side," he trills, forgetting to invite me. "Which, lucky for everyone, is every side."

Chase lights up. He's definitely noticed every side of Darius.

I hastily leave the dessert and nod to the table, not meeting Captain Rossi's eyes. I weave toward the display area, and relief flickers through me. I escaped dinner without messing up too horribly.

Rows of photos glow on the screen—Maggie Jo blowing theatrical kisses, Baron blinking stoically like he's posing for a passport, Darius mid–tuxedo twirl with Chase laughing beside him.

But mine?

Mine isn't there.

Every couple has a photo... except us.

Except *me.*

"Hey, I'm going to check out the Glacier viewing with Chase," Darius says over his shoulder as they skip away. My human shield flutters away on a cloud of glitter and flirtation.

The crowd thins around the display. The laughter drifts off. Soon, everyone wandered back to their rooms or the lounges—everyone except the Captain.

She's there.

Waiting.

She steps closer—*too close*—and sharp citrus, warm musk, the clean crispness of snow on navy wool tickle my nose. The festive lights in the Atrium flicker, scattering hypnotizing colors across her white uniform in a way that I can't look away from.

"Well," she murmurs, her voice soft velvet with an edge, "it is just you and me now, *Cara mia.*"

My stomach flips so hard I swear it hits my ribs.

I'm a disaster at lying.

If I just avoid eye contact—just breathe—I can do this.

Probably.

Chapter 6

Mistletoe Mocktails & Midnight Problems

Day 1: At Sea

Captain Rossi leans in.

The deck doesn't tilt—*I* do. My knees perform a swooning interpretive dance as the warm glow from the string of lights crowns her in this unfair, dazzling halo. The wind, sneaking in through the cracks, mixes with her, smelling like pine, ocean, and something expensive that has no business smelling this good in subzero temperatures.

Her face is close.

Too close.

Close enough that the last time we were at this distance, she was kissing me under mistletoe and short-circuiting every self-preservation instinct.

I step back, then touch the button to open the door, stepping into the cold night and away from the hot mess I'm creating.

She steps with me.

My breath catches—quietly.

She hears it.

Of course, she does.

"Cara mia," she murmurs, accent low and sinfully warm, "Why do you blush every time I look at you?"

"I—I'm naturally red," I squeak. "Like my hair. It's genetic."

Her mouth curves. Slowly. Dangerously. The kind of smile I'm going to regret seeing.

Our breaths mingle in visible puffs, the space between us shrinking with each heartbeat. Her amber eyes track my mouth with precision.

And suddenly... I ache.

Not just wanting.

Not just flustered.

Something real—something I haven't felt since Alexis. Something like being *seen* and *wanted.*

The couples around us are no help—newlyweds wrapped around each other, champagne glasses clinking, soft laughter drifting from the heated lamps. Everyone is touching someone else. Everyone is being held by someone.

And me?

The newlywed shivering in a tropical dress with itchy rhinestones, who is trying very hard *not* to make out with the Captain.

"Captain," I whisper, my voice cracking like thin ice. "This is a mistletoe-free zone. I shouldn't... I can't..."

She steps closer anyway. Her hand brushes mine on the railing—on purpose, deliberate, controlled. A feather-light touch with the weight of a promise behind it.

"Is it?" she muses. "Perhaps I should issue a new protocol. I'll put mistletoes everywhere you go."

My brain swirls, and my lips start trembling.

"P-protocols are great. Love protocols. I'm all about rules."

Her laugh is low and warm. "Certo che sì. Adorable."

No one flirting with the intensity of a lightning strike gets to call me adorable.

"You're very..." I start, and swallow. "Intense."

"*Intense,*" she repeats, amused. "Is that what you call it when someone sees the real you?"

"No," is all I can manage to whisper.

"Maybe," she says softly, "I want to see more of you, Cara."

My panic spikes.

She cannot see the truth.

She cannot see that I'm terrified, that our little marriage fiction is a ploy to blend in. She can't find out, not with my job hanging in the balance, and my dad believing in me.

And especially not when she looks at me like she'll devour me, no matter what I tell her.

She steps closer, and my back bumps the railing—cold metal against bare skin. My breath shortens. My pulse stutters.

"Tell me something true," she says.

My throat closes. "W-what?"

"Something real, *cara mia.*" Her voice dips. "You hide your real self... very well."

"I'm not hiding—I'm just—bad at being a person, talking without rambling. I once hid and fell asleep during hide-and-seek on the playground. The police were called to search for me."

She smiles, slow and knowing. "No. I think you are good at hiding, but I don't want you to hide from me."

That hits too close to the bone. I want to step back. I want to step forward. I want to run. I want—*I don't know what I want.*

"I can't do this," I blurt out.

Her brows arch. "Do what?"

"This. The... intensity thing. The..." I wave at the crackling air between us. "Whatever this is."

Her smile deepens. "This."

"I have a marriage to—" I stop myself, swallowing hard. "—to respect. Boundaries. Marital boundaries."

She studies me with a focus that feels like being held in place. "*Hm.* Boundaries." She says the word like it amuses her. "And tell me. Does your husband give you everything you want? Everything you need?"

My heart stops.

She steps in closer, her voice dipping into a velvet murmur.

"Sometimes," she says, "a woman may find she wishes to explore experiences her husband cannot offer." Her eyes flick down, then up, slow and knowing. "Interests he cannot understand."

My mouth goes dry. "Captain—"

"It is only fun," she says lightly, though there's nothing light about the look she gives me. "Perfectly natural."

A beat. "Especially when someone else sees her more clearly."

I may actually faint.

Before she can get even closer, a couple stumbles past us—laughing, kissing, practically glued together—and I use the distraction to duck under her arm, away.

I bolt.

Not gracefully. Not powerfully.

More of a frightened rabbit escaping a skilled fox.

By the time I reach the upper deck hallway, my heart is fighting my lungs in my ribcage. The holiday deck lights shimmer off the dark water. The night is pure Alaskan magic—gorgeous and vast.

I scan for refuge. A bar. A crowd. Noise.

Anything to drown out the echo of her voice and calm my racing heart.

That's when I spotted a small white sign taped beside an ornate door, "FRIENDS OF BILL – TONIGHT – ALL WELCOME."

I blink at it.

Bill who?

Probably some cruise club or family reunion.

Probably a crowd and snacks.

And snacks sound safer than risking seeing the captain again. My stomach growls in agreement. I'd drunk too much champagne and eaten too little at dinner—too busy pretending to be blissfully married, and dodging Captain Rossi's questions.

I slip inside to safety.

The room is warm, quiet, softly lit—the opposite of the chaotic cruise energy outside. A small circle of chairs. Maybe twenty people. Santa hats. Casual attire. No buffet table like I'd hoped... but there is a tray of cookies. And—praise the gods—a bar. Everyone looks unnervingly calm.

"Hey," the bartender says gently, sliding me a sparkly pink drink. "Cranberry fizz."

I take my emotional support beverage. "You had me at fizz."

A woman in a corner chair smiles. "First meeting?"

"Yeah," I admit, already eyeing the cookie tray. "I came for the buffet distraction. But I'm staying for the vibe and snacks."

A laugh ripples around the room—warm, kind, absolutely nothing like what I expected from Bill's friends.

A man stands and addresses the circle. "Welcome. This is a space for honesty and being real. No judgment. No pressure. Speak or just listen."

Oh.

Oh no.

I cannot do "honesty" or "real." I am an undercover tropical liar hiding from the ship's captain. I am the definition of a lie.

Friends of Bill is not a family reunion.

I have once again wandered into an AA meeting. Are the gods telling me something?

My cheeks heat, but no one stares. People smile. They introduce themselves and welcome me with no requirements.

I sat. Because I absolutely cannot risk running into the Captain again.

I curl into a back-row chair with my mocktail and two cookies—I deserve emotional support cookies, too.

People talk about themselves. Making mistakes. Breaking bad patterns. Not running from your problems.

Something inside me cracks open, just a little.

When it's my turn, I don't intend to speak.

But I do.

"Hi. I'm Aurora. I, uh… I'm living a lie. I don't talk to my mom. I broke up with the person I thought I'd be with forever. And I'm just trying to make my dad proud and do the best I can."

Heads nod. Not shocked, just listening.

I laugh nervously. "I'm not, like, a villain-liar lying. More like, I'm pretending to be someone I'm not. The truth is messy. Complicated. And I'm terrified of messing up. I'll mess up my job. I'll mess it up with my dad. I'll mess it up with my friend. I won't fit in. I'll prove that I'm not worthy of anything or anyone. I'm one giant messy liar wearing a sundress and drinking too much champagne."

A woman nods softly. A man wipes a tear. Someone murmurs, "Amen."

"And honestly," I say, shrugging, "I just snuck in here to escape and eat cookies."

The room laughs warmly.

I feel… lighter.

The bartender slides another cranberry fizz toward me with a nod.

When I leave the meeting, snow starts falling again—soft flakes catching the light outside the windows like glitter. The deck lights glow, and beyond them the glacier rises like an ancient cathedral, silent and impossibly still.

"Cara mia."

I jolt so hard I nearly drop my cranberry fizz.

I whirl around mid-stride.

Captain Rossi is there—leaning in the shadowed archway of the hallway. Her posture is relaxed, her gaze anything but. The overhead lights catch in the strands of her perfectly coiled hair beneath her cap.

It hits me—she didn't happen to be here.

She was waiting.

She somehow knew exactly where I'd be.

The realization sends a shiver skittering down my spine that has nothing to do with the cold.

"I thought you left," I breathe.

"I did not." Her gaze is steady. "You ran."

"I... briskly exited our conversation."

She steps closer—not as close as earlier, but close enough that her perfume curls through the cold air.

"You fascinate me, Aurora," she says softly.

My pulse attempts a backflip.

"You are hiding something," she adds. "I can feel it."

Panic pricks at my ribs. I clutch my cranberry fizz.

I make a noise. A terrible tiny wheeze.

She smiles—a slow, knowing curve. "Perhaps," she murmurs, "I have found a clue."

Oh no.

"It's nice to see you again. Good night," I blurt—much too loud—and spin on my heel before she can respond.

Then I run.

A full-speed, no-dignity-left run.

Straight toward the sanctuary of my posh, romantic newlywed honeymoon suite.

Chapter 7

Couples Massage Meltdown

Day 2: Seward, Alaska

The ship's horn blares—loud, dramatic, and absolutely unnecessary at whatever ungodly hour this is. Apparently, we've arrived in Seward, Alaska, which I somehow slept through.

Darius, also, slept-in. He's starfished across his side of the bed, wearing an eye mask labeled 'Queen' and noise-canceling headphones.

To add to my morning disorientation, an aggressive knock jolts me.

I practically fall out of bed as a chipper butler bustles inside, waking us up with actual espresso shots and a silver tray of breakfast–mixed fruit and bakery treats.

He hands us our itinerary with a too-bright smile. "Good morning, winning newlyweds! Your spa excursion upgrade is in twenty minutes!"

Twenty minutes.

I need a gallon of coffee, a good hair day, and roughly an hour of mental preparation before public interaction—but apparently today we're on spa time.

I stumbled to the balcony window. Docked in Seward, I stare out—stunning, chilly, with mountains so close I could probably hit them with a snowball if my aim didn't resemble someone who's never played sports.

And me?

I'm in a thin tank top and pajama bottoms.

My outfit says I'm heading to a sunrise yoga retreat, not the hypothermic, ice-kissed coastline of Alaska.

Thank God we're in port. I need real clothing. I'll survive the spa, then sprint to a store for wool socks, jeans, a sweater, and an electric blanket.

An hour later and two coffees and a croissant on the small tender/boat ride over, I haven't seen a store, but we did see two sea otters and a playful harbor seal.

We check in at the luxurious spa yurts.

"They don't have any waxing services here, only restorative body-positive la-di-dah." Darius frowns looking up from his phone. "Sorry, Girl. I guess your kitty cat will be Alaskan style until I can rebook our appointments at the ship's spa."

"Bummer," I say, while trying to hold back a laugh. Only someone like Darius, with 110% confidence would bemoan a body-positive relaxing spa experience. This is the first perk I'm going to fully enjoy.

"Couples massage, this way, newlyweds! In your private yurt, go ahead and remove your clothes and put on the robes. We'll give you two lovebirds some extra time before we enter," she says with a smile.

My relaxing day is causing an anxiety attack. Right. *Newlyweds.* To Darius, my *lovebird.*

Being naked in front of someone isn't exactly comfortable to me, even if it is my best friend who has seen me in dressing rooms. I glance at my fake husband—my adorable, sparkly best friend—and he is absolutely radiant. Despite missing his torture session he calls grooming, he is giving beauty pageant Spa Day Superstar vibes. Last night he even pulled out his personal nailcare kit and spa slippers to bring with us. With his buzzing about our spa day today, I somehow was unable to yuck his yum and tell him how abandoned I felt after dinner.

And I'm not ruining this spa day experience for him, even if I don't exactly want to share a yurt or get naked.

I plaster on a smile and pull out the finger guns.

"Pew pew," I whisper. "Let's do this."

The spa itself isn't the arctic rustic style I expected—it's a Nordic-style retreat built outdoors along the snowy shoreline. Steam coils from cedar hot tubs like dragons waking up. Frosted lanterns hang from pine posts. Heated stone walkways snake between yurts, making me a queen in a bougie Viking village.

The yurt smells of eucalyptus and a holiday spice scent—warm, soothing, very relaxing. Outside, mist curls off the icy water, giving Alaska her own glittery winter scarf.

"How are my favorite little honeymooners?"

Maggie Jo's Southern voice rolls in behind us—full of warmth, sass, and confidence. She's fanning herself with a sequined clutch. She actually brought a sequined clutch. To a spa. In Alaska. "We didn't think you'd make it out of your room this morning to the spa."

Baron stands beside her, arms crossed, glasses low.

"You cannot be flapping that purse around. It's a safety hazard, dear."

"We are doing the cold plunge with steam today, Honey," she says to me pointing to the nearby pools.

"That sounds invigorating. Maybe we should do that, wifey poo?" Darius says, wanting to ruin my relaxing day.

"Dear, here's a towel for the sweat," Baron says, holding two towels.

"We are glistening, babycakes, glistening," Maggie Jo says, waving her clutch dramatically. "These hormones don't care about the climate. Hot, cold, happy, nostalgic for no reason. Hormones are the worst." She nods at me for solidarity.

Baron sighs. "Love is booking a cold plunge instead of a massage." He looks longingly toward our yurt that the attendant is waiting for us to enter.

Darius jumps in, delighted. "Girl, I'm sure that the hot and cold pools will help. Shock the system, reboot your vibes."

Maggie Jo claps her hands. "Honey, that's what I told Baron. *You are a treasure.* Enjoy your massages."

God, they are the perfect couple, joking, and so sweet. I want them to adopt me and feed me gumbo along with unsolicited life lessons that end with "Bless your heart" and "Honey."

Darius blows them a kiss. "Thank you!"

We shuffle to the "Exclusive Winning Newlyweds Spa Retreat," our luxurious outdoor Scandinavian yurt. A crystal chandelier hangs inside the heated yurt. Warm golden lighting glows through frosted windows. A fountain pours steaming eucalyptus water out of an artisanal seashell.

Darius is wrapped in a plush robe so fast, I wonder if there's some sort of Guinness Book Record for removing clothing.

"Aurora," he whispers reverently, looking born into Nordic royalty in his robe, holding a pine branch. "You are about to witness peak luxury. Prepare your pores."

My pores are already retreating from hypothermia, and I turn to shrug out of my Bride hoodie, tank top and capris.

Then walk across the heated stone floor to the armchairs that have herbal waters beside them. Two porcelain soaking bowls filled with rose petals. Two pristine massage tables with blankets so fluffy they look like delicious marshmallows.

A serene woman in white linen knocks and greets us. "Congratulations, winning newlyweds. Your Love-Knot Healing Massage includes our deluxe hot-stone, and scalp treatment, Himalayan salt scrub, moose-milk hydration mask, and an optional polar bear plunge to increase virility for our couples."

I choke on the herbal water. *How is it I'm always mid-sip when people drop conversational bombs?*

She lifts a brow, worried, and I scramble to say something that doesn't involve my fertility status. "Moose... milk?"

She nods serenely. "Very hydrating."

Darius whispers, "Wifey poo, don't ask questions. Let the moose milk bless you."

She ushers us to the massage table, and another attendant appears with a small tray of oils, potions, and what looks like authentic Viking bludgeoning instruments. The freezing Alaskan air seeps into my soul, making me shiver as I hurriedly remove my robe and quickly slip under the fluffy blankets. I burrito myself and try to breathe like someone who belongs here and is not naked waiting for a stranger.

The masseuse touches my shoulders, I make a sound.

Not a cute sound.

A weird, dying-bagpipe wheeze.

Darius whispers, "You sound like you're giving birth to a walrus. Relax, Girly."

"Relaxing is stressful!" I hiss.

She brushes my hair back, murmuring, "Deep breaths."

I inhale. Breath out. Inhale a piece of fuzz or *is it my own hair?*

Snort.

Choke.

Cough.

Wheeze.

Try to move under the weight of the blankets to no avail and give in to the fate of dying a naked Viking death.

She pats my back as if I'm an infant. "Very good."

Darius sounds like he fell asleep.

Then she starts applying something warm and sticky to my shoulders.

"What... what is that?" I ask, already bracing for the hair removal Darius talked them into doing when I wasn't listening.

"Reindeer-sap energy balm," she says calmly.

Reindeer-sap. At least it shouldn't hurt.

Is that... like reindeer snot?

On my skin?

At least it smells like mint and pine, not a wild, dirty animal.

Relax, Aurora. Breath. I pep talk myself.

Who is harvesting sap from reindeer? Is that a job? Do they unionize? Is it ethical?

Before I can unravel Alaska's reindeer-industrial complex, she moves to my calves and brushes on something oozier and freezing.

I jolt so hard my towel does a dramatic cape flutter. "Gah!"

She pats my ankle, and turns on soothing music. "This is the moose-milk cooling gel."

Moose... milk.

Great. Perfect. I prefer my dairy in coffee but why not toss it on my legs?

"Oh. Thanks. Love this," I murmur instead, counting the minutes.

On the next table, Darius is awake since he says, "Yes queen, milk me!"

I bury my red face into the pillow.

After twelve excruciating minutes of sticky relaxation, the attendant steps back and announces in a serene voice, "We will return momentarily for your synchronized hot-stone couples seaweed wrap."

Synchronized.

Couples.

Hot stones.

I am not built for relaxation or nakedness while trying to perform my newlywed role.

Before I can strategize how to fake a massage injury, footsteps crunch outside the cabana.

The flap bursts open without warning,

"FUN FACT—Alaskan moose migrate to the Bahamas for winter!"

Chase!

In shorts. Shorts!

In December.

In Alaska.

I shoot upright so fast I forget I'm naked, so I immediately have to scramble back onto my back to get the blankets.

"No worries. I'm gay," he says with a wave, as if that's the problem.

"And I'm married," I retort, performing quite well under pressure.

Chase beams like I've just complimented his IQ. "God, I love your energy."

He wanders like he owns the spa, sniffing the eucalyptus air and sitting in the big chair. "You two getting blissed and blessed? Since you are my favorite newlyweds, I wanted to check on you and share some great Alaskan facts, real indigenous nature stuff, from TikTok."

There's no escape and Darius is blissfully relaxed, smiling encouragingly to Chase. I burrito myself back into the blankets with a groan. "Please stop talking." I mumble but no one hears me through the muffling blankets.

Chase taps his temple like there's a functioning Alaskan encyclopedia up there. "Did you know glaciers are made of frozen saltwater?"

I physically peel my face out of the pillow so I can glare at him with my whole soul.

"No. They're compacted snow," I say.

Chase nods like I've shared a bold political stance. "Huh. I'll send you the reel. Interesting opinion."

"Not an opinion."

Darius pats my arm. "Breathe, girl. Remember—chill. He's beautifully clueless." He clears his throat and sits up slightly, shooting Chase his subtle-not-subtle flirty smile.

"We'd love to hear more, Chase."

I turn to Darius with a look that could sink a cruise ship.

But Chase continues like we're all on a very educational field trip. "Love the passion in here."

He turns toward Darius and casually asks, "Anyway, drinks later and I can tell you more?"

Darius lights up like he doesn't need that virtually polar plunge. He nods and gives him a wink, as if his wife isn't within arms length away.

Chase waves and blushes.

Blushes.

Before Chase leaves, he pulls out a tiny digital camera. "Oh! Smile, honeymooners!"

We freeze—then snap into our practiced performance.

I lean my head dramatically toward Darius and he sits up and grabs me and my burrito'd blanket, wrapping his arms around me like we are blissful newlyweds.

Click. Click.

Another shot of the world's most chaotic newlyweds.

"These'll be posted in the gallery tonight!" Chase beams, then slips out.

"Hot," he says, instantly.

I slap my hands over my face. "Darius."

"Ho-phase, wifey poo," he murmurs. "This is healthy coping. Let me spread my wings."

"If you spread anything in this tent I will smother you with a eucalyptus towel," I whisper through my fingers.

Peace finally settles.

For about three seconds.

Because I feel her before I see her.

Captain Rossi stands framed in the yurt entrance. Snow dusts her shoulders. Her pristine uniform unfairly glows in the soft spa lights. Her amber gaze pins me exactly where I lie—as if she's checking her favorite constellation.

"Our special newlyweds," she purrs. "Enjoying your treatment?"

I squeak—an actual broken musical instrument noise.

Darius toe-kicks my ankle. "Smile, bride."

"I didn't realize this was an open-to-anyone private newlywed massage yurt," I grumble, pulling my burrito around me tighter.

"Good Morning, Captain," Darius sings.

"We're so relaxed!" I babble. "Physically. Spiritually. Emotionally moisturized!"

Her eyes drag over me—slow, rich, devastating.

"You look tense, Cara," she says.

"I am... *super* tranquil," I squeak. I'm more zen than a meditating mountain goat."

Her smile is pure sin. She knows I'm lying and loves that I'm lying.

She steps inside. Too close.

The cold from outside follows her, sharp.

My soul jolts, and I try not to react.

"Surrendering to relaxation," she murmurs, "sometimes requires guidance."

Darius whisper-hisses, "Girl, she is devouring you with her eyes. Should I leave?"

"Hush," I whisper back. "I'm doing serenity."

"Do you want some moose milk or sap water?" I ask her, loudly.

"No. I'm just checking in on our winning newlywed couple," she says, silky but stern. "Many newlyweds on board would kill to trade slippers with you two. This is quite the treat."

Then she looks at me—one last molten, devastating look—before stepping out into the snow.

I collapse onto the massage table.

"Girl," Darius whispers. "You are not built for espionage."

"I can lie!" I whisper-yell, adjusting the wedding ring.

"You are sweating—or as Maggie Jo says 'glistening,'" he says in her adorable Southern accent that instantly makes me giggle.

"It's a romantic glow."

"It's fear juice."

Our masseuses return, serene as ever.

CRACK.

"OW!" I yelp as my spine performs a Viking battle cry.

"You have many emotional knots," my masseuse says calmly.

"Understatement," Darius whispers.

By the time I stumble out of the spa—sticky, sparkly, and spiritually unstable—I'm pretty sure I should have stayed in bed.

I'm a damp noodle in borrowed slippers, suddenly very aware of how cold it is outside in my capri pants.

"We have to stop in town," I tell the nearest cruise van driver as we sit down. "Like, urgently. There's a pants emergency. My legs are freezing. I may get hypothermia."

The staffer—perfect teeth, perfect parka—gives me a sympathetic smile. "Our apologies, ma'am. The Newlywed Spa Excursion is a direct shuttle to and from the ship. There's no time. No detours."

"What about a tiny detour?" I try. "A casual, life-saving pants detour?"

"We're on a tight schedule. The next activity on board starts soon."

As if summoned by my dread, another staffer bounces over, wearing a Holiday Princess parka and the cruise-staff enthusiasm that must be a job requirement.

"We can't be late for the next activity on the ship!" She sings. "The Holiday Princess Newlywed Game!"

Chapter 8

Newlywed Games & Northern Lights Lies

Day 2: Seward, Alaska

Darius turns to me with reverent horror, his blue suit jacket shimmering under the lounge lights. "Aurora."

"No," I say, immediately. My heart is already doing the panic tap dance against my ribs.

He clasps my hands dramatically, his touch warm and familiar. "Wifey-Poo, I have waited my entire life to be the star of a game show. This is my moment—our moment!"

"Darius! We just got fake married to *blend in*! This is the opposite of blending!" I gesture vaguely at his diamond sparkle lip gloss, which he's pausing to apply just to give me his puppy-dog eyes. He does look perfectly game show-worthy, which only makes him harder to resist.

"Okay," I relent with a sigh that sounds suspiciously like a groan. "I'll do it for you."

"Yasss, Girl!" He squeezes my hands so tight I might need a professional re-alignment. "Besides, you know everything about me, from my thirteen-year-old tragic fedora stage to wearing that pink dress to our prom."

"Okay, first of all, let's agree never to speak of that bright pink tulle monstrosity, again," I say, climbing into the shuttle that will take us back to the ship. "I had almost wiped it from my memory, and now the nightmares are going to come back. Second, it's going to be hard to pass as a heterosexual newlywed couple if all our shared memories start with, 'At the LGBT club in high school, we decided to storm prom...' or any obviously not-cis-standard stuff. I want to support your game show dreams, but what if they ask about—" I lower my voice to a conspiratorial whisper "—marital intimacy."

Darius grins, a flash of pure mischief. "Girly, just channel Queen B and say we are 'Crazy in Love' then wink and giggle."

I laugh, despite myself, or maybe it's the funny shimmy he's giving me. God, I love Darius! "We do sing *wayyyy too much* Beyoncé and Britney karaoke. So, that means that you ask me to marry you by saying, 'I'm putting a ring on it.'

"For sure, girl. We will channel all our usual karaoke goddess inspo!"

"I'll do it, but no 'Hit Me Baby One More Time,'" I warn him. It's way too on the nose for my current state of anxiety.

"Deal! It's all 'I'm Too Sexy' and Backstreet Boys, then we'll dance away with all the prizes."

The shuttle rumbles back toward the pier. Through the fogged-up windows, the ship glows, a floating Christmas mall—twinkle lights and wreaths hanging on every rail.

Back up the gangway, we funnel into the atrium, where a buffet has magically appeared. Long tables are loaded with soup, fancy rolls, salmon sliders, and tiny desserts in tiny wine glasses. Darius and I grab trays and eat among the other happy couples.

Everyone is glowing. Everyone is smiling. Everyone is friendly, saying, “Oh my gosh, I love your hoodie!” “You two are adorable,” and congratulated us on winning the cruise newlywed prize.

And slowly—like, really slowly—the panic in my chest loosens a notch.

We eat, wedged between Maggie Jo and Baron. She loads up her plate, and he is methodically working his way through the dessert table.

“You look much calmer than this morning, sugar,” Maggie Jo declares, spoon halfway to her mouth. “The spa did you good.”

“Reindeer sap and moose milk,” I say dryly. “The cure for all anxieties.”

Baron adjusts his glasses. “Placebo effect,” he says. “But having this dessert, and an all-you-can-eat holiday buffet is scientifically proven to help anxieties. Chocolate is known to be therapeutic.”

I nod with a spoonful of the chocolate moose melting deliciously on my tongue. I'm in heaven.

Darius leans in. “Are you two playing the Newlywed Game?”

Maggie Jo smirks. “Honey, we live the Newlywed Game. We've been together for thirty years. This is our second honeymoon. These baby newlyweds don't stand a chance.”

My heart sinks. “Wait, you mean, you're signing up too?”

She beams. “You don't sign up. They've picked a mix of couples to make it entertaining. We're goin' for the grand prize, Honey.”

I look at Darius, but his sparkle doesn't dim with the news of them as our competition. I hope they have very poor memories... I mean, it has been decades since their first kiss and proposal.

By the time we finish eating and follow the crowd into the main lounge, I'm buzzing—not just from sugar, but from nerves.

The Holiday Princess lounge is transformed into something between a game show set and Santa's glitzy living room. Garland wraps around the railings. Twinkle lights drip from the ceiling. A giant fake ice sculpture of a reindeer stands in the corner, looking like it's one bad day away from unionizing.

Rows of chairs fill the space, all draped with fleece blankets printed with tiny snowflakes and wedding rings.

Onstage, six sets of loveseat chairs are lined up, each with a small side table and a whiteboard. Above us, a big screen loops candid photos from around the ship—couples kissing under mistletoe, people in hot tubs. One picture is of Darius and me, in the yurt that makes my lungs seize. Luckily, the towel is covering all my nakedness, and we look soft and happy together.

And smack in the middle of it all is Chase, in a velvet blazer and sparkly bow tie, holding a microphone, beaming.

"WELCOME, LOVEBIRDS!" he booms through the lounge. "It's time for the much-anticipated, Holiday Princess Newlywed Game!"

Applause. Cheering. Someone wolf-whistles.

I turn to Darius. "We can still back out."

He's already halfway to the front of the room, where there's a stage with six chairs. Maggie Jo and Baron are already sitting in one set.

Maggie Jo spins toward me as I follow Darius to our chairs. Her sequined sweater is even more dazzling than Darius's scarf.

"Don't get too excited, Honey," she declares. "I may look nice, but I'm leaving this stage with a trophy and braggin' rights."

Baron adjusts his glasses, already in full analysis mode as he scans the clipboard. "Statistically, we have a ninety-three percent advantage over the other couples," he says. "Experience, communication, and the ability to remember the exact year we got married should clinch this victory."

Darius whispers, "They don't have Queen B and a patented shimmy like us. We got this!"

"I'm totally nervous," I whisper. "Can I fake a heart attack?"

He wiggles his perfectly plucked eyebrows. "Don't kill my dream of winning a holiday cruise boat newlyweds game show."

His tease makes me laugh, and Maggie Jo's thumbs up helps me to relax enough to breathe.

My gaze drops to the sign on the table in front of us. Our names stare back at me in neat block letters. "Newlyweds: Aurora & Darius – Anchorage, Alaska." Seeing it written out makes the lie feel heavier. Realer. Permanent, in a way, it *absolutely* is not.

Before I can start hyperventilating, Chase bounces onto the stage, being his excited peacock self.

"Okay, snowflakes," he announces, clapping his hands, "We have couple number one—Maggie Jo and Baron from..." he squints at the card, "Baton Rouge, Louisiana!"

They lift their joined hands like seasoned champions. The crowd cheers. Maggie Jo does a little hip shimmy–*so much for my patent shimmy giving us a winning advantage.*

"Couple two is Gary and Lionel from Vancouver, British Columbia!"

A silverfox pair of men blow synchronized kisses to the crowd, as they take the stage with glasses of wine in their entwined arms. *I saw him playing Jazz last night, and he was telling jokes at the breakfast buffet.*

Chase presses a hand dramatically to his chest, milking the moment. "And finally," he says, drawing it out, "the couple that stole the ship's heart on night one..."

My stomach drops.

"...give it up for our cruise's winning and favorite newlyweds, Aurora and Darius from Anchorage, Alaska!"

The lounge erupts in clapping, and I wonder if there's a lit-up applause sign I can't see.

My entire body flails internally, but muscle memory kicks in. I paste on my best smile, and wave with Darius at our fans.

The stage lights are brighter than I expect—hot and a little blinding.

Chase struts to the center of the stage. His elf shoes have jingle bells. Every step tinkles.

"Okay!" he says. "Here's how it works, cupcakes. I'm going to ask a question, and each of you will write your answer on your board. No peeking. No sneaking. When I count down, you flip your boards. Matching answers get a point. The couple with the most points wins our Very Exclusive

Newlywed Excursion. Ready to see which of these couples will shine the brightest."

"We will," Chase says, dropping his voice to a stage whisper. "We got that prize in the bag!"

I glance toward the back of the lounge—and my heart stutters.

Captain Rossi is standing near the bar, arms folded, white uniform immaculate. She's half in shadow, half in twinkle light glow, expression unreadable. She's just... watching.

Watching me.

I whip my gaze back to the whiteboard that a staffer hands me, like it's suddenly the most interesting thing in Alaska.

Chase lifts his mic. "Question number one!" he calls. "This is an easy warmup. Where did you share your very first kiss?"

The crowd coos.

I choke a little. I scribble a word on my board and flip it over on the side table, hoping for the best.

Chase's jingle bells tinkle as he paces. "Time's up, lovebirds! Let's see those answers!"

Maggie Jo and Baron flip theirs, "Fishing Pier, 1988" on one and the other "Daddy's Old Fishing Spot on The Dock."

Awes from the audience.

Gary and Lionel flip simultaneously with one reading, "In the green room after a community theater production of Cabaret," and the other "on our Whistler ski trip." And they laugh, with Gary saying, "A peck on the cheek doesn't count."

Chase turns to us, his eyes sparkling with anticipation. "And the crowd favorites, Aurora and Darius! Where did you two crazy kids lock lips for the very first time?"

We flip. My board reads, "The Dive Bar where we discovered the magic of karaoke." Darius's board reads, "The only place we can properly belt out 'Don't Stop Believing.'"

A couple of chuckles bubble up. "Close enough for cruise ship work!" Chase declares. "One point for Maggie Jo and Baron and one for Aurora and Darius! You two are certainly... *unique*!"

"Question two, this is for the person on the left!" Chase booms, looking at Darius. "What would your partner say is your best feature?"

I immediately write down the answer that Darius has sung to himself in the mirror on more than one occasion.

"Flip!"

Maggie Jo and Baron, with Baron sitting on the left. "His heart of gold" and "My ability to fix anything."

Gary and Lionel try answering with "My wit" from Gary and "his perfectly sculpted beard."

His beard is epic with shine and thickness.

"Aurora and Darius, what did you come up with?"

We flip, "His Booty" and "I'm bootylicious!"

The lounge bursts into laughter. Darius preens, executing a small, perfect hip thrust from his seat, then turning to show off his booty. "I'm a winner!" he stage-whispers into my ear.

"Moving on, because I'm obsessed!" Chase grins, pointing the mic at me. "How did your partner propose?" This is the one. The moment I know we will win.

I write with the urgency of a woman who needs a point.

"Flip!"

Maggie Jo and Baron have the same answer, "Under the Eiffel Tower."

Gary and Lionel get a point for writing similar answers. *The first day same-sex marriage was legal in BC.* It earns them a round of emotional applause.

My Board says, "He told me straight up that if I liked it, I should put a ring on it."

The crowd is humming the song now.

Darius's Board says, "I told her that I'm putting a ring on it!"

"A matching set of Destiny's Child inspiration!" Chase claps. "A point for sure! This is what I call Crazy in Love!"

The audience cheers, and I feel a rush of adrenaline. Maybe this isn't about blending in—maybe it's about *outshining*.

"Next question, lovebirds!" Chase calls out. "What's the song that ALWAYS gets you two emotional?"

Maggie Jo has too many answers crossed out to read, and she shrugs. "I couldn't decide." Baron pats her leg and shows his board, "Unchained Melody."

Gary and Lionel both wrote, "I Will Survive."

We also get a point with the obvious answer of "Wind Beneath My Wings," one of Darius's favorite songs to sing.

"Alright, let's get to the nitty-gritty of *love*," Chase announces, leaning into the mic. "How would you describe your partner on the right's personality in one word?"

I don't even hesitate. There is only one answer Queen B would pick.

Flip!

"Fierce!"

"A perfect match!" Chase shouts. "A point! And I concur!"

"Last question to win the VIP prize!" Chase builds the tension, his eyes wide. "When did you know they were 'the one'?"

The lights feel even hotter. I recall the first time Darius and I stayed up until 4 AM singing our hearts out and realized I never wanted that night to end.

"Wait to flip! Let's do it one by one. Couple number one, go!"

Maggie Jo wrote, "When he changed my tire in the rain." And they won a point since he said, "Changing her tire."

Gary and Lionel flip and win the next point by writing about a Jazz club date.

And that leaves us under pressure. I look at Darius and wonder if I chose the wrong answer.

Chase puts the mic to my mouth. "So Aurora read your answer to us."

With my heart in my throat, I say, "When I realized I didn't want to say bye-bye to him at the end of the night."

The crowd laughs, and Chase asks Darius to show his board.

I heard a hoot before I read his answer.

When I didn't want to say BYE-BYE to her.

A collective "Aww" ripples through the crowd, quickly followed by the infectious beat of the song being whispered around the room.

We got it. We are the cheesy, hilarious winners.

After what feels like forever, Chase presses a finger to his ear like he's listening to the producers of this severe cruise game show.

"Okay!" he says. "The results are in. Our runners-up, with seven points, are Maggie Jo and Baron!"

Thunderous applause. They stand and bow like royalty.

"And our winners, with eight points, winning by only one point, are the famous and very funny couple that makes me believe in romance–give it up for–Aurora and Darius from Anchorage Alaska!"

The room explodes in applause and a wave of energy and support!

I freeze.

We... won?

We stand automatically, hands lifted as the crowd cheers. A staff member hands me a giant golden certificate.

> Exclusive Newlyweds Only VIP Excursion —
> Private Whale-Watching & Glacier Calving Tour with Captain Ophelia Rossi.

My stomach drops straight through the floor and into the ocean.

That's a tour my dad, our employer, asked us to review.

The universe is mocking me. Aggressively.

Chase thrusts the mic at us. "How does it feel to be our Holiday Princess Newlywed Winners, again?"

"I'm too sexy for this win! Too sexy for this boat! So sexy it hurts!" I blurted, quoting the song Darius and I love to butcher.

The crowd laughs at my joke.

Darius throws an arm around my shoulders, pulling me close. His velvet blazer is shockingly soft. "We're honored," he says smoothly, the consummate performer. "We love this ship. We love romance. We love... whales."

"Love whales," I echo weakly into the mic.

Maggie Jo hugs me tight as we leave the stage, smelling like sugar cookies and triumph.

"Honey, you two are hysterical," she says, pressing my cheeks between her hands. "You got good hearts."

Baron pats my shoulder. "You deserve the win. Have fun on your trip and enjoy the bragging rights."

After the game, the lounge shifts into cozy mode. The lights dim a little. Christmas jazz plays softly. Staff bring around trays of cocoa and tiny cookies.

We sit with Maggie Jo and Baron for a while, basking in the kind of giddy, exhausted post-performance haze that reminds me of stepping offstage after a high school play.

It's the first time this whole trip that I don't feel like I'm drowning or hiding.

People stop by our table just to say hi.

"You guys were so funny."

"You remind me of my niece and her husband."

"We love you!"

Every kind word adds another layer of guilt... but also something else.

Belonging.

Maybe this trip doesn't have to be a disaster.

Maybe I can make it work—for Grant and the family business, and, most of all, for me.

At the bar, I start to order, but don't see a menu beyond the top-shelf bottles of alcohol. "Uh, can I get a peppermint... thing?"

The bartender, a guy with kind eyes and an elaborate robotic tattoo on his wrist, leans in. "Mocktail? I got you."

He winks.

I blink. "Oh, I'm not—"

He nods, all solemn understanding. "Proud of you, hun."

A bright pink drink with cranberries and sugar on the rim appears in front of me. A small note on the printed receipt with my name reads, "MOCKTAIL ONLY."

Darius elbows me. "How can you be cut off before you even get crazy stupid?"

His phone dings with a notification at the same time mine buzzes.

I glance down.

A voice message from Lisa.

I hit play.

"Girl," Lisa's voice crackles through my phone speaker. "Saw snaps with you tagged on my socials. You two are ICONIC. Also, funny thing, I saw your ex, Alexis, at my office, my Alaskan Dating Service office. She asked about you? Like with *interested energy*??! WTF, right? Call me. Love you, BYE."

My soul liquefies and melts onto the wood bar. The pink drink suddenly tastes like betrayal.

Darius's jaw drops. "Your ex asked about you?" He claps his hands. "Oh, someone has massive regrets. You know what they say about dating in Alaska... *the odds are good, but the goods are odd.* Get ready for the expensive gift, like Manolo shoes you can't walk in, and the inevitable hook-up when you get back to Anchorage."

"I can't do that heartbreak, again," I whisper, clutching the pink glass. "Luckily, I don't have to, now that I'm *happily* married!"

He sips his champagne, completely unbothered. "Ugh."

I glare at him. Before I can retort, I notice a shift in the vibe of the room. A subtle energy change, like the air temperature just dropped twenty degrees.

I *feel* her before I see her.

Captain Rossi approaches, and the other guests subtly step aside, parting naturally to bring her closer to me. The white of her uniform starkly contrasts with the dim, cozy lighting.

"You performed well," she says when she reaches our table, her voice velvet and dangerous. "The ship adores you."

I almost inhaled a cranberry from my cranberry fizz.

"I'm... uh... relatable," I stammer, the lie catching in my throat.

Her mouth twitches, a faint, almost imperceptible curving of her lips.

She steps a little closer. The scent of sea salt and expensive cologne is immediately overwhelming. "Your joy draws attention," she says. "It's intoxicating, *Cara mia*."

Guilt punches me square in the sternum.

Fake joy. Fake wife. Fake marriage. Fake *everything*.

She studies my face like she's reading a map, only she understands the treacherous terrain.

"You are tense, again?" she asks, the simple question a direct hit.

"Nope!" I chirp, practically vibrating with tension. "Perfect! Married bliss! Yay! Whales and... feelings." *I am a mess.*

Her eyes soften, the tiniest crack in the armor. "Marriage is not always bliss." There's an unexpected, deep resonance in her voice, a hint of history and pain. *Her* history.

Before I can ask, she nods formally, her attention refocusing, the armor snapping back into place. "Rest. Tomorrow, I will see you for your private glacier tour."

She walks away before I can respond, leaving a lingering chill in her wake.

Darius leans in, his eyes dancing and his love radar practically audible. "Quick question," he murmurs. "Are you falling in love with the hot captain, or just spiraling?"

"Maybe," I whisper. "*Yes*."

Chapter 9

Breaking the Ice (and Darius's Stomach)

Day 3: Valdez, Alaska

Glaciers gleam around me like ancient gods. Sea lions bark on rocky outcrops. A faint billowy cloud brushes snow peaks like powdering a donut.

The perfect Alaska day. The kind my father advertises and sells to tourists. The kind I should be thrilled to enjoy, while I'm here reviewing this whale watching tour for the family business.

I turn to share this movement with Darius, just in time to see him pitch forward, as if he's aggressively flirting with the Pacific Ocean.

Then he vomits.

Violently.

"Death! Release me!" he wails between heaves, clutching the railing as the tiny sightseeing boat bobs gently on the water—barely rocking, honestly.

I pat his back, trying to be supportive and not laugh, but a laugh escapes anyway. "Why didn't you tell me you get seasick?"

He groans, unable to talk.

"When have I ever been on a boat? I don't fish and I'm more of an indoorsy, Netflix and Chill kind of a guy."

"On a scale of one to The Exorcist, how are you feeling?"

He dry-heaves, then weakly glares at me. "This is worse. I hope at least this is toning my abs into a chiseled six pack because there better be a silver lining."

"True," I say, smoothing his hair. "And your eyebrows are still absolute fire."

"You better put that in my eulogy."

"I'll embroider it on a pillow."

I inhale—salt spray and crisp glacier breeze. It hits my lungs with a crisp, clean feel. I exhale, and it fogs white in front of me because Alaska loves to remind you it's winter even when you still haven't accepted it.

Darius groans and leans over the rail again, giving the fjord another breakfast regret monologue. Meanwhile, our eager cruise naturalist, Chase—who was ignoring us in favor of narrating loudly to another couple—finally notices Darius is dying.

"Calving is named from the First Native, err.. Indigenous word, Calvinichatta, meaning water goddess birthing... Oh my gosh!" Chase yelps, waving his hands like he's trying to catch the attention of deaf people. "I thought you were gasping in awe, but nope—that's vomit!"

He rushes over, his orange puffer and shiny boots squeaking with each movement. "Okay champ, let's get you inside where I can warm you up. Fun fact, even though it looks gross, Alaskan water is full of electrolytes because—"

"It's... salt water," I offer.

Chase winks like I'm part of his talk, giving me my finger guns. "Exactly! So super hydrating."

"No," I say, appalled. "The opposite. You can't drink any sea water."

"Who's the Naturalist?" He grins like Florida invented science. "I love a spirited debate! C'mon Darius."

He loops Darius's arm over his shoulder and helps him toward the cabin.

"Wifey-Poo?" Darius croaks dramatically. "Don't... remarry until my body is cold."

"You'll be fine," I promise. "Also, it's freezing out here, your body is already cold."

Chase brightens. "Oh, don't worry, I'll take excellent care of him." He winks again. I'm ninety percent sure we are going to be the best of friends.

I am not!

Darius tries to whisper to me, but it comes out as a damp croak. "Save yourself. Go on without me..."

Then he disappears inside with Chase, leaving me alone on the stern deck, breath puffing in little clouds, bundled in my one warm-ish piece of clothing—my white bride hoodie, sequined BRIDE sparkling with each tilt of the boat, layered over... summer clothes. Because I am unprepared in every conceivable way.

I rub my bare, shivering hands up and down my arms and try—TRY—to look normal even though I can feel eyes on me.

Not just eyes.

Her eyes.

Control. Command. Cinnamon warmth and ice melt in a single look.

Captain Rossi stands at the railing like she was carved from the wind itself—coat navy and perfectly tailored, hair tucked under her cap with aristocratic precision, the Alaskan gusts swirling around her like they know better than to mess with her. She looks like the kind of woman who could command armies or make you apologize for existing in the softest, most devastating way.

I pretend I don't feel her gaze.

I absolutely feel her gaze.

It's like swallowing a glacier that thaws sharp and slow inside my ribs.

She steps toward me across the observation deck—measured, grounded, confident. Each footfall looks intentional, like she's aware the whole ship pauses to watch her be extraordinary.

"Cara, my Holiday Princess," she says in that Italian-lilt voice that pours fuel on my racing heart.

"Your husband is... seasick?"

"Oh, that." I gesture vaguely toward the boat's cabin, which is probably faintly echoing with Darius's dramatic retching. "Yeah, he's basically recreating Titanic in there. The one-woman version. Without the awkward nude drawing scene. Or, uh... the buoyancy."

Her lips twitch—a tiny upward shift I immediately treat as a personal victory. My heart almost leaps across the deck.

"Good," she says.

"Good?" I blink.

"He will be resting," she clarifies smoothly. "Which means he will not be here to... hover."

Hover?

My stomach swoops and drops.

"I don't think he hovers—"

"You," she interrupts gently, stepping closer until her breath is visible between us in soft white clouds, "are shaking."

I glance down. I am indeed. My fingers are stiff, pink, borderline tragic.

Before I can excuse myself or invent yet another lie—

She lets out the softest sigh, one that feels more frustrated at the universe than at me.

Then she shrugs off her coat.

Her immaculate, wool-lined, heavy, warm, smells-like-cedar-and-expensive-adult coat.

And she drapes it over my shoulders.

Before I can protest, she adjusts the collar at my neck, gloved fingers brushing my skin.

Everything inside me electrocutes.

I make a sound. I hope it sounds human. The sound is more of a confused orca squeal.

"Captain," I start weakly, "I can't—"

"You will wear it," she says simply, as if this were a royal decree.

Wrapped in her coat, I feel small, ridiculous, safe, and faintly like I'm about to commit a crime.

She turns to the glacier ahead—massive, cathedral-blue, haloed in silver light—and her voice shifts.

"This is Columbia Glacier," she murmurs, reverent. "One of the largest tidewater glaciers in Alaska."

I swallow hard.

She's close enough that I can see the snowflakes catching on her eyelashes.

Close enough that if I breathed wrong, I might accidentally kiss her shoulder or her collar or something catastrophically embarrassing.

"A glacier looks solid," she says quietly, eyes fixed on the ice, "but eventually, it breaks. And when it does, it makes a terrible groaning. A moaning."

Her voice dips. My spine does a full electric wave.

I am no longer thinking about glaciers.

I'm thinking about her hand brushing my neck.

And Alexis.

And how Alexis hated talking about her emotions or anything that wasn't scheduled.

And how the Captain looks like she schedules storms.

"You are not dressed for this climate," Captain Rossi says.

I look down at my thin hoodie. "I'm dressed for a tragic honeymoon surprise."

Her mouth twitches. "Indeed."

A chunk of ice calves from the glacier—thunder cracking across the Sound. I flinch, shivering.

"Romantic, yes?" she asks softly.

"Depends on your vibe," I whisper. "Some people love a dramatic breakup. Nature just ghosted that glacier chunk really hard."

Another micro-smile. I'm collecting them like rare Pokémon.

"You are... strange," she says.

"Thank you," I beam. "I think."

Silence settles between us—not the awkward kind, a still, comforting silence. Everyone else has slipped inside, leaving just the Captain and me on the deck.

Then—quietly—

She steps closer until our elbows brush.

"You are quiet today," she says.

Words are dangerous. Words crack lies open. Words uncover truths.

"I'm thinking," I manage.

"About?" she prompts gently.

"Whales," I lie.

Her gaze slices clean through me. "No. Something else."

Snowflakes drift around us like glittered secrets. My chest feels too thin to hold a heartbeat.

"I'm glad you are here," she murmurs, "It's just us now."

And suddenly it is.

Just us. At the edge of the world.

I lift the binoculars to hide my face and gasp.

"Whale!" I blurt, pointing.

She leans in—shoulder brushing mine—to follow my line of sight.

Her presence is a gravitational field. My pulse stumbles, then races.

"Ah," she says. "A humpback."

"I love them," I breathe. "They're mysterious and beautiful and gentle, but if you disrespect their space they will absolutely slap you with their tail."

Her laugh is low and smoky. "You see the world in... in an interesting way."

"I'm consistent," I mutter.

She tilts her head, studying me like she's memorizing my freckles, my blush, the way my hands clutch her coat.

"Tell me." She says at last, "about your wedding. And the rest of your love story I did not hear. At dinner."

A pause.

"Or during the newlywed game."

I choke on air.

"Our—our what?"

"You are newlyweds, no?" Her voice stays soft, but her gaze sharpens. "So... tell me how you fell in love."

Oh no.

I should have kept notes. Our lies are out here free-range and unsupervised.

My panic-brain takes the wheel.

"Well," I say, "we met in school. But we fell in love... at... Target."

She blinks once. Slowly. "Target."

"Yep! We reached for the same jumbo bag of Cool Ranch Doritos. Very Notebook mashed up with snacks and retail therapy..."

"You wanted chips," she says, dry.

"They're a cornerstone of American romance," I insist.

Her face remains still, but her eyes spark.

"And then?"

"Then we bonded over hating decaf coffee."

"Decaf."

"It's an abomination. You drink it when you've given up on life."

She steps closer, gaze slicing right into me. "For a newlywed, you don't seem to mind being away from your husband. I notice you don't stand close together or hold each other."

"I stand close to him. He knows my heart is always with him."

"Your eyes," she murmurs, "are not."

I freeze.

She lifts her gloved hand and brushes a stray hair off my cheek. Slowly. Deliberately.

My breath stutters.

"Tell me." She whispers, "why you avoid your husband's touch. If you were mine..."

Her fingers drift down—brushing my jaw, the line beneath my chin—"I would never get enough of this soft skin. This silky hair. This blush..."

Her fingertips graze the column of my neck, feather-light.

My knees nearly give out.

"I—" I gasp, a sound scraping from somewhere deep.

A massive crack thunders through the fjord as another block of ice calves, splitting from the glacier into a white explosion.

The sound jolts me, and I stumble backward, words and secrets and panic exploding inside me.

And she watches.

All calm.

Waiting for the truth I can't give.

"Captain, I have to be honest with you about—"

My throat closes. My brain panics and yanks the steering wheel of the conversation off a cliff.

"—chocolate!" I blurt.

She blinks, the slightest tilt of her head. "What?"

"Both the solid chocolate and hot chocolate," I ramble, too fast, too bright. "I—uh—I love them. I make the best non-alcoholic and alcoholic hot chocolate. Ever. Seriously, like—award winning. If there were awards. Which there should be."

Her brows lift slightly, amusement flickering like the soft glow of her cabin lights.

I keep talking because apparently my fight-or-flight includes rambling about chocolate.

"Okay, picture this... white chocolate, milk chocolate and butter cream with freshly grated cinnamon—not the sad dust you get at grocery stores—the actual sticks that you buy. Then you add this—"

I'm babbling so fast I might actually leave my body.

Her lips curve. Slow. Devastating.

"You hide behind talking about chocolate?"

"It's a—skill," I squeak.

Her gaze drags over my face, down to the mug in my hands, back up again.

"You are sweating," she observes.

"I don't sweat," I insist, mortified. "I glisten."

A soft huff of laughter—not quite a laugh, but the warm exhale of someone who finds me... charmingly unhinged—leaves her.

Then she reaches into a small inside pocket of her jacket and removes an insulated container and pours the steaming liquid into my empty mug.

"Hot chocolate," she says, low and gentle. "Perhaps you are hiding something sweeter than hot chocolate recipes, *Mrs. Newlywed.*"

My brain short-circuits. I nearly dropped the mug. My hand brushes hers—warm glove brush against my cold fingers—and my entire nervous system throws sparkles into the air.

"Y-you know," I croak, trying not to die, "fun fact, Rudolph was originally—"

"Do not," she interrupts, her voice velvet-wrapped steel, "fill silence with anymore meaningless rambling."

My mouth snaps shut so fast I probably chip a tooth.

She looks pleased.

Snowflakes drift between us, tiny white sparks. The glacier ahead cracks again, an echoing boom rolling through the fjord.

She turns slightly toward the ice. "A glacier does not pretend," she says softly. "It is honest. Brutal. Beautiful. It shows its truth eventually. It cannot help it."

Her words melt something in my chest.

"I wish I was a glacier then," I whisper.

She studies me for a long, steady beat. "Are you an honest woman, Aurora?"

My name in her accent steals the air from my lungs.

"I... want to be," I manage. My voice is thin, trembling.

She watches that truth land inside me. Watches me struggle with it.

Her coat dwarfs me, and I curl deeper into it, sipping hot chocolate that tastes like melted snowflakes and childhood holiday movies and—safety.

My throat feels thick. I should confess. She can tell I'm hiding something. She *feels* it.

Before I can open my mouth—

My phone DINGS. A satellite miracle.

A tidal wave of notifications floods in.

Dad says, "Great work reviewing the spa. And congrats on the game! Call me."

Lisa's text, "HELLOOOO ARE YOU IN LOVE WITH THE CAPTAIN YET because Darius gave me ALL the tea."

Another Lisa text, "I stalked the ship hashtag. You look like the cutest newlywed. Obsessed. Also, if you and Darius ever get REAL married, I'm planning that wedding."

My heart slams so hard my ribs complain.

Captain Rossi watches, her gaze sharp as a glacier's edge. "Important messages?"

"Just—family," I croak. And Lisa. Human tornado. Disaster prophet. Threat to my entire operation.

Rossi's eyes narrow, reading far too much.

I panic-babble. "I wish the photographer was here to get a picture of the whale. But it's weird I haven't seen any of my pictures in the gallery yet. Or—me in any of them."

Her expression shifts. Not shock. Not confusion. Something else—a quiet click of decision.

"I will inquire," she says immediately. "The ship photographers should have captured many pictures of you, *Bella*."

The word hits me like heat under my skin.

"You will have beautiful memories," she adds, voice softening. "Even next to the wrong person... you are a beauty."

I choke on hot chocolate so violently that I almost baptize the polished deck in cocoa. "S-sure."

Her gaze holds mine—warm, intent, unbearably intimate.

Then she nods toward the glacier. "Everything that appears solid breaks eventually, Aurora."

My pulse stutters.

My ribs constrict.

She's not talking about ice.

"I—uh—I should check on Darius," I stammer, stepping backward like I'm escaping gravity's pull. "He's probably arguing with Chase about... moose... something."

She doesn't stop me.

She doesn't touch me again.

But her voice follows—silk and promise and something far too dangerous.

"We will continue our conversation later."

Not a threat.

Not a request.

A certainty.

I stumble inside the cabin, swallowed in her coat, my phone lighting up with Lisa's chaos, my heart thundering like I've sprinted through a blizzard.

I hear Darius and Chase arguing down the hall about whether Moose Tracks ice cream counts as culturally authentic.

I am absolutely going to die of romantic anxiety before this cruise ends.

How is my *relaxing holiday* the least relaxing thing in my entire chaotic life?

Chapter 10

Back to the Holiday Princess for More Trouble

Day 3: At Sea

We step off the Zodiac onto the gangway, and Darius collapses. I bite down on a giggle because his flair sits at an eleven today, though guilt pokes at me since I got glacier views, a breaching whale. He got... seawater and gravity punting his dignity overboard.

"I swear on Beyoncé's left earring," he wheezes, sliding down the rail, "if one more molecule of ocean mist taps my lips, I'm filing a lawsuit."

"You can't sue the ocean," I say, patting his back like he's ninety-three.

He sharpens a glare. "Watch me. I'll subpoena Aquaman. He'll swim in here with his tris—" he stops, swallows, grimaces, "—and I'll glare at him too."

"You wouldn't show weakness in front of Aquaman."

"I threw up seven times and died at least twice," he corrects, hand splayed on his chest. "I am weak. Spiritually. Emotionally."

Chase hops off the Zodiac behind us, majestic as a PBS host, cheerful as Santa on espresso.

"Fun fact!" he announces. "Whales vomit too sometimes!"

Darius's soul leaves his body. I grip his elbow before he folds again.

"Why would you tell him that?" I hiss. "Why?"

"I love science!" Chase beams. "And fun! And sharing my knowledge! Also, puking? Super normal. Navy SEALs do it. I do it every time I get Botox."

He shimmies toward the ship like he's hosting *Queer Planet Earth*, and Darius mutters, "Take me, Lord. Pride left hours ago."

I hook my arm through his and guide him toward the atrium doors.

Warmth smacks my frozen face. Pine garlands. Piano music twinkling like holiday sugar. The gingerbread smell is thick in the air. Red bows are exploding everywhere like Christmas sneezed on the ship.

And on the massive atrium LED screen—

Us.

Us, on the screen during the Newlyweds Game. *Us in HD.* Us, in the exact moment Darius yelled, at a volume that could shatter glass, "HER SECRET IS SHE LIKES TO ROLE PLAY A BOSS POWER DYNAMIC—AND NOT JUST IN THE BEDROOM!"

"And there I am, fifty feet tall on the screen, choking on my mocktail."

"Oh no," I whisper.

"Oh yes," Darius replies, suddenly upright again.

Passengers turn. They spot us. They start applauding like we're the cruise mascots. Or a circus act. Or both.

I freeze so hard I might be forever broken.

Darius executes a full bow because he's apparently not sick now.

A random woman screams, "CONGRATULATIONS, LOVEBUGS!"

Another yells, "KISS! KISS! KISS!"

"No!" I blurt, waving my arms like I'm traffic control at a small-town airport. "We're... uh... saving intimacy for later. After Dramamine."

I cringe immediately at the mental image of Darius's post-vomit mouth anywhere near mine.

Darius fans himself. "My fandom understands. My stomach rebelled today. No kisses."

The clapping ramps up. Someone starts a chant. I contemplate dissolving into seawater.

Through my teeth, I whisper, "Why can't I just blend in with the crowd?"

"Because your amazing wifey-poo and I'm a sparkling peacock," he whispers back.

I want to scream. Whoever decided public humiliation counts as entertainment is getting a complaint card so big it qualifies as a novel.

Maggie Jo bustles toward us in a leopard-print coat that radiates Southern holiday chaos. Baron trails behind her.

"HONEY!" Maggie Jo bellows. "Y'all looked PRECIOUS! And poor Darius! I ain't seen a groom look this sick since my aunt's fourth weddin', when her fiancé realized they were second cousins. Georgia family, not Louisiana family!" She raises a hand, as if geography clears it up.

Baron assesses Darius with clinical precision. "You appear pale. We can send ginger ale to the room."

Maggie Jo claps. "Y'all comin' to karaoke tonight? We're doin' 'Islands in the Stream,' but with more Southern spice and more vocals."

"We can't—" I start, already imagining trauma.

"Yes," Darius answers instantly, straightening like karaoke resurrected him.

"We were going to nap and hydrate," I hiss.

"These people need art," he whispers urgently. "My Beyoncé medley offers joy. Holiday joy."

Baron adjusts his glasses. "You two continue to perplex me."

My soul unplugs itself and floats toward the ceiling.

We inch toward the elevators. I whisper, "I need to call Lisa and Dad. And return this coat—"

I tug the huge Captain's jacket closer. It smells like cedar, salt, and pure authority.

Do not think about the authority kink Darius broadcast to half this ship.

Great. Thinking about it more.

Chase materializes behind Darius.

"Pre-karaoke cocktails? I know a bartender who does peppermint-mocha margarita shots!"

Darius lights up. "Yes!"

"No," I beg. "Please don't abandon me—"

He pats my cheek. "My love, you'll survive ten minutes. Growth!"

"Through abandonment?"

"Growth-through-abandonment!" he sings, following Chase away.

I slide into the glass elevator—even in here the mirrors, sparkles, pine garlands hug every corner. As if right on cue, Captain Rossi steps in behind me as the doors seal.

Oh no.

The universe dislikes me. Fair.

The elevator glides upward through the atrium. Glittering trees glow below, along with guests taking ugly-cry selfies, as if public romance keeps them alive. I clamp my palms on the rail, gripping for emotional survival.

Rossi stands military-still, hands behind her back, gaze like glacier steel blended with melted chocolate. Disaster combo for my dignity.

Her voice hits soft, nearly a whisper. "You fled after the glacier tour."

A squeak escapes my throat. A squeak. "I didn't want to interrupt... the ice vibes."

Her eyes dip to me. "Ice carries no need for permission, Cara."

"I... uh... also exist without permission?" My mouth throws that out. I regret everything instantly.

She steps closer. Too close. Snowflake glitter twinkles on her sleeve. My pulse turns into a hyper otter doing aquatic backflips.

"You ran," she says.

"Nope!" My voice cracks. "I had to check on my sick husband. There were recycled liquids and sickness coming out of him..."

I need an arrest for public awkwardness.

"You stand nervous." Her head tilts faintly. "Newlyweds are at peace near each other. They do not tense up or get sick."

"We tense supportively?" I attempt. This helps nothing.

Her stare stays locked. "Your body betrays you."

Something in her expression softens, which ruins me further.

"You did not plan for this marriage," she adds. "You please others by reflex... then end up paired with the wrong partner. And a man."

A swallow scrapes my throat.

Silence drops—heavy, cold, crushing.

Rossi's voice drops. "Marriages fail when lies crack under winter pressure."

My bones nearly puddle. "We're fine. Super fine. Full joy. Bliss."

"You hold no want for him. You refused a kiss."

"I—uh—avoid vomit!"

My brain short-circuits. This transforms into a power-dyke interrogation, and I flunk every vibe metric.

Rossi studies me. Something flickers behind her gaze—loneliness.

"When someone draws your heart," she murmurs, voice low enough to melt metal, "you crave closeness. Even in discomfort. Avoidance signals fear, not devotion."

Alexis flashes through my mind—her perfect posture, her airtight schedule, her curated emotions. A life with little space for my chaos. Letting her go was like stepping off a cliff on purpose, convinced wings would grow. They didn't. I'm still midair, still grabbing at anything that feels like truth.

My voice comes out tiny. "What if they don't... need you?"

Rossi's eyes lift to mine—piercing, sure.

"Then they are a fool."

Oh.

Heat surges up my neck. My cheeks burn so fiercely I'm surprised the elevator doesn't fog over.

The floor hums beneath us.

The elevator slows.

Rossi steps closer—barely half an inch.

Her coat slips from my shoulders as I instinctively lean into her space, into her warmth, into the gravity she radiates. Our breath mingles. Her hand rises, almost touching my jaw, fingers hovering with devastating precision. My heart trips over itself.

"Aurora, my Bella," she whispers, like my name is a secret.

The elevator dings.

The doors slide open.

And standing right there—wide-eyed—mouth open—camera raised—is a cruise photographer.

He freezes.

I freeze.

Rossi does **not** freeze.

Her smile curves slowly, like she planned this.

FLASH.

The camera goes off the bright flash blinds me.

"Oh my *gosh!*" the photographer squeals. "That was adorable. The coat! The leaning! The whole—everything!"

"I—WHAT—NO—WAIT—DELETE—"

I flail to the side, nearly knocking over a decorative poinsettia. "My face was a panic smile, not a holiday cheer smile!"

But he's already scampering down the hallway on a mission.

Rossi watches him go, her posture relaxed, her expression smugly composed.

"An intriguing image," she murmurs. "No doubt."

My insides collapse into warm, panicked pudding.

Rossi steps just slightly into my space again, gaze tracking every micro-emotion in my face.

"You care deeply," she says softly. "Public judgment crushes you."

I swallow hard, pulse shaking my ribs. "Only when it's—complicated."

She leans in just enough that I feel her breath against my cheek.

"Bella," she says, "it doesn't need to be complicated."

I stare at her. "The alternative equals chaos."

"Chaos often equals truth," she replies.

The doors nudge shut again. Trapping us in eye contact. Frozen. Breathe sharply. Air thin.

My chest throbs. Words climb my throat. I nearly confess everything.

"I—" My voice cracks. "Captain, I'm not—"

"Your floor." Gentle. Precise.

Saved. Ruined.

I stumble out with zero coordination. My pulse pounds in my ears, and I wonder if she can hear it too.

Rossi holds the door, steady as stone.

I fumble with the coat. "Here, um—thanks—I—"

Her fingers brush my arm. Electric sparks fire straight through my ribs. "You need this more than me."

My insides implode.

"I'm fine." My voice cracks again.

I swallow hard and try to return the coat. My hands shake.

"Thank you," I whisper.

"Keep it," she says.

My heartbeat stutters. "I can't."

"You return it when this voyage ends." Her tone drops to something oath-like. "Not a day sooner."

A sharp truth punches through me—she stands lonely in a way I recognize. A way I relate to. Captain. Isolated.

Softly, nearly lost under elevator holiday music, she adds, "It's nice not to stand alone."

My chest tilts sideways. "Okay," I breathe.

She steps back inside the elevator, then glances through the narrowing opening.

"Aurora."

My name dissolves me. "Yeah?"

"Stop running from the truth trying to surface. Ice cracks, yes. Light enters through cracks."

The doors slide shut. She disappears.

And I remain in the hallway clutching her coat like it anchors every chaotic spark inside me.

My phone buzzes.

Dad messages, "I can't wait to hear about the tour! Was it worth the $1200 price tag?"

A $1200 glacier excursion. Free.

These newlywed perks mean this lie is a big savings for me and the company.

I slump against the wall. My chest cracks, thaws, shines, sinks, spins—everything at once, like chocolate chunks tossed into boiling cocoa.

"I'm not making it through this cruise," I whisper into the hallway.

A shorebird screeches outside across the harbor like nature delivers commentary.

Footsteps echo. Darius sweeps around the corner holding a peppermint martini like he's hosting a holiday drag brunch.

"Great news," he declares. "I rise from my own ashes. Chase thinks I'm mysterious. Also, he told me whales sweat glitter. Do you think he believes that or drops lines like that to flirt?"

I blink at him with dead-inside accuracy. "Whales sweat zero glitter. Chase? Full belief. Zero hesitation."

Darius shrugs. "Who are we to crush his sparkle?" His eyes narrow. "Why is your face flush?"

"Captain Rossi interrogated my entire soul in an elevator."

He sips. "Hot."

"I think she KNOWS."

He gasps. "That you crave a nude-twister power-dyke showdown?"

"About *everything.*"

He tilts his head. "So, we'll kill it at karaoke to confirm we are the perfect couple.."

"I'm about to implode."

He presses my arm, voice softening. "No implosion until after our duet. Couples cruise, couples rules. We need a song together. Will you be the Will to my Grace? Rachel to my Ross? Milo to my Stitch?"

My brain spins. "Yeah."

Darius starts humming "All I Want for Christmas Is You," pitch-perfect, dramatic, full joy, like Mariah possessed his lungs.

Chapter 11

Glitter Nights, Karaoke Fights

Day 3: At Sea

The karaoke bar smells like spilled sugar, peppermint syrup, and something vaguely middle-school-dance-traumatic enough to make my nose twitch. Disco lights skitter over the ceiling, ricocheting off tinsel Christmas garlands like they're trying to trigger festive seizures. Someone hung a real wreath above the stage, and it's doing its best impression of me on a treadmill—drooping, struggling, barely surviving the cold sea air.

"Welcome to The *Christmas Couples Princess Holiday Night Mic!*" Chase bellows over synth beats, arms flung wide like this is the Super Bowl.

"Sorry—I have to say that for the recording." He points at the ship photographer, who is inexplicably holding a vintage camcorder. "Okay, holiday crew, let's sing like no one's pitch matters!"

The crowd cheers. Chase is a better emcee than he is a naturalist—which is alarming because his job involves knowing things to keep passengers safe.

"We're all family here on the Holiday Princess!" he yells.

More cheers. The room glows dark and sparkly and tacky-perfect. The portholes are fogged with breath and weather, and beyond them the Gulf of Alaska churns black and glittering, lit by the ship's outline of white bulbs and red trim. A carved black bear in a Santa hat guards the stage. The TV loop above the bar cycles through snow-capped mountains... sled dogs... an orca pod... then lingers *way* too long on two moose rutting.

"Romantic," I mutter.

Darius slips into our two-top and fans himself with the songbook. "Ah. This is where we were meant to be, Babes."

"It's *Wifey-Poo* to you," I say. "Husband-Poo."

He winces. "Okay, absolutely workshop that nickname. Workshop it like... urgently."

I peel off my fur-lined Bride hoodie and drape it over the back of the chair, and decide to tug Captain Rossi's wool-lined officer's coat back around me. The coat smells faintly like cedar, expensive soap, and international power imbalance.

Don't think about the Captain.

Oops. Now I'm thinking about the Captain. Aggressively thinking.

"How are you even upright," I hiss, "after throwing up for, like, four hours and then sitting through a two-hour dinner where Chase explained how Cleopatra invented Alaskan gold panning?"

"He had charts," Darius whispers reverently. Then shakes his head. "I purged all the negativity from my soul, and now I will sing."

"Great. I'll order my guilt—on the rocks to calm my nerves."

"Order two," he says, wiggling his eyebrows. "Also something with peppermint. And sugar crystals. And a mini candy cane stirrer. But like... classy."

"I can't walk up to the bar with a Starbucks holiday drink order for a nightcap. And you have to stop flirting with the bartender. And with Chase. And with anyone who is a man."

He gasps. "I *am* trying. This is my post-breakup cardio recovery plan, babe. Let me thrive."

"Cardio is stairs, not men whose name is Chase or whose cologne could kill mosquitoes."

As if summoned by the universe—or pheromones—Chase appears with a stage-crew lanyard and a necklace made of blinking Christmas bulbs.

"Fun fact," he says, slapping down new menus, "in Alaska, karaoke is legally required to include at least one Shania Twain song."

"That's not a law."

"It is in my heart," he says, leaning toward Darius. "You up first, superstar? I saved 'Born This Way' and 'Santa Tell Me.'"

Darius fans himself. "Tempting. But my best work happens in keys invented by goddesses. How about 'Bad Romance'? 'It's Raining Men'? Maybe... 'S&M'?"

Chase vibrates as if he's a Labrador seeing his favorite ball. "Say the word, and I'm pulling out the money gun."

"Money gun?" I echo.

"Oh yeah," Chase beams. "Full of Santa's Reindeer Bucks. You can cash them in at the gift shop for something extra special."

Darius preens. "Chase, Sweetie, I have never been more motivated to hit a high note."

I loudly clear my throat, trying to snap the love-bubble around them.

Both turn, though neither breaks eye contact with the other.

Then Chase sashays off toward the DJ booth, trailing peppermint glitter in spirit if not in fact.

Darius watches him go. "Wifey-Poo, did Santa just give me a Florida man with dimples?"

"Do not unwrap him," I warn.

I sink lower in my chair like I'm trying to fold myself into the table's decorative garland.

I'm still anxious from the glacier tour, from the Captain's voice echoing in the elevator—*lies always crack in the cold.*

The lies crack from trying to be five different Auroras at once: perfect honeymoon bride, undercover cruise reviewer, dutiful daughter, dependable friend-wife, and... me.

The me, who desperately wants to relax on my first actual vacation, not perform.

The me who still dreams of a honeymoon on a tropical cruise with turquoise water and zero secrets.

The me who is tall, awkward, and so tired of being observed like I'm an exhibit titled *Lesbian in Her Natural Habitat (Beware, Skittish).*

A server sets a hurricane glass in front of me—three umbrellas, two cherries, a pineapple slice doing Olympic-level balancing, and a plastic penguin staring straight into my soul.

"Your *North Pole Glow*," she chirps, hands clasped.

I blink at it. "Is everyone... getting this?" Because everywhere else I only see champagne flutes, and apparently marriage makes bubbles compulsory.

She leans in conspiratorially. "Nope. Just for you. And the penguin is commemorative. You can pop him into your wedding scrapbook."

I pick up the tiny hunk of plastic joy. It has "Royal Caribbean Princess Newlyweds Cruise" printed on the back in sparkly blue. "You know Alaska doesn't have penguins, right?"

Darius does not come to my defense. He is swamped, waving and hooting at Chase, who's putting on a Santa hat to kick off karaoke with "All I Want for Christmas Is You," because apparently the gig economy never sleeps.

"Are you sure?" She asks innocently, then lowers her voice. "No alcohol in that, sugar. We're keeping your secret. It's all mocktails. Even if they look boozy." She winks. "We support you."

"Oh," I say. What else can I say? Someone thinks I'm an alcoholic in recovery and is trying to keep me safe. Add that to my Jenga tower of lies.

"Bless you."

I sip. It's a slushie mix of weaponized Christmas joy. The chill surges into my sinuses into a brain freeze. I choke so dramatically that I might qualify as a drowning incident.

Darius doesn't notice. He's too busy giving Chase the kind of flirty grin that should come with a fire warning label. I wheeze into my drink until the brain freeze retreats.

On stage, Chase croons into the mic, encouraging couples to sway, and points randomly at people while laser-locking onto Darius. A woman near the front claps so far off-beat it should be illegal.

I lean my chin into my hand, letting the disco lights scatter across my face, feeling the acid rise in my throat like I swallowed a regret volcano. Maybe my cabin would be more relaxing. Or a glacier. Or an iceberg. Anything quiet.

A pair of colorful Converse walks by—black shirt, cozy Alaska fleece—and that tiny, stupid, tender longing rises again. Alexis should be here.

No. She shouldn't.

She chose her company. Her plan. Her future wife, who will stay home with her two future children and her perfectly organized calendar.

Not me.

But wanting isn't rational. It hits soft and aching, like a bruise you forget until someone leans on it.

I want to be desired.

To be someone's first choice. Not a fake wife. Not a cover story. Not a spy. Just... wanted.

"Okay, Mrs. Wifey-Poo," Darius says, nudging me. "What's our secret plan tonight? Which other events are we attending and reviewing for your father's tourism empire of joy?"

"We're going with the flow," I say. "Trying to be invisible. And maybe take some notes. Quietly."

He kisses my cheek, leaving a faint shimmer of his highlighter. "I know you hate the wife bit, but you can play at being anyone for two hours. After this vacation? You never have to be anything but yourself again. Also, pretending we're married is good practice for us."

I smile despite myself. He is infuriating. He is my favorite person alive.

"Next up!" Chase yodels. "Please give it up for our holiday royalty—Maggie Jo and Baron—with a special *seasonal* number!"

The room erupts. Maggie Jo struts onstage in cranberry-sequin glory. Baron adjusts the mic with Rotary-meeting precision. Maggie Jo sees us and blows a kiss.

I catch it like I'm doing mime improv. Surely that's straight. Or maybe, very not. I overthink it immediately.

"Honey," Maggie Jo drawls, "we're singin' 'Santa Baby'—but our version is our personalized version."

Baron clears his throat into the mic. "We have restructured the verses to honor our Southern culture." He pauses and adds, "please do not turn this into a hoedown."

The crowd cackles like it's the funniest joke ever written.

Darius turns slowly toward me when Baron emphasizes "ho," and I mouth, "*That's you,*" at him.

I sip my frozen sugar explosion again and let the ridiculousness soften the edges of everything. Outside, the Gulf is calm—too calm, the black water licking the ship.

It's only a few hours. I can do this. I can be a wife. I can cruise. I can lie convincingly.

By the time Maggie Jo purrs, "Slip a sable under the tree—for me," the room is swaying along. Baron harmonizes in a low alto that gives me sophisticated queer goosebumps. They're not raunchy. They're romantic and gentle and familiar with each other's breath.

The love I want someday. The kind that whispers between lines, *you're doing great, babe.* Not fragile. Not conditional. Just steady.

"Future us," Darius whispers, blinking fast.

"I wish," I say. My heart pings an SOS.

The server leans over as I scribble in my tiny notebook. "You takin' notes on your favorite server to tip extra?" she teases.

"God, no," I blurt. Then backpedal, "I mean—yes. Wait. No—uh—I just take notes during... music." I flip the page, but she is absolutely reading upside down.

"'Evening karaoke with oddly chosen songs and an annoying fake Naturalist as MC. Ventilation A-, bar team A+.'" She smirks. "Ooooh. Are you a secret influencer?"

"I'm a student," I say, which is technically accurate. "Collecting data for... an English paper."

"Right. Well, don't forget us when it's tip time." She slides me a coaster with another penguin on it. I make a mental note to remember later that this ship has adopted a penguin mascot and that Alaska deserves better.

"Next up!" Chase calls. "My favorite newlyweds! Give it up for Darius and Aurora!"

The room swivels. Applause echo. My heart sprints off the ship and into the frigid Bering Sea.

Darius grabs my hands. "Okay, we can't do the duet I signed us up for because it was 'Santa Baby,' and we can't repeat a song that was another couple's hit—"

"I have a song," I say.

Suddenly I'm onstage. The mic is cold, heavy, and alive.

The intro starts. It's "All By Myself."

My emergency karaoke song. My truth song.

"You want me to—?" Chase asks, for once, seeing through my fake smile.

"No," I say. "Let it play."

The lights warm my face. The room blurs soft shapes and sparkles. I inhale.

And I sing.

Not big. Not a diva. Truth-sized. Glacier-sized. Cracked but shining.

Every line is the ache I've been swallowing for months. Every note is a confession. I'm tired of pretending. I'm tired of hiding. I want to be wanted for me.

Halfway through the first chorus, I feel a shift. A cold current behind me. A hush under my ribs.

The back door opens.

Captain Rossi steps inside like she's entering a chapel—coat collar up, hat in hand, shadows clinging to her like obedient soldiers. She does not belong in this tacky holiday bar.

But she belongs in this moment.

Our eyes meet. Her officer's coat—still carrying her scent—suddenly burns against my skin.

The note in my throat scrapes raw. I lift my gaze to her. My voice steadies, then sharpens.

She doesn't move. Doesn't blink. Her jaw ticks. Her mouth—normally smugly perfect—softens into something dangerous. Something too close to the unpredictable moods that lived in my mother—beautiful one moment, volcanic the next.

Jealousy, fascination, hunger, anger. My bones know her expression. And I'm terrified of it. And drawn to it. And confused by it.

I finish the last note to a roar of applause. A whistle. Darius screams. My chest shudders with the aftermath.

I laugh-cry into the mic. "This song was sponsored by my very stable marriage and the staff's generous drinks."

Laughter erupts. I bow because what else do you do after emotionally unraveling in public?

From the back of the room, Captain Rossi steps forward—just one step—eyes locked on me like she's already deciding what she plans to do next.

Chase's voice detonates the second I step offstage, "WHEW! Give it up for my girl—excuse me, Darius's girl—Wifey-Poo AurorAAAAA!"

I pass him the mic like it's a bomb. My brain is static. I can't look at the back of the room where she stands, and I also can't stop looking. Captain Rossi watches me with that expression—*the truth is inside you, and I will extract it with a spoon.* Italian spoon. Silver, probably engraved.

"How about a duet?" Chase points at Darius.

Darius preens. "Oh absolutely, darling. Anything for ratings."

Chase laughs. "You can't let your partner upstage you!"

Darius leans in, sparkly menace in his eyes. "Time for me to shine."

"Take your phone," I whisper. "If this ends with you in a walk-in freezer with a hot Entertainment Staff guy, I'm not calling Search and Rescue."

He scoffs. "What am I, a complete horny slut? We'd go to an unused coat closet or storage room." He pockets his phone. "Safety first."

They launch into a holiday medley—Chase harmonizing badly, Darius singing like Beyoncé's competitive cousin.

A server slides a champagne flute into my hand. "Looks real. Alcohol-free," she says proudly.

"Thank you." I want the real version. I'd drink warm champagne at this point. I tuck my review notebook into my pocket and wonder if anyone will notice if I sneak out and sprint directly into the void of the night—I mean, my stateroom.

"Live a little," she says, chin-tipping toward the shadows. "Also, uh, the Captain sent that umbrella pineapple slushy thing earlier. I forgot to tell you."

My heart pirouettes into a wall.

I look up.

At the back rail, Captain Rossi lifts a champagne flute at me. The faintest toast. A silent *I see you,* or worse... *I know!*

I tip my mocktail back at her because my anxiety has hijacked my motor skills. Her mouth twitches upward. A millimeter. Enough to ruin me.

Maggie Jo appears. "We sounded sensational, honey," she shouts, peppermint breath swirling. "But your ballad? Lawd have mercy, you wrung me out like an ol' washcloth."

Baron appears beside her, sipping club soda like it's bourbon neat. Maggie Jo eyes the backstage door where Darius vanished. "Your groom's powderin' his nose with the naturalist?"

"He likes talking about... nature," I say. "And men named Chase."

Maggie Jo gasps theatrically. "Open marriage?" she stage-whispers at a volume audible in Juneau.

I sigh. "Sure."

Baron pats my arm. "If you're new to it, keep it closed year one. Build that core romance. Avoid future tax issues."

Maggie Jo wags her bejeweled finger. "Too many love connections is how I ended up married three times. But you two look solid. Whatever you're doin'—keep doin' it."

I fold over the bar. "Maybe I shouldn't have come. I'm living..." *a lie* "...in the past."

"Impossible," Baron says. "Your energy is aggressively present."

The backstage door swings open.

Darius and Chase reappear—glowing, giggly, suspiciously disheveled. Darius's lips are glossy, Chase's hair is doing interpretive dance, *and Darius is now wearing a sparkly Christmas scarf that absolutely did not exist five minutes ago.*

It's shimmering red-and-green, covered in sequins, and tied around his neck in a way that says *someone very flirtatious* styled it for him.

My stomach drops.

He tries to casually smooth it like he's always owned a stripper-elf accessory. The more he fusses, the guiltier he looks.

He's happy.

He's also going to blow our cover.

And the awful whisper in my brain, *You're blowing it too. Your face. Your singing. The mistletoe kiss in front of everyone. The almost-kiss in the elevator. The—you know—everything.*

Chase practically levitates to the DJ booth, hitting a fader with enough enthusiasm to summon Santa himself.

"Family!! Guess what!! Today's cruise photos just dropped in the Atrium Billboard Bonanza! If you made memories, go see 'em!!"

My internal organs seize.

Time halts.

I hear snowflakes scream.

In my mind—Elevator doors. Flash.

Rossi's face inches from mine.

My hands are in her coat.

The photographer gushes, *"Adorable!"*

"Nope," I say. "No thank you. No memories today."

I move fast—but immediately slam into a solid wall of human Christmas sweaters, joining the sweater pub crawl. Great. My life's falling apart, and the entire cast of Rudolph blocks the exit.

"Excuse me—sorry—my impending doom is time-sensitive—"

Maggie Jo cackles. "You get caught stealin' the silverware?"

I choke. "Bathroom."

Across the bar, Rossi's gaze sharpens. Not the playful toast now. Predator-knows-prey-is-panicking sharp. She takes one step down from the rail.

I freeze. If she sees that photo before I can delete it, everything collapses—Grant's trust.

Our job.

This entire free trip.

My tuition.

My cover story.

My sanity.

"You look like you'll faint," the bartender murmurs. She slides over a new drink—another umbrella monstrosity. "This one's also from the Captain."

I look up from the tangle of sweaters barricading me.

Rossi raises her glass again. Her smile curves. Slow. Confident. A little wicked. A lot of knowingness.

Is she taunting me?

Does she think I'm flirting back?

Is she about to throw me overboard?

Why am I blushing?

Her eyes say—*You are a prize.*

Her smirk says—*And I win.*

My entire being says, *Oh no.*

Darius slips behind me, glowing. I slump into our booth because escape is futile.

"Don't go anywhere," he whispers. "We're up again."

"You're glowing," I hiss. "Like you swallowed a string of LED lights."

"We'll talk later," he says, dreamy and chaotic. "Promise."

I want to be mad.

I want to scream.

I want to be honest.

Instead, I bride-smile. It tastes like aluminum foil.

Chase hits the talk button. "Alright, my holiday sweet snowflakes! *Community Song Time!*

Get your butts up here—we're doing a full-cabin singalong. Everybody knows, "We Are Family!"

Cheers. Groans. People surge forward in a festive stampede. The Christmas sweaters lead the charge, clinking flaming reindeer mules.

"We're—what?" I croak.

"Family," Darius says, dragging me into the glittering mess. "For three minutes and thirty-six seconds."

Bodies press in. Someone's antler headband stabs me. Baron claps on two and four with terrifying precision. Maggie Jo belts like she's performing for Miss Universe.

The ship rocks underfoot—the sea reminding us it owns us.

Rossi doesn't join, but ever so slightly sways with the music.

She stands at the edge, watching me through the human tinsel forest. The lights skim her cheekbone. The shadows swallow the rest. When I stumble, her chin tilts up—a tiny command.

The chorus crashes.

"We are fam-i-ly!"

I sing. I dance. I lie.

My mouth chants togetherness while my brain plots a heist on the Atrium photo screens, and my heart yearns for connection.

Halfway through the second chorus, my phone buzzes—two sharp vibrations.

Lisa texts, "Your cruise photos are online. I saw the photo. Are you still pretending to be married to Darius or are you all in on the Capt? CALL ME."

Then the next from Dad. "I'm glad to see you having fun. Don't work too hard!?"

OMG. They saw it. A chill creeps over my body, and my pulse races.

Did the entire cruise see it?

Does Rossi know?

Of course she did. She sees everything.

"Breathe," Darius whispers in my ear.

"I can't," I whisper back.

Chase whoops. "Family! Take a bow!"

The song collapses into laughter and squeals. Bodies swirl, shove, and clog the hallway. The Atrium might as well be Antarctica.

Rossi lifts her glass one last time and gestures subtly toward the exit.

A dare.

Or a warning.

Or a message, *come tell me the truth.*

My drink sweats in my hand, ridiculous and pink, umbrellas drooping in solidarity.

Maggie Jo leans in. "Honey, listen. If you're gonna do an open marriage? Pick a better cover story. And do NOT choose such a high-profile guest."

Baron pats my shoulder. "Honesty is the cornerstone of any good marriage."

"I know," I say. I don't.

Across the room, Rossi's eyes don't leave mine.

The crowd surges toward the next bar. Laughter spikes. The deck tilts.

My confession is almost to my lips.

I open my mouth—but clap it closed, knowing what I need to do.

I need to get the picture of me kissing the captain under the mistletoe and the picture of me leaning in for another kiss today. I need to destroy them along with the digital evidence.

I can't fall in love when I am in a fake marriage, while trying to impress my dad with my cruise review.

Chapter 12

Midnight Lights & Gingerbread Flirting

Day 3: At Sea

"The northern lights," I breathe, because my lungs literally forget how to do anything else. "They're—oh my gosh—they're being painted live."

Green watercolor ribbons spill across the sky, dripping into the black ocean like some moody artist is dragging a brush across the horizon. Purple flickers at the edges. White shimmer dances like lightning, too shy to commit. Even the ship's wake looks magical—glitter shattered behind us.

I've seen auroras from parking lots and midnight walks of shame to sneak back in my bedroom window, but never like this. This feels alive. Like the sky's making eye contact.

Couples crowd the Observation Piano Bar. They're snuggled into tiny alcoves, hot cocoa steaming, noses touching, matching sweaters glowing under twinkle lights. A fake fireplace flickers behind the piano, wreaths everywhere. Romantic. Cozy.

I?

I am not cozy.

I'm buzzing inside Captain Rossi's wool-lined coat, marching toward the Atrium because if even *one* picture from that elevator moment exists, my entire fake life detonates.

I power-walk to the photo wall. "Where are you, stupid elevator mistake?" I mutter, swiping through the stack of glossy memories.

Nothing.

More nothing.

An artistic photo of Darius smiling like he's auditioning for a toothpaste commercial. But not me.

"What?" I whisper. "Where am I?"

I check screen after screen. Still nothing.

It feels wrong.

I choke on a half-formed thought of Alexis, but tonight that memory is soft and far away, like it's underwater. The panic eclipses everything. Did someone buy those photos? Where are they?

I step back, dizzy, ready to cry in public.

"They are as beautiful as you," a voice murmurs—velvet and warm, sliding right into my chest. "This must be why you are named Aurora."

I jump. My lemon tea nearly waters a poinsettia.

Captain Rossi stands behind me, and I swear the sea calms just for her. She's all sharp cheekbones, dark eyes, and that confident, effortless posture that makes the tide look like her intern.

"You'd think my name was inspired by the lights," I say, scrambling for sarcasm, "but nope. Disney Princess. My mom expected golden hair and fairytale vibes and got... me."

Rossi's smile curves like the aurora trained her personally. "She received something far more rare."

Heat crawls up my neck. I suddenly cannot remember anyone named Alexis. Or Darius. Or me.

I retreat to a loveseat. Rossi sits beside me—invited? Who knows. Expected? Yes. Her thigh brushes mine. A spark zips up my leg like static with emotional consequences.

I pretend to sip tea. "Um... could you help me with a cruise issue?"

"I am in charge of everything on this ship," she says, voice low and steady. "Tell me what you need, Princess Aurora."

My organs malfunction.

"My photos disappeared," I say. "Every time the photographer takes one, it vanishes. I checked the Atrium. Nothing."

Her smile deepens, slow and deliberate, with a flicker in her eyes that makes my heart roar.

"I will find out," she says.

And somehow that sounds like *I already know.*

Then lightly, with a wink soft as a dare. "What happens at sea, stays at sea."

Her hand glides to my thigh again, lingering—a warm, claiming touch disguised as comfort.

My breath catches. "I—I don't want more secrets. I already feel like... like a fraud."

"You prefer honesty," she says thoughtfully. "Even when it hurts."

"How do you—who told you that?"

"I observe everything on my ship." Her gaze sweeps over me. "Especially the people I find intriguing."

My heart slams into my ribs.

"It is unusual," she continues quietly, leaning in just enough to make my brain evaporate, "to be with someone who does not choose you. Someone who chooses everyone."

I freeze.

She knows.

Not about Alexis. Not about Darius.

About *me.*

I swallow. "We... make it work. I guess I'm just used to being the person who isn't enough. And it's easier to hear the truth than to—than to be blindsided again."

Her expression softens—not kind. Controlled softness. Purposeful.

"You are with someone who cannot meet your needs," she murmurs. "And I could."

Heat blooms in my chest—dangerous, too bright. Her nearness makes every nerve spark.

"Thank you for listening," I whisper.

She tips her chin subtly toward the ceiling cameras. "When I am not beside you," she says, "I am always on duty. Always watching."

That sends goosebumps everywhere.

I tell myself it's hot.

I tell myself it means she cares.

I ignore the tiny voice saying, *That's a lot of watching.*

"Very older-sibling energy," I laugh weakly. "If the older sibling were a hot Italian captain with a... um... strong leadership personality."

Her laugh is soft—pleased. "Leadership simply means I know what I want."

Shiver. Full-body.

Rossi steps closer, casting me in her shadow. "Is this life—the one you're pretending—what you truly want?"

My throat closes.

"I—can't answer that."

"You pretend you do not want something," she says, voice velvet-lethal, "but I think you are waiting for permission to want it."

I stand abruptly. "I need air."

"You have the entire Pacific," she answers. "Breathe."

I inhale shakily at the window. The lights ripple white. I whisper, "I feel small."

"The ocean makes everyone small," she says. Then adds with a chuckle, "except me."

I choke-laugh. "Confident."

Her smile sharpens. "Truthful."

A hum buzzes between us. Something is shifting. Something I'm not ready for but also absolutely prepared for, which is a problem.

"Fine," I say, turning back to her. "Help me. If there's a photo, I need it gone."

"Because it shows the truth," she says.

"Because it makes a mess," I correct. "My dad, my job, my... everything falls apart."

Rossi considers me, that calculating glimmer returning. "I have already retrieved it, but I can make sure the digital copies are erased."

I stare. "You—what? How?"

"I protect the things I care about," she says simply. "If you cannot be honest, then be smart."

I try to make sense of what she is saying. Why does she have my pictures?

"Tell me, Aurora Disney Princess," she murmurs. "Are you running from a photograph... or from what it proves?"

I swallow. Hard.

"You can still find love on this cruise," she adds. "Love that chooses you."

My heart stumbles.

"I'm not looking for a secret romance," I say fast. "Even if I... even if it's allowed."

"Are you sure?" she asks quietly.

The elevator flash slams into my memory.

I hate how warm it makes me feel.

"I need air," I mutter, standing too quickly.

"You have the whole Pacific," she says. "Breathe."

I go to the glass.

The lights ripple white, then light green, across the sky, leaving streaky colors that fade into the darkness.

"I feel small," I whisper.

"The ocean makes everyone small," she says behind me. "Except me. I make the ocean behave."

My snort escapes before I can stop it. "Who needs a God complex when you can boss around the sea?"

Her eyes flash. "I do not rent the sea. I own it."

Something in me fizzles and melts all at once. I turn to her, pulse stuttering.

My pulse jumps. For a moment, it feels romantic.

But a tiny warning flutters in my ribcage.

A radio crackles at her hip. She doesn't look away from me. Not for a second.

"We will speak again," she murmurs. "You will tell me the truth."

"Unlikely," I breathe.

Her smile slices sharply. "I enjoy a challenge."

Then, softer—almost tender, almost possessive, she says, "And I always win."

"Of course you do," I mutter—

—and that's when Darius appears, glitter scarf and all.

"There you are!" he sighs. "I've been looking everywhere for you. Wait, am I interrupting something here... Are we doing interrogations or flirtations?"

Rossi looks at him once, then back at me with a silent message—*Later.*

"Good night, Mr. Newlywed," she says. "Do not fall overboard."

"No promises," he singsongs, then whispers to me, "Why do I feel even more energy between the two of you than before?"

"Because she's... something," I say, heart pounding. "We need to talk—"

He interrupts instantly. "But the midnight cookie bar—"

He doesn't even finish the sentence before sprinting toward the gingerbread trays.

I blink after him, floored. He's actually eating again. He's actually abandoning me *again.*

I glance back at the northern lights—but they've vanished, slipping behind clouds like my bestie-husband into a cookie-fueled void.

A prickle crawls up my neck.

I turn—and Rossi is suddenly there behind me.

Waiting.

"Walk with me," she says. Not a question.

"I'm staying here," I manage.

Her eyes flick with interest. "Very well. Then we speak here."

She steps close—closer than before. The air shifts.

"There is a very compromising photograph," she says quietly. "In the digital queue."

My breath catches. "Where?"

"My photographer is careful," she says. "Careful who sees what. Careful who gets to keep what."

"You paid them off?"

Her brow arches. "They work for me. And tell me—who else would pay for a photo of you looking irresistible after kissing the most powerful person on this ship?"

My heart thrashes.

Nobody. The answer is nobody.

"This ship is small," Rossi continues. "Secrets don't survive here unless the right people keep them. If you choose an ocean fling, I'd be the discreet choice, Bella."

"I'm married," I whisper. "On my honeymoon."

"You're pretending," she counters softly. "And you're starving for something real."

Heat flushes my face. "You don't know what I want."

"I watch," she says softly.

Too closely. Too well.

I swallow. "I just need the photos gone. I want to enjoy this cruise without everything falling apart."

"Then let me make it easy," she murmurs. "It is the most honest thing you can do."

Something inside me snaps.

A truth.

A fear.

A need.

"You don't actually want me," I blurt. "I'm intersex. Tall. Awkward. TSA scanners panic. I'm complicated. I'm not—I'm not the girl people choose."

She studies me. Then—

"None of that," she says slowly, "changes what I want from you."

My heart stops.

Her gaze warms, darkens.

The aurora reappears, glowing behind her.

She steps even closer.

"I will have all images of you sent to my private office," she says. "To review personally. To protect you."

My knees wobble.

"I don't need—"

She leans in, catching the end of my sentence.

"You need my help, Aurora."

My breath catches.

A beat. A pull.

A spark like the first crack of ice breaking on a lake.

She lifts her hand, brushing a stray curl from my cheek with slow, devastating precision.

"Let me help you," she whispers.

"I..." Words fail.

Her fingers linger on my jaw.

Her breath ghosts across my lips.

The air between us is electric—charged—dangerous.

"Aurora," she murmurs, voice like velvet smoke, "stop running."

And then—*she kisses me.*

Soft at first.

Then firmer, claiming, dizzying—heart ricocheting, aurora blazing so bright it burns behind my eyes.

The world narrows to heat

and salt

and wool

and her.

I kiss her back.

Because for a heartbeat, a breath, a flicker of impossible hope—it feels like maybe this is the person I've been waiting for.

Someone who sees me. *Chooses* me. *Wants* me.

When she finally pulls back, her lips still ghosting mine, she murmurs, "Good girl."

My pulse quickens and I think my heart is about to detonate.

She steps away just enough to look into my eyes with quiet triumph.

"We will continue this," she promises. "Soon."

Chapter 13

The Gingerbread Pact

Day 4: At Sea

I yank Darius from the elevator so fast he nearly faceplants into his *new sparkly Christmas scarf from Chase.* It sparkles and jingles. It actually JINGLES.

The hallway echoes a violin rendition of "Silent Night," making everything feel ten times more dramatic.

"WAIT—I'll drop a cookie!" he yelps, balancing a plate stacked with Christmas tuxedo gingerbread men like it's a newborn.

"WIFEY-POO—NOT MY SWEET GINGERBREAD TUX!" he cries, clutching one of the sweet treats.

I swear this man cares more about seasonal baked goods than the minor detail that my entire life is collapsing like an igloo in a heat wave and taking our new careers down in the slush avalanche.

"Forget the cookie, you drama llama!" I hiss, swiping the keycard so aggressively it nearly bends, then dragging him into the room as dramatically as if the hallway was on fire. The door shuts behind us with a fancy whoosh, and I finally inhale a full breath in the sanctuary of our suite.

"The Captain asked me to meet her in her room later to retrieve the pictures." My voice squeaks. "She knows. Darius—she knows everything."

I throw my arms in the air and flop onto the bed, defeated.

Darius marches to the door, twists the deadbolt shut for *extra* security, then starts pacing the room. The towel swan on our bed looks deeply judgmental, like it's ready to report us to the staff.

Darius pauses mid-prowl, adjusting his sparkly scarf with the confidence of someone giving a glamorous red-carpet interview.

"Knows what?" he says. "That I am *serving* peak 'hot man in a holiday scarf' energy? Or that you've been spiking your tea with actual champagne instead of that artisanal sob-story lemon water everyone thinks you're sipping?"

"No! She knows the real deal!" I throw my hands up. "She knows we're not in love! She thinks we're in an open marriage! She knows I'm a liar and—I may have gone a bit dramatic trying to get the photos back—AND I told her I'm intersex!"

Darius freezes. "Hold up. Photos. Plural?"

I groan. "It's not my fault! She keeps... appearing! And leaning! And being all—Captain-y!"

He gasps. "Is there a *Kim Kardashian-style* video I should be aware of? Because if so, girl, get ahead of it. Kim *made* it work. But lighting is *important*."

"Darius!"

"This is because you're the worst liar alive," he snorts, not even remotely concerned.

"I have a soft spot for alpha women," I moan, sitting up and then flopping back against the headboard. "You *know* that. And you keep abandoning me! I need you *glued* to my side before all these married people cheering for us figure out we're NOT the blissful honeymooners they think we are—and I get thrown off the ship for kissing the Captain."

"Oh, Wifey-Poo," he says, fanning himself with a cookie. "We are halfway through this cruise, and *no one* has figured out we're not married, are here on a work assignment, and our flamboyantly, *not* straight neon signs above with arrows above our heads."

"What if we get charged for all these bougie prizes we've won?" I babble. "What if I disappoint my dad? What if I'm falling in love *again* with the wrong person?"

His face shifts—surprised, soft, worried. "Aurora. Are you... catching actual feelings for Captain Rossi?"

"I don't know!" I squeak. "Maybe! Probably! She knows things, Darius. About me. And she listens. She smells so good. And she—*leaned*."

He throws his hands up. "This was supposed to be 'ho-phase mode' after the breakups! Not 'Aurora finds a new emotionally dangerous soulmate' mode! Lesbians move fast, sure, but girl—you're already *married!*" He gasps in mock horror.

I bury my face in my hands. "I told her I was intersex to scare her off."

"Oh girl." He winces. "Your nuclear honesty bomb?"

"Yes! And she just called me 'Bella' and told me I was a 'good girl.' *Who does that?!*"

I stand and march to the window. Outside, the Alaskan night hangs the velvety darkness velvet hiding the towering mountains.

"I wish someone wanted me. The *real* me without any conditions," I whisper.

Darius bumps my shoulder. "Someone does."

"Someone who is my soulmate. Not someone that is my adorable, fake husband," I murmur.

He gasps dramatically. "Rude. I am *absolutely* still your soulmate."

"You're my walking, sequined soulmate," I correct.

He beams. "That's better."

My phone buzzes—*Lisa.*

Darius lunges. "Put her on speaker! I need emotional back-up *and* fresh gossip."

I answer. "Lisa—"

"*Honey*!!" she screeches. "Why is the Holiday Princess cruise trending on my feed?! Did you *kiss the captain?* Did Darius get seduced by that pretty-boy Entertainment Director in a Santa hat? What is happening?! SPILL THE TEA!"

Darius clutches his scarf. "*I did not get seduced*—okay, maybe a little—but it wasn't *totally* my fault."

"Lisa, it's a total disaster," I groan. "There are photos. Plural. And they basically out me without my consent."

"PLURAL?!" Lisa shrieks. "Aurora, are you making a scandal on a cruise ship? I'm so proud."

"Lisa—this is my *job*," I remind her. "My dad is trusting me! I need everything under control! This was my chance to prove myself."

"Oh, Aurora," she says, warmly, "You've never had anything under control. That's why we love you. Now listen, I have news about your exes—Alexis *and* Richard—and you're *not* ready, but—"

The phone crackles violently.

Darius shouts, "*Don't you dare hang up*—"

Static.

Beeeeep.

Call failed.

"NOOOOOO!" Darius collapses to his knees like he just watched his favorite drag queen get eliminated.

"Try her on WhatsApp!" he shrieks, flapping his scarf.

"Okay, okay—wait." I jab at the screen. "Now it says LTE and... no bars. Great. I think we skimmed the edge of a satellite coverage area or something because there is literally *nothing* now. Sorry."

I stare at the dead phone, dread spiraling.

"I think I'm going to throw up."

He grabs my shoulders, shaking me lightly. "Focus. Now let's recap and strategize. You attracted the most powerful woman on this ship. There is a compromising photo or photos that could expose EVERYTHING. You've been summoned to her private quarters for a photo 'retrieval' that is absolutely going to end in a kiss—if not a steamy hook-up."

"Darius!"

He wiggles his eyebrows. "Did she offer the meeting agenda? Should I warn Chase we're about to replace him as cruise gossip royalty?"

"I think she wants to... teach me things. Things a man can't teach me," I whisper.

We burst into hysterical laughter, collapsing onto the bed.

Darius wipes his eyes. "Well. Chase thinks he turned ME gay too!"

He snorts. "He told me he was honored to be my *first guy.*"

I gasp through my laughter. "Did you tell him—"

"No! I didn't have the heart! He was so excited I thought he'd throw confetti and give me a rainbow participation ribbon!"

We explode with laughter again, ridiculous and unhinged in our panic.

And somewhere on the ship, the Captain is probably smiling, waiting for me.

Darius escorts me down the officers' hallway like I'm a contestant being marched into a finale she didn't study for. His sparkly Christmas scarf glitters with each step, throwing red and green disco flecks on the walls.

"You *cannot* be distracted," he whispers, gripping my shoulders dramatically. "Repeat it."

"I cannot be distracted."

"You *must* get the pictures. Repeat it."

"I must get the pictures."

"And *delete* the digital copies before you kiss the hot Italian captain! Promise me and repeat that you'll do it!"

I sigh. "That's a little excessive."

He grabs my face. "*Excessive? Girl, listen.* Kissing before completing the mission is like paying the plumber *before* the leak is fixed. It NEVER ends well."

"What plumber are you hiring who kisses—"

"FOCUS!" he hisses. "You flirt *after* the photos. *After* the deletion. *After* the metaphorical hostage situation is resolved. You have the *rest* of the cruise to be a hopeless romantic disaster."

"I'm not a hopeless—"

"Aurora, you made out with her in an elevator, *a glass elevator!*" He shakes his head. "You are a walking disaster with great legs."

I smack his arm. "I do *not*... Look... I'll get the photos. No kissing, no leaning, no swooning. Strictly business."

Darius narrows his eyes. "Good. Because the second you're alone with a sexy authority figure you get this... face."

"What face?"

He imitates me—lips parted, eyes hazy, head tilting.

It's rude but accurate.

"I do NOT look like that."

"You do. You look like you're about to ask her to ruin you and rescue you in the same breath."

I groan into my hands. "Darius!"

"Stay focused." He points to his eyes. "My ex cheated on me. Your ex left you for her corporate five-year plan. We are here for our new job and your family's business. We *need* those photos gone so we can keep the suite, the free swag, the exclusive excursions, and maybe, *maybe* my chance to get Chase to be my epic vacation fling."

He stops outside the Captain's private door, smoothing the scarf and looking around to make sure no one else is listening.

"Aurora Thompson," he says solemnly, hands on mine. "Promise me you will *not* kiss her until the photos are secured."

"I promise," I say, trying to look sincere.

"Say it again with less lip-biting."

"I PROMISE!"

He nods, satisfied. "Good. Now I must disappear before the Captain sees me and assumes you brought your chaperone."

"I got thi—"

"Hush!" He waves me off. "I'll be at the end of the hallway by the elevator pretending to read a brochure about shore excursions. If something goes wrong—cough twice. If it goes *really* wrong—*run!*"

"What if—"

He shoves me gently toward the door. "Remember... Mission first. Makeouts later. Now *go*."

He sprints away around the corner so fast his scarf catches air.

I barely have time to inhale before the door in front of me opens—

—and Captain Rossi fills the doorway, all uniform, authority, and molten dark eyes.

She smiles.

I immediately forget how walking works.

"Cara," she purrs. "Come."

Darius' voice echoes in my head, "Focus. *Focus!*"

Captain Rossi invites me into her private suite like she rehearsed it. All dark wool, clean lines, and warm smirk.

She looks at me like she's getting ready to unwrap her Christmas gift.

"Come," she says again.

I follow her inside.

The door clicks shut with a heavy sound—expensive privacy.

Her quarters aren't what I expected. Warm light. A low lamp. Deep navy walls. A decanter of something amber. It smells like cedar, sea salt, and danger.

"Thank you for coming," she says.

"Of course. But did I... have a choice?" I ask.

"Always." She tilts her head. "You chose me."

My heartbeat does a weird hiccup. "I—I chose the pictures."

Her smile deepens. "Mmm. Of course. The pictures."

She walks past me, brushing my arm so lightly it feels intentional.

A firework goes off in my ribs.

"So," I try again, "the pictures... Where are they?"

Rossi opens a drawer in her desk and pulls out a small, blue, official-looking folder. But she doesn't hand it over. Instead, she holds it lightly between two fingers.

"Before business," she murmurs. "May I offer you tea? Or... something stronger?"

"No," I say too fast. "No alcohol. Please."

Her brows rise, but her smile is soft. "Then nothing at all. Come, sit."

I sit on the small sofa. My knees knock together.

She sits beside me—close. Too close. My brain fails me, short-circuiting.

"You look nervous," she says.

"I'm not nervous," I lie.

"Your hands are shaking."

"I'm cold."

She leans in. "I know when someone is trembling from cold... and when it is something else."

Heat rises to my cheeks. "Okay, maybe I'm nervous."

"Why?" Her voice dips lower. "Do you think I will bite?"

"I don't know what you'll do."

A warm laugh erupts. "Cara mia... you come to my room at night, and you do not know?"

"That's not—I'm just here for—photos!"

"Yes," she murmurs, "we keep returning to the photos."

She sets the folder on the table.

Still unopened.

Still out of reach.

My eyes flick to it.

Her eyes flick to me.

"Oh," she says, "you want them that badly?"

"Yes!" I blurt.

She leans closer, her knee brushing mine. "Perhaps you will have them."

"Great."

"In time."

Less great.

"Captain—"

"Rossi," she corrects quietly. "When we are alone."

"Rossi," I breathe, "please. Can I please have the photos?"

She studies me, eyes sweeping across my face. "You should not ask for things in that voice."

"What voice?"

"The voice you use when you want someone to kiss you."

My soul just leaves my body for a moment.

"That is *not*—"

She moves closer, her breath brushing my jaw. "You lean into me in the elevator. You look at me wanting, and then *you* run."

"I didn't run!"

"You ran tonight."

"That was because of the elevator photo embarrassment!"

"Mmm. Yes," she says. "The photo of you in my coat. Leaning close. Blushing."

Her hand hovers near my cheek. "You looked beautiful."

I am definitely going to combust. "Stop doing that!"

"Doing what?"

"Saying things you don't mean!"

She cups my cheek—barely, fingertips warm. "I mean everything I say."

My breath catches.

She leans in—

I lean back—but then my back hits the sofa.

She whispers, "Tell me no."

I open my mouth.

Nothing comes out.

She smiles—small, victorious.

Then she kisses me.

Soft at first—barely a brush. Then firmer, deeper, warm, and sure. Her hand slides behind my neck, tilting me toward her.

I gasp into her mouth. Her lips taste like mint tea and confidence. My heart is sprinting laps around the globe.

Then—A pounding on the door snaps us apart.

"CAPTAIN!" someone shouts. "We have a situation. We need you on the bridge!"

Rossi pulls back slowly. Her thumb ghosts along my jaw. Her eyes burn with a mix of frustration and amusement.

"Duty," she says. "Unfortunately."

My lips feel swollen. "Rossi—the photos—"

She grabs the folder—not giving it to me—and locks it in a drawer. She places the minor key in her chest pocket.

"You will have them," she promises. "But not tonight."

"Wait—what? Why?!"

She stands, smoothing her uniform. "Because I want you to come back."

My entire nervous system fizzles. "That's manipulative."

"Mmm," she says, smiling. "And yet... you will still return."

I choke on air. "I—no—I won't—maybe—okay yes—NO—"

She touches my chin—gentle, but firm enough that I feel the promise underneath. "You are safe with me, Aurora."

The word *safe* hits wrong. Before I can figure out why, A hard knock, again, rattles the door.

"Captain—urgent!" an officer calls.

Rossi straightens instantly, slipping into command like she never took it off. Her gaze flicks back to me—warm, possessive, knowing.

"Until next time, *Cara*."

She steps out, and the door swings shut behind her with a soft thud that feels louder than a slam.

I stay there, completely still. Kissed. Dizzy. My heart is doing cartwheels.

And somehow... still missing the pictures.

Chapter 14

The Polar Bear (Bare) Plunge Uncensored

Day 4: Yakutat, Alaska

Chase calls enthusiastically into the mic, wearing a beanie with antlers and the blinding confidence of a man who has never met a temperature below eighteen degrees. "Fun fact!" he announces, already half-wet and fully committed. "All Alaskans are prepared to participate in the annual Polar Bear Plunge. It was an Indigenous tradition to celebrate the winter solstice!"

He raises his arms. "Let's go on three!"

"One!"

"I hate three," I announce, wrapping my arms around my goose-pimpled chest.

Everyone crowds close to the pool, steam curling upward in wild white ribbons against the freezing winter air. The ship glides past Yakutat, slicing through a world made of crystal breath. The cold is so sharp it feels like it could carve me into snowflakes.

"At least you wore the perfect outfit for this, Wifey-Poo," Darius says, adjusting his sequined scarf and expertly keeping himself out of the splash radius.

"Two..."

I do *not* willingly jump.

Instead, I step backwards towards the ship railing. My foot slips on the rime-frosted deck, my hand skids off the freezing railing, and gravity decides my fate. There's a collective gasp—then I hit the ocean water with a splash.

The black-blue ocean roars in my ears. My limbs flail. My brain forgets verbs. My heart does a moose stampede.

From the deck, Darius yells, "She was NOT prepared! And I can't jump in with my swimmer's ear—I'm a high-maintenance newlywed!"

"Three!"

Chase—bless his oblivious heart—cannonballs in after me to "help." A wave of salt spray blinds me, and his waterlogged robe (which he forgot to take off!) drags both of us downward.

Then my right swimsuit strap betrays me. My bikini top—in its first and last test of subzero seawater—slips right off.

Perfect.

I slap a forearm across my chest and scream-laugh, "I'm fine! I'm fine! I'm—oh my gosh, I can still swim! My lungs still work!"

"I've got her, folks!" Chase sputters loudly beside me. "Don't worry! You're amazing and sweaty!"

"STOP saving me!" I shout, shoving his heavy arm away. "You're pulling me down! And I'm NOT sweaty—that's seawater and panic!"

"She's glistening like an Alaskan mermaid!" Maggie Jo hollers from the deck. I spot Baron hustling forward with towels.

Strong arms haul me toward the metal ladder—efficient crew members working. The deck erupts into cheers, jingling bells, and someone yelling, "That's our favorite newlyweds! They *consummated the plunge!*"

I scramble up the ladder, grabbing towels and yanking my bikini top back into place with negative grace. That's when I see the photographer. Red knit cap, lanyard, camera raised—eyes gleaming with Christmas-paparazzi joy.

Click. Click. CLICK.

"Nope!" I shriek, stumbling forward, clutching the towel. "*Delete!* That is *not* an authorized, public nipple! This is not a clothing optional French Riviera cruise! *No nipple pics!* My dad will disown me! Consent is *not* given!"

The photographer lowers his camera just enough to look offended. "Ma'am, we capture the *authentic* cruise experience. An Alaskan holiday always includes a few unexpected frostbite moments. You can purchase these later."

"My authentic cruise experience does NOT include my wardrobe malfunction living in every family's memory album," I snap, teeth chattering so violently my jaw clicks. "Please—can I have ONE honest moment on this trip that isn't terrifying or humiliating?"

"Sorry," he says, shrugging. "No deleting without approval."

"Whose approval?"

He steps back as I swipe at the camera with my frozen noodle arms. "Captain Rossi, of course."

Of course.

"Absolutely not," I hiss, already marching, towel dragging behind me. "No one sends BOOB PHOTOS to the Captain for review without my consent!"

Darius jogs after me, stage-whispering, "Calm down, Wifey-Poo! Are you SURE you didn't give her consent yesterday? Or when you kissed her under the mistletoe? Or when you almost accidentally kissed her in the elevator? I'm just connecting dots here."

I glare at him so intently that the air warms by a degree.

"Do you *really* object to the Captain reviewing those photos?" he asks, raising an eyebrow. "There've been... a lot of incidents between you two." He snaps a picture of my horrified face. "For documentation."

"Fight him!" I yell, pointing wildly at the photographer, who is now fast-walking away, muttering about "policy."

The photographer vanishes around the corner before either of us can retaliate.

Chase jogs at our heels, dripping and grinning. "She's fine, y'all! Polar bears do this for breakfast with only a *little* sweat!"

Darius rounds on him. "Can you help us here? Aurora—my wife—did *not* consent to nudes being posted for sale on the ship."

Chase blinks. "Honestly? This was unexpected. Usually, the Polar Bear Plunge is in the *heated pool,* not the actual ocean... but hey, I admire the gusto!"

Around us, staff guide the *other* participants toward the pool ladder, handing out warm towels and heated blankets. Most guests are here for the "standing in a swimsuit next to a glacier" photo-op—not the full subzero horror I just survived.

My phone buzzes from the towel pocket.

A message from Lisa lights up, "Aghhhh! Your plunge is online. I saw your freckle—your *private* freckle. I'm serious. It's censored but still. Are you ok?? Do I sue a boat or the entire cruise line?? Do you need a lawyer?"

Fantastic. The digital queue has already made it to land.

I text back with fingers that barely bend, "Don't sue the boat. Yet. I don't want more drama!!!"

She sends, "NP."

A crew member intercepts us near the elevator. "Aurora? Captain Rossi would like to see you in her office. Immediately."

Darius squeezes my hand. "I'll come. We've been to the principal's office before. I'll make sure she's fair."

The crew member glances pointedly at my dripping bikini under my towel. "The Captain requested... just Aurora."

Darius drops my hand like it's radioactive. "I'm flattered *and* jealous. She only wants you? Bold."

"I'm humiliated and being sent to detention," I groan. "Stay in the lobby. Pretend you're my doting husband. I'll handle this—for real this time."

He salutes. "Worried-husband rage is activated."

Then immediately turns to Chase, who's hovering with towels. "Two champagnes. For morale."

"Darius!" I bark.

He zips his lips. He absolutely does *not* lock them.

I step into the elevator alone, towel clinging, stomach swirling. As the doors glide shut, I mutter to myself, "If I die of embarrassment, bury me in a hoodie. Not this bikini."

The crew member leads me through the officer's hall to Rossi's office—silent, elegant, intimidating. It smells like coffee, old leather, and authority.

The windows stretch wide, framing the bay as the ship turns—blue-white bergs gliding past. Slate water. Cutter lines of ice. And the massive Hubbard Glacier is glowing in impossible layers of blue.

The door closes behind me with a soft click.

Captain Rossi is waiting.

She stands behind her desk, hat off, hair smooth, gaze piercing my soul.

"Cara," she says evenly, eyes taking in my damp towels, my swimsuit peeking out, and the single rebellious curl stuck to my cheek. "You need something warm and a discussion about protecting your privacy."

"Accidental toplessness," I say brightly, forcing a joke to deflect the fact that my teeth are still chattering. "Newlywed tradition. Thanks for the quick chat."

The corner of her mouth considers a smile and declines. "Sit. But first, take this."

She doesn't wait for me to object. She grabs a large, ridiculously expensive-looking soft white robe, embroidered with a discreet silver crest, from a hook and hands it to me. Then she pours a steaming hot cup of coffee and passes it to me. I hold the cup to warm my hands. I'm shaking too hard to take a sip.

"Wet clothing on a winter day on a cold ship is an invitation to illness. Remove that wet towel. Now."

Her tone is a command disguised as care, and I can't find the energy to argue. I shiver, drop the damp towel, and quickly pull the robe on. It's cashmere or something equally absurd. It smells like clean linen and has an impossibly plush softness that melts around me, engulfing me.

As I sink into the plush leather chair, a crew member silently appears, places a fresh tray with another mug, sugar, spoons, and all the accoutrements next to me, along with a coaster, then moves my mug of coffee onto it. The steam smells heavily of dark chocolate and bright citrus.

"Hot chocolate," Rossi says, folding her arms. "With Italian orange zest. It cuts the bitterness and warms the hands faster."

Rossi comes over, pours another mug of the chocolate liquid, and hands it to me. I take a greedy sip. The combination of the rich cocoa and the warmth of the robe melts my physical resolve. This is why people fall for narcissists. They see the need you didn't know you had.

She picks up my coffee cup and takes a sip, then slides a screen toward me—thumbnails from the digital queue.

The photo of me with my body exposed for all to see fills the display. I sharply inhale and wonder if it's evident to everyone that I'm intersex, the sharp angles that seem to be lacking the complete roundness of a woman's body.

She taps the screen again—another thumbnail. It's the original pictures that I fear would expose me—in the elevator with her coat around my shoulders, our faces too close with intimacy and passion, "almost" written in the air like steam. It's just as damning as I imagined. The elevator, the low, intimate lighting, her leaning down, and me looking up—my eyes wide, my lips slightly parted, a flush on my cheeks, the "Bride" hoodie entirely forgotten under the wool coat.

"I prefer we take care of this situation efficiently, Captain," I say, trying to channel the ice-queen boss energy that I admired in Alexis. "I did not consent to have the photos taken of my body or the photos of intimate moments between us taken."

She smiles, a slow, predatory curve of her lips. She doesn't flinch at my coldness. Instead, she opens a frame with a mounted 8x10 photograph.

My breath catches. It's the photo from the mistletoe kiss.

Next to it, a stack of smaller, standard print photos rests. I realize with a jolt that these are all the pictures I thought had vanished. I see the seasick one with Darius on the glacier tour, a funny one of me making a face at a menu, a nice candid shot of me holding my lemon tea. Rossi didn't just steal the bad one. She secured all of them.

"See?" she says, watching my face. "No need to worry. They are all here. The photographer is very loyal." She taps the incriminating photo. "But this one... this one tells a much more interesting story than any of the others."

I reach for the photo, but she covers it with her hand—a gesture of ownership. Her touch is immediate, sharp, and confident.

"I am a collector, Aurora. I do not give away my treasures easily." She leans forward, her eyes catching the reflection of the falling snow outside. "And as I said, I want what I want."

My lungs hold still. "That one," I say, my voice small, betraying the truth of the previous night's kiss. "Please also... never."

Rossi's gaze doesn't leave my face. "It is... compelling."

"It is a mess," I say, meeting her gaze. "It looks like I'm a woman who can't decide what she is. It also makes me the villain of my own honeymoon. I don't need any more lies complicating my life."

"Or it makes you a brave and beautiful human," she says softly.

Then, cockier, "Or it makes me the villain, for hiding who you really are and not allowing your husband to know your betrayal."

She pauses, letting the statement hang in the air. "What else are you hiding, *Bella*? What is it you really cannot afford to lose?"

I clutch the mug tighter, a flash of panic hitting me—she's getting closer to the real reason I am on this cruise. "Nothing! Just my reputation. And my deposit on the room. My husband and I don't need a scandal, either." I deflect with a lie about Darius.

Rossi doesn't press. Instead, she slides a thin legal folder across the desk. "For that reputation, and to ensure all our... private discussions... remain protected, I need you to sign this Non-Disclosure Agreement. It is a standard privacy measure for those I invite into my office."

My blood runs cold. An NDA. If I sign this, I can't use anything on this vacation in my family's Alaskan Cruise & Travel business, either to review or refer clients—the whole reason I'm here. It would effectively sabotage my entire mission.

"Oh. A contract," I say, my voice light and far too cheerful. "My father taught me never to sign anything without reading the fine print first. Especially when my hands are shaking from near-hypothermia."

She pushes the photo a half-inch closer to me on the desk. "The exchange is simple. I will give you the photograph and the negatives. You give me one moment of truth."

I narrow my eyes. "What kind of truth?"

"The truth your body is telling you right now." She rises, walking around the desk slowly. Her power isn't in her uniform. It's in her certainty. She stops right next to my chair, too close. "You told me you were wanting to be honest. I want you to be honest about the desire I see when you look at me."

I try to stand, but the space is too confined. My back is to the wall, and she is a wall of wool and Italian heat.

"I told you my truth! I'm intersex! That's my truth. I'm not the girl you want! My husband and I have an open marriage, yes, but I don't want this kind of complication."

Rossi doesn't argue the point. She simply reaches out, gently cupping my chin, forcing me to look up into her intense gaze.

"I do not care about your biology, Princess Aurora. I care only about your honesty." Her voice drops, a command disguised as velvet. "I want one kiss where you are not thinking about your father's approval, your husband's needs, or silly pictures. A kiss that is just you. Give me that, and I will give you your life back."

Her eyes are dark, gleaming, challenging me to step off the ledge. The pressure is suffocating. The photo, the lie, Alexis's judgment, the fear of ruining the deal with my dad—it all crashes down. This woman is offering a moment of pure, selfish release, a moment where I don't have to be the perfect, dutiful, newlywed daughter. She offers honesty wrapped in a toxic, irresistible package.

She's narcissistic, like Mom... she's controlling, my mind screams at me to run from all the red flags she's waving.

But she sees me. She sees all of me, and she still wants me. My body whispers.

I lift my free hand, the one without the ring, and place it on her upper arm. My touch is hesitant, but my intention is clear. I don't know if I'm trying to push her away or pull her closer.

"You are a bad idea," I whisper, the words breaking on a shaky exhale. "A truly terrible, boundary-crossing, selfishly motivated bad idea."

"Si. Now be selfish with me."

She closes the remaining distance, and her lips meet mine. It's not the soft, hesitant kiss of a tentative admirer. It's the firm, decisive kiss of a Captain taking command of her ship. It's warm, demanding, and utterly intoxicating. The world narrows to the taste of salt, expensive coffee, and her intense confidence.

And I kiss her back.

Focus—Darius's words come back to me, and I pull away.

"Captain—umm, Rossi. The photos?"

Rossi leans back, fingers steepled, the picture of effortless control. "Ahhhh, yes. I would *hate* for these photos to continue circulating or become available."

My stomach drops to the floor.

"Aurora," she continues, voice silky and dangerous, "if you don't want your... your *seeming* bisexual tendencies exposed—along with your beautiful breasts—you can sign this document, and this doesn't go any further."

My heart stabs itself. Is she threatening me?

She pauses, eyes glittering. "Or," she adds lightly, like offering a dessert menu, "you can come back to my room tonight and we can work out an arrangement. Discreetly. I find you compelling, and your secrets... I have a very specific thing in mind for us. It will require that you bathe before you arrive."

My jaw unhinges. She's blackmailing me for some kind of—Oh God.

Sexual. Power. Thing.

"I—I appreciate the attention, Captain," I stammer, standing up so fast the robe nearly slips. I yank it tighter, trying to cover every insecurity I've ever had. "I'm flattered. But I can't. My boundaries are... I'm married..."

"I do hope you will change your mind, *Bella*." She drags a finger down my arm.

I flinch hard, jerking away. The goosebumps aren't from the cold anymore.

"We're done," I manage, though my voice sounds hollow, like it doesn't believe me. "My husband and I will not be having any more... time apart for private meetings."

She leans back in her chair. "For now. But you know where to find me, Princess Aurora."

I turn, practically *bolting* for the door, holding onto an incriminating photo.

I make it one step past the threshold when her fierce whisper stops me.

"*Cara bella*," she says, "I am in charge of this ship, not your husband. I know you'll be back. And I'll be watching. Waiting."

My skin crawls. My pulse thunders. I grab the NDA folder with shaking fingers.

"I will take this back to the cabin," I choke out. "My husband and I will review it. Tonight. And... thank you, for the cocoa, but—I need to go."

I don't wait for her response.

I flee.

Her sharp gaze follows me.

I haven't signed the NDA.

I have some of the pictures.

Victory?

The PA system crackles—then chirps with Chase's offensively cheerful voice, echoing through the hallway.

"Fun fact—glaciers are like ogres! They have layers! And they move slowly. Coming up tomorrow is the highly anticipated newlywed ice sculpture contest! Captain Rossi herself has offered a very special grand prize!"

I freeze, my hand on the doorframe.

Behind me, Rossi purrs, "Cara... that prize is *very* personal. Perhaps a very special candid photo of myself... with a popular guest. I hope you win. I wonder what you'll be competing for next?"

I look back at her—part rage, part heartbreak, part fear.

"You are evil," I whisper.

Her smile is smug with her victory.

"*Sì.* Now go. Your husband is waiting. *And so am I.*"

Bzzt. BZZT. BZZT.

The hallway outside blurs as my phone erupts with notifications. The phone is trying to crawl out of the towel pocket.

It's not just Lisa.

It's a full-blown emergency alert.

I swipe. It's a screenshot. A polished, corporate, glossy announcement.

Lisa texts, "omg are you seeing this??? she is stepping back."

She adds, "holy. moly. She must have cancer. There's no way Alexis would give up CEO willingly."

The photo loads.

Alexis—perfect posture, perfect hair, perfect life plan—standing in front of a steel-and-glass corporate sign.

> ALEXIS, CEO of Alaska Temp Agency, STEPS DOWN—Official Press Release

My heart stutters painfully, like it's forgotten the choreography.

Alexis is stepping down?

In the middle of her five-year career plan?

The plan she chose over me?

The plan I wasn't "compatible" with?

Does she—Is she sick?

Does she need—?

My breath vanishes.

The warmth from Rossi's cocoa.

The rush from her kiss.

The dread of her threats.

All of it collapses under a new tidal wave—fear, regret, and one stupid, hopeful flicker that maybe—maybe—I didn't actually lose Alexis the way I thought.

I bolt down the hall.

I need Darius asap!

Chapter 15

Glitter, Gossip & Glacial Drama

Day 4: Yakutat, Alaska

I throw our suite door open like I'm escaping a Kodiak bear.

"Darius! Emergency—level ten—maybe eleven."

I pause to take a breath. "Alexis stepped down!"

He's sprawled on the couch, a sequined scarf still perfectly draped. He sits up so fast a cookie launches off his chest.

"*What?!*"

He snatches my phone with a gasp. "Oh no. OH NO. Did she perish? Did she look around her office after we left and realize she was emotionally supported entirely by your spreadsheets and my charm? Did the silence take her OUT?!"

"I don't know!" I shriek. "Lisa texted. She thinks it's cancer. Or a coup. Or a cult situation."

"Back the truck up. Did Lisa text you *before* me?"

I drag both hands down my face. "Darius… that's not the point. Alexis would *never* step down. She schedules bathroom breaks into her calendar."

He stares at the screen, eyes wide. "Well, this is definitely not because she misses you."

I glare. "*Rude.*" Beat. "Also possibly true."

He drops the phone on a pillow like it's radioactive. "Okay, babe, put a pin in this. Your ex's corporate meltdown is *not* our main emergency right now."

"What do you mean? This is huge. The Captain trying to blackmail me into sleeping with her and signing an NDA *barely* compares—"

"Hold up. You still don't have the photos, and now you're signing an NDA? You are the opposite of a successful spy. We should be joined at the hip from now on."

"I may need to catch you up on the meeting I just barely escaped."

He patiently listens, munching Christmas cookies while I unload everything.

"...then Lisa texted and I knew it was serious and I needed to talk to you about the Alexis thing, and then Rossi literally tried to blackmail me into—"

"*Yes,*" he cuts in, "and *that* is what we're dealing with. Not our ex-boss's existential crisis."

I flop onto the bed. "That meeting was a disaster and I kissed her. Again, Darius."

"Wow, color me, shocked." He drops down beside me, eyes huge. "Okay, fine, not shocked. But, Aurora—NDA?? Pictures?? The world's hottest Captain trying to force you into a Fifty Shades nautical spin-off?? *That* is the fire we're putting out."

I groan into a pillow. "If I sign that NDA, I can't use anything from this cruise in our official review. My dad will kill me. And if I *don't* sign, she releases the pictures."

"Yeah—your 'leaning-toward-women' pictures," he air-quotes dramatically, "and your, uh... bare Arctic boob situation."

"My breast betrayed me," I whimper. "It went rogue in international waters."

He pats my head. "Sometimes nipples just want to breathe."

I bolt upright. "What if the cruise finds out we're not actually married and they make us pay back *everything*? The suite? The prizes? The chocolate-covered strawberries? Will we get banned from cruises for life?? Do you know what happens to cruise-banned people? They go on land vacations, Darius. Like Greyhound bus vacations."

He gasps. "We'd have to travel in buses or trains. No more Holiday Midnight Chocolate Buffets."

"Mass transit with the riffraff. We can't live like that!"

"No, Wifey! WE are way too glam for that. *We really can't get banned from cruises.*"

We sit in shared horror for ten whole seconds.

Then Darius snaps his fingers like he's cracked a code on *CSI: Honeymoon Edition*. "We need counsel."

"What, like an attorney?? We don't *have* an attorney."

"We have something better." He springs to his feet, eyes blazing with chaotic purpose. "We have Baron... and Maggie Jo."

I blink. "The veteran cruisers? The married couple from Louisiana?"

"Yes!" He points with the conviction of a man naming prophets. "Baron is a rock. A *business* man. He definitely owns stocks. Maybe a boat dealership. Or an island. He gives big 'has a lawyer on retainer' energy."

"And Maggie Jo?"

"Maggie Jo," he whispers, almost reverent, "was Miss Louisiana Runner-Up two years in a row. She's a beauty queen and she's no quitter. You don't get to that status without master manipulation skills and learning to read people."

I stand, breathless at the brilliance. "Maggie Jo did tell me to call her if we ever needed anything."

I dig into the pocket of my Bride hoodie and produce a wrinkled napkin with her phone number on it.

Darius snatches it like it's the final rose at a Bachelor ceremony and immediately fires off a message.

Ding.

"They're expecting us for cocoa and dessert," he announces triumphantly.

"Of course they are."

He grabs my shoulders, eyes wild. "Here's the plan. We meet with them, pretend we need marital guidance, and *casually* slip in that we might be accidentally committing cruise fraud. Then—this part is crucial—we butter them up with a brownie. Then we ask for their *wisdom.*"

"And we do *not* mention my intersex status or the kiss with the Captain. Really, let's try not to spill any more secrets."

He shakes his head so hard his scarf shimmers. "Absolutely not. Rule one of crisis is to disclose *nothing* except what earns pity."

"Wait, what? How does pity help us?"

"It gets you extra whipped cream," he says, sagely. "And usually a lot of Southern grace."

I rub my forehead. "Darius, do you really think they'll help?"

"I think Maggie Jo has attorneys on speed dial. And Baron? He is painfully competent. That man could negotiate peace treaties."

I nod slowly. "Okay. Baron and Maggie Jo. Cocoa. Legal strategies."

"And Aurora?"

"Yeah?"

He squeezes my hand, warm and steady. "We're going to fix this. The NDA, the photos, Captain Horny-on-Deck—everything."

I laugh shakily. "Thanks."

"Now," he says, marching toward the door with heroic determination, "let's go talk to the couple who might be slightly crazier and much wiser than we are."

Together, we head out into the hallway—toward dessert, alleged wisdom, and two people who have definitely survived scandals requiring lawyers and holy water.

We hustle down the promenade, my sandals squeaking on the polished deck, the air so cold it tastes blue. Snow-dusted fairy lights rim the railings, each bulb wearing a tiny frost halo.

"Faster," I whisper, clutching two steaming cocoas like life support.

"Faster?" Darius wheezes. "Girl, I am moving at a holiday power-walk."

"You're at a holiday sashay," I correct. "We're late for our legal consultation."

We slip through the aft doors into the Sky Lounge—warmth hugging us. Pine and peppermint swirl from garlands roping the ceiling. A pianist noodles "Jingle Bell Rock" like the keys are marshmallows. The panoramic windows show the ship's wake unspooling in silver ribbons, and my heart does its little ache-proud thing because Alaska is showing off again and I am not emotionally stable enough for it.

"I yearn," I blurt. "Capital-Y Yearn. For uncomplicated. For a Caribbean vacation with no glaciers and zero lesbians in charge of things."

"Oh my god," Darius bumps my shoulder. "Build a bridge. And I yearn for you to stop giving the Captain bedroom eyes. You swear you're uninterested and then look at her like she's a limited-edition Stanley cup."

"My attraction to women in charge is a medical condition!" I shove a cocoa into his hand. "I am my own worst enemy."

The lounge hums with newlyweds in matching snowflake sweaters, everyone glowing like they swallowed a Hallmark movie. Through the glass, I see the Inside Passage breathing steady, the faint milk-glow of Hubbard Glacier.

A server glides by with caviar canapés. Darius reaches—I swat his hand. "No. We are here for business. Not for roe."

We beeline to our usual corner—a semicircle of plush chairs under a wreath large enough to house a small family. Maggie Jo and Baron are already there, naturally early because they are overachievers in love and punctuality.

Maggie Jo pops up in a whirl of glitter earrings and Southern warmth, pulling me into a hug that smells like cinnamon-sugar and triumph. "Honey, did you thaw out from that plunge? I swear your hair had actual icicles."

"It did," I sigh. "And that's not even the worst thing that happened."

Baron rises more slowly, offering me the accountant stare-down. He's wearing a Santa hat that does not match his serious vibe. "We brought paper," he says, patting a folder. "And a calculator. I assume you didn't summon us for our dinner conversation, but I do hope this is not a preliminary divorce hearing?"

"Be still my heart," I breathe. "Numbers."

"Don't tease her with spreadsheets," Darius warns. "She loves spreadsheets more than me."

"Okay, old marrieds," he continues, flopping down dramatically. "We need guidance. The Captain is radiating alpha-lesbian energy. Aurora has a terminal case of I-don't-want-to-want-her-but-I-need-her eyes."

Maggie Jo claps. "Spicy, Honey!"

Baron adjusts his glasses. "Define 'other issues.'"

We intended to tell them only about the NDA. Instead, we word-vomit everything to them. They listen to our fake marriage, the elevator almost-kiss, the breast exposure catastrophe, the job review mission, the NDA threat, the unethical seduction attempt, the entire "newlywed" lie, *all of it.*

We stop only when Chase, the Cruise Director, appears with his tanned Florida smile, puffy vest, beanie with a pom-pom the size of his ego.

"Ayyyyy! My favorite newlyweds and my resident cruise champs!"

"Hi, Chase," I say in a measured, cold tone.

He tosses Darius a wink bright enough to tan wood. "Chocolate buffet later? I'm hosting 'Name That Holiday Tune.' Winner gets a caviar tasting for two! With me as your plus-one to explain how Alaskans pronounce smørrebrød."

"That's Swedish, baby," Maggie Jo says.

"Love that for me," Chase grins. "I'm multilingual in vibes."

Darius mirrors my *please-not-right-now* face. "We're... in a meeting."

"Cool, cool, cool." Chase hums off-key, sauntering away.

"Bless his confident heart," Maggie Jo sighs.

"Bless his commitment to incorrect information," Baron mutters. "Now. To business."

We settle at a private table with our mugs and desserts.

I gulp cocoa. "Okay. Here's the crisis, the captain is trying to blackmail me because I'm 'devoted to my fake husband.' She has an unreleased photo of me almost kissing her in an elevator. And I have a meeting with her tonight in her office to 'decide my future,' which sounds like she wants... something in return. Maybe the truth. Maybe a kink. Probably my soul."

"Ooooh," Maggie Jo says, delighted. "Romance with terms and conditions."

"Romance with financial liability," Baron corrects. "Let's evaluate."

"And..." Darius says, pointing at me, "we're reporting everything back to her dad for their cruise review business. And now the cruise line wants us to sign an NDA, which is ridiculous because literally *everyone* overshares on vacation."

I slump. "In my defense, when we accepted the Newlywed Package, there was no NDA. Just a big room, champagne, and a free robe. And I am weak for robes."

Maggie Jo pats my knee. "We've all been seduced by a quality robe."

Baron writes NDA in tidy, terrifying block letters. "Worst-case scenario is if they decide you violated the Newlywed Package terms, you owe the value of the perks."

Darius whips out his phone. "Let's do the math! The upgrade is three grand. A spa day is five hundred. Tours are variable. And I'm not even going to look up the caviar, robes, and hoodies."

Baron taps the calculator. "Call it five grand. Minimum."

My stomach drops through the deck. "Five thousand dollars," I croak. "I'd have to sell an organ."

"You cannot," Baron says dryly. "Organ donation requires informed consent and zero compensation."

"Then I'll sell Darius to the highest bidder."

Maggie Jo wheezes. "Honey--"

Baron folds her hands. "You just need a strategy. Stay married or at least appear married. Stall all paperwork. Lean *hard* into wholesome couple activities. Avoid private meetings with the Captain. And absolutely no bedroom eyes."

"I'm not giving her bedroom eyes!"

"You *are,*" Darius insists. "Your eyes are saying 'make me your first mate,' and your brain has completely abandoned ship."

A server appears with drinks Chase invented. They look like holiday-themed chocolate crime scenes topped with whipped chaos and served with a whiskey chaser.

We do not drink them.

Maggie Jo does.

"Mmm!" she sighs, delighted. "This tastes like I'll be dancing the macarena later tonight."

Baron pretends he did not hear that and calmly slides me a crisp checklist that resembles an Advent calendar for legal survival.

> Stall signing anything ("We need time to review").
> Get written confirmation that all photos stay unpublished or destroyed.
> Boost wholesome newlywed visibility.
> Do NOT be alone with the Captain.
> Darius suggests limiting exposure to your kryptonite, Captain Rossi.
> Aurora suggests that Darius listen to his own advice and limit his time with Chase.
> And STOP mentioning your 'open marriage' & flirting with cruise staff.

Maggie Jo squeezes my hand. "You deserve someone who wants you for you, not for leverage."

Darius pats my back. "Boundaries. You control the narrative with the Captain. We're your glitter-covered backup."

The pianist slips into the *sad* version of "Have Yourself a Merry Little Christmas"—the one that turns your throat into a fist. A hollow ache blooms in my chest. Every secret I'm carrying presses harder against my ribs, crowding out my breath.

Then I see her.

Across the lounge, Captain Rossi stands concealed by the shadow at the end of the bar–the brass on her uniform glints, catching some of the soft gold light, her posture unmistakable.

She does not look at me or acknowledge that she sees me.

It is somehow worse. Like punishment. Like a promise.

My phone buzzes.

A chill slides down my spine.

Before I can inhale, it buzzes again.

Lisa texts, "Heads up. I'm not the only one who saw your photos. Alexis asked me about them. Also, she liked your dress/jacket combo. And I saw your dad getting coffee. He was bragging about you. Full 'proud papa' mode. You have the best dad, *omg*."

Warmth floods me—my father's pride, Lisa's chaos comfort—something soft and hopeful trying to unfurl inside me.

Then under that message.

Unknown Number. "Don't be late."

And suddenly the Christmas lights are too bright, the room too small, and the Captain's unseen gaze, *ominous*.

Chapter 16

Chainsaws & Ice Sculpture Dildo

Day 5: Valdez, Alaska

"I can't believe I fell asleep," I groan, half-awake and barely dressed appropriately for the morning buffet.

"I tried to wake you," Darius says, trotting to get around me to the warm croissants. "You gave me a hand-flap and whispered, 'Not now, Wonder Woman'."

"Captain Rossi is going to murder me by throwing me overboard," I say. "New plan, total avoidance. We are stealth. We blend as if we are snowflakes."

"Girl, you are a six-foot-tall ginger giraffe in a bedazzled bride hoodie," he says, kindly. "*Stealth* is never going to happen for you."

We walk through the aft doors into Deck Eleven, trying to make as little entrance as possible.

Why is Darius still wearing that glittery holiday scarf that draws obligatory compliments from other passengers?

The Valdez Deck Day banner flaps, speakers croon "Rockin' Around the Christmas Tree," and the scent of cocoa and salty breeze hangs in the air—holiday cruise meets icy Alaskan harbor. A row of chainsaws sits on a tarp, ominously. Blocks of ice rise chest-high, chalked with cartoon reindeer outlines. Guests in puffy jackets cluster, cell phones up. And at the mic, wearing a puffer vest and a red beanie with a pom big as a clementine, is Chase.

"Ladies and gentle-honeymoons and other cruisers!" he booms. "Welcome to our Ice Carving + Cocoa Contest!"

"Didn't he tell us we were carving butter last night," Baron asks as we sidle up next to him.

As if reading out thoughts, Chase adds, "It was supposed to be butter carving—" He sweeps a hand toward a table of croissants "—but we annihilated the butter at breakfast, so we're doing it Alaska-style with chainsaws and ice. Safety goggles are the new sexy!"

Baron, in a herringbone cap and the resigned aura of a business professional on a cruise, raises a dry hand. "Have you done this before? And more importantly, is this... safe?"

Chase beams. "Probably! The Eskimo tribes have been doing it for centuries—"

"We haven't had chains for centuries," I start, but Darius shushes me.

"—and I personally took a class online. It was very technical, an almost hour-long tutorial," Chase finishes.

I whisper, "If I lose a finger, I'll never forgive you, but at least the Captain will feel sorry for me and forget about the blackmail or NDA."

"We can only hope, Wifey-Poo," Darius says, nudging me.

"I just want," I say softly, watching sea otters bob like punctuation near the pilings, "a day where I can relax and not worry."

"Not on this boat," he says, and kisses my temple. "Sweetheart, chin up."

Maggie Jo materializes, hard to miss in her glitter earrings and humidity-defying southern hair. "Sorry I'm late!"

She turns to Baron. "Sugar cakes! And friends! I signed us up." She waves at the blocks of ice and chainsaws.

Chase's hawk eyes spot us. His smile widens when he notices that Darius is wearing the scarf. He cup-hands the mic. "And entering the arena, our star newlyweds—the couple to beat—the ship's own Aurora and Darius!"

The crowd cheers. My stomach dives over the rail.

"Goodbye to having ten fingers," I hiss, smile glued on.

"Aurora says, wave your fingers," Chase sings, while giving exuberant jazz hands, and for good measure, he points to a videographer. "We are filming for the Highlight Reel for the Holiday Princess Newlyweds Cruises! Say 'sled dogs'!"

"Sled dogs," Darius says, teeth flashing and blinding me for a millisecond.

"Help," I whisper through mine.

From the upper catwalk, I notice the flash of a white hat and black uniform. Captain Rossi is up there, hands clasped behind her back, hat perfect, gaze a sweep of horizon—then, unmistakably, me. Heat flares under my hoodie like I swallowed a heat pack.

Darius follows my eyes. "Remember our plan—*Avoidance.*"

"I am avoiding," I lie. "With my eyeballs."

Chase claps. "Teams, goggles on, mittens off, chainsaws at the ready! We've got reindeer, Orca, sled dog, and—" he checks his list "—freestyle, for the brave."

"Freestyle," Maggie Jo tells the onlookers, winking. "Art is the opposite of rules, honey. I think we'll be doing abstract ice art with our eyes closed. My eyeballs are getting cold."

Baron leans toward me. "Maybe there's a fire alarm I can pull. I actually like all ten of Maggie Jo's fingers."

A crewman hands me a cordless chainsaw with a little Holiday Princess sticker on it. The purr and vibrations only confirm that this isn't a dream. We shuffle over to our block of ice. The thing glitters glacier blue-white and is as hard as a slab of concrete.

"Okay," the knowledgeable crewman says, leaning in. "We are going to create an object that is unmistakably a reindeer. I will let you start the carving, and be here to assist. Then I will do the fine tuning. I want you to have fun but know that I'm here to assist and to wrap my scarf around it when you're done."

"So I'm doing all the carving, and you are adding a scarf?"

"Razzle Dazzle–that's what I add," he says, dead serious.

Chase struts by, whispering with maximum volume, "Remember—winners get a gift-shop mega-credit and a spot in this afternoon's cocoa blind taste test. Losers get… memorialized on the cruise film."

"Gift shop," Maggie Jo gasps. "I am sensing a shopping spree. Baron, you can't say no to that penguin hat and sasquatch slippers if they're free!"

Baron shakes his head and stares at his un-sashquached feet.

A whistle trills. Chainsaws snarl to life like angry bees. The block before me shivers under the first bite of the small chainsaw. Ice dust hits my face like powdered sugar, and I refuse to close my eyes or give up on shaping the dense ice.

I follow the stencil drawn on the block of antlers in three dimensions, which is hard with the motor and vibration. A very loud motor. There's rhythm and resistance, a music I learn in microseconds—push, let up, glide. It's actually not that different from using an electric knife that sounds like a lawn mower. My breath fogs my goggles. Valdez's sun glances off the saw teeth and throws little rainbows off the ice.

Someone whoops. Someone else drops a saw, in frustration—their crew member swoops in to help. The cameraman walks around us at a safe distance to get all angles.

I look up to see that the Captain doesn't blink her eyes, with her intense gaze.

"Gentle, gentle!" Maggie Jo yells at her crew member, who has completely taken over the creation of her abstract ice carving.

Darius yells to me over the motor, "You got this, think of the finished product and start shaping it!"

I angle the blade. An antler emerges, delicate, curling, maybe too… smooth. The other one… not so much. I step back. The right "antler" leans, glossy, bulbous. The antlers are so big, I'm unsure if I can make a head under them. Maybe I should have tried something easier. I can hear the other blades slowing as the other four ice sculptures approach completion. I make some finishing touches, and my crew member, who has been hands-off, examines it.

"I don't think I need to add any dazzle, you did a great job!" He flashes me a fake smile.

Darius chokes. "Is that—"

"It's an antler," I say too fast, realizing that my antler has the shape of a particular male organ.

He leans close, whispering. "It is not an antler. Now I know it's hard to play heterosexual, but this is a little over the top, don't you think, girly?"

Maggie Jo has moved away from 'her' creation and evaluates mine, hands on her hips. "Honey, art is brave. I think you should call your Christmas morning surprise!"

Chase jogs over, eyes widening. He looks at the sculpture. He looks at Darius. He looks back at the sculpture. "Impressive! I can see you have been inspired by your husband. I think I see a winner." He winks.

Baron pats my arm and adds, "The human brain seeks patterns and tends to humanize even inanimate objects."

"I hate it here," I mutter.

"At least you haven't lost a finger," Darius says. "Yet. Maybe tilt that part. Less... spike and more angled antler..."

I tilt and turn on the blade to make a few minor adjustments. The antler... persists and grows even larger and more prominent. The crowd giggles. My face matches my hair.

"Time!" Chase sings, and the chainsaws die. The silence after the sound is absurdly loud.

We step back. The Orca whale next to me is noble and sleek.

Team sled dog turned their ice block into a lump and millions of splinters. I'm guessing their design didn't work out.

Maggie Jo's is a block of ice with an abstract heart that looks like someone stabbed it repeatedly, and it wouldn't die. Even her crewmember couldn't fix the design she started. If pain had a name, it would be her abstract sculpture.

Our reindeer is... at least an attempt at carving something. There's a boxy head and his large antlers, proud. Unapologetic.

Chase waves the mic. "Give it up for our brave artists!" The onlookers start clapping and begin to walk closer to the disastrous blocks of ice.

Chase continues, "Judges will tally while we pivot to our cocoa contest. Grab your tasting spoons! We've got five cocoas for you to identify between the traditional, spicy, holiday spirit, mystery chef's kiss, and vegan bliss. Guess the secret ingredients in each and give each sweet holiday beverage a fun name!"

Darius squeezes my elbow. "You got this one in the bag. We aren't getting off the ship today so with that credit you can buy a turtleneck and wool coat. I have confidence because you consume chocolate like it's a food group. Your palate is practically a professional ingredient detector at this point."

"I do like every type of chocolate, even vegan white," I say, wiping ice dust off my jacket. "At least this gives everyone something to do instead of looking at my dildo deer anymore."

"Reindeer dildo, honey. And it's magnificent!"

"Thanks."

"Yeah, Wifey-Poo, it's a good thing you aren't team hetero because that creation is a little unrealistic in size, especially if you take into account the cold."

I laugh and punch him. *I did have a fun time!*

We move inside to join the crowd at a tasting table. Steam rises in soft columns off the hot chocolate. The cups are labeled A through E with snowman stickers. People murmur ideas as they sip. "Cinnamon... Marshmallow... Nutmeg... Cardamom?"

"Cup A," Darius says, sniffing. "Peppermint, obvious. They always have to make the first one too obvious. This is a candy cane invasion."

"Cup B," Maggie Jo says. "Spicy! Cayenne."

"Cup C," Baron says. "Oat milk. Vanilla. Sweetened with maple. This one is vegan, for sure."

"Cup D," I say, holding it under my nose like I'm proposing. The aroma is warm citrus and dark corners. I taste. The chocolate is deep, not too sweet. There's a bright thread like sunlight, and a licorice whisper. The familiar taste floods the memories of being in Captain Rossi's office and feeling helpless. I close my eyes. There's—

I open them. She is watching me. Captain Rossi, at the edge of the crowd. No smile. Just intent.

"Orange zest," I say. "Zested from a Seville or at least a not-sweet orange, right into the pot so the oils bloom. Star anise, not too long or it goes medicinal. And..." I take another sip, chase it with air. "A single whole clove, pulled early. And a pinch of sea salt."

Maggie Jo fans herself in her southern belle over-the-top way. "Well, marry me. You sure do know your spices."

Baron nods, impressed. "Agree. And... black pepper as the twist?"

I test again. "You're right. One trick ingredient. It adds some warmth, not heat."

Baron gapes. "How are you, like, a cocoa psychic... the beverage whisperer?"

"Chocolate tasting skills," I remind him. "Actually, that last one tasted a little like the one I drank with the Captain when I ended up tongue-tied in her office."

"Your tasting skills are great," Maggie Jo quips.

I look up to see the Captain's mouth tilts, the smallest private look. Her eyes say, *I see you*.

Darius sees me see her seeing me and steps neatly between us, a human blizzard. "And cup E?"

I sip from cup E. "Coconut milk. Cardamom. Nice, but the cardamom pod suffered a death by overboil. It's not my favorite."

"That's my fault!" Chase yelps, coming up behind me. "I got excited and forgot time."

Baron murmurs, "Enthusiastic and careless. Thank god he's not navigating this ship."

"Wait, we have to name these after we listed the ingredients," I say, grabbing my paper to make up some cute names quickly, but Darius snatches it from me.

"I got this," he says, biting back his grin as he scribbles.

"Okay!" Chase yodels. "Time to turn in your sheets."

A crewmember takes our papers, and Chase flips through them and says, "Time to reveal our winner. Peppermint was A, spicy B, vegan E, maple C, and the mystery chef's kiss is our Captain's recipe was D. The winner with the best names is..." He pulls out a piece of paper to read them.

"The new hot chocolate tasting menu names are Candy Cane Invasion, Naughty List Winter mix, Oat Daddy Me Please, Sexy Italian Cocoa Kiss, and Cardamon Commitment Cocoa."

I clap, and Darius hoots, "That's you, Aurora!"

"Winner of the palate prize," Chase grins.

"For her tongue skills," Maggie Jo yells, trying to be helpful but only making me cringe.

I feel the weight of Captain Rossi's look.

Chase continues, "For nailing the names and correctly guessing the very complicated special ingredients in the hot chocolate, Aurora!" He holds up a snowflake trophy. "And winner of the ice carving—drumroll please—"

"Not us," I whisper. "That whale is the only identifiable ice sculpture of the four."

"Our favorite, well-endowed, *apparently,* newlyweds," he hollers. "Aurora and Darius!"

I die. I genuinely perish on the deck.

The crowd roars.

Darius bows like he won an Oscar. Maggie Jo blows kisses, and Baron claps enthusiastically, probably since he won't have to wear sasquatch slippers.

"Prizes!" Chase trills. "A gift-shop mega-credit and a private VIP cocoa flight named by our palate queen."

Darius leans in, sotto voce. "Take the credit, it was your tongue that did the work."

Chase claps his hands. "I went ahead and scheduled the shopping spree for this afternoon at two—just Aurora—so our groom can attend my Seal Facts & Fudge seminar!"

Baron, deadpans, "There will be no facts."

"Wrong!" Chase says, radiant, "Seals are full of fun facts, like they are only dogs of the ocean. Try throwing them a stick, and you'll be amazed. For more fun facts, come see me on the Forget-Me-Not stage at two pm, folks."

I whisper to Darius, "He's separating us on purpose. Chase is much more devious than we give him credit for. He might try to undo this marriage before the captain does."

"I'm sure it's just logistics," he says.

"Remember your kryptonite. And be careful," I warn, trying to sound authoritative.

He waves to Chase as he moves around the crowd to invite others. I sigh.

From above, the Captain descends the steel stairs confidently. The crew instinctively clears a path.

She stops in front of me with Valdez sparkling behind her, a black wedge of ship and mountains.

"Brava," she says, for me alone. "Orange and anise stellato. Perfetta, cara."

"Lucky guess," I say, heart, sprinting.

"And the name?" Her mouth tilts. "Very nice."

Darius slides in, smiles politely, eyes warning. "Captain, we appreciate the culinary thrill ride. We also need to stop by Guest Services ..."

She doesn't take her eyes off me. "Guest Services can wait. We have other matters to discuss."

"Which matters," Baron walks up at the perfectly timed moment. He is ready to be my wingman.

"Just some forms and paperwork for the winning couple," she says. "And any... misunderstandings."

Maggie Jo hums. "Do we need to fill out paperwork too? It is odd to have extra paperwork."

Chase bounces at her elbow. "Captain, are we doing the Valdez sea otter talk now?"

"Later," she says, and finally looks at him with her steady gaze, "And no more chainsaws without consulting a safety officer."

He salutes with two hands. "Yes, ma'am! Safety is my middle name."

"His middle name is 'Stanley,'" Darius whispers.

The Captain shifts back to me. "Two o'clock. Shopping. Da sola? Alone?"

"I—" I start.

Darius coughs. "She's busy at two. We have... bedroom duties to enjoy."

Chase gasps. "So romantic! It's terrible she'll have to do that alone. Come on Darius. You'll need to do a mic check with me as you are my co-host this afternoon."

"Sorry," Darius mouths, as he's dragged away by Chase.

"Rude," I say, cheeks hot.

Rossi leans in, whispering, closer than propriety and a camera drone would recommend. "I missed you last night," she says, voice velvet-warm. "Tonight you will not miss our appointment."

"I'm not—" I start.

"Your truth," she says, softer. "Talking, I mean. You owe me nothing else."

Maggie Jo inserts herself. "Captain, honey, aren't you needed at the wheel."

Rossi's gaze flicks to Maggie Jo, then back to me. "I am but I always am sure to make time for you, Aurora."

The Captain's radio crackles. She lifts it without looking away. "Sì? ... Sì. I'm coming." She tips her head, all commands again. "Congratulations on your... sculpture." Her eyes tease. Then she's gone, cutting through the crowd, leaving cologne and static in her wake.

I exhale like I've been holding my breath since Ketchikan.

Maggie Jo beams. "Time for a group photo with our antler friend."

"Hard pass," I say.

"Can you take our picture?" She passes me her phone. I follow her towards the door.

"Baron," Maggie Jo says, calling him to pose next to her. "He's going to the seal talk and will assure Darius' safety."

Baron nods. "I enjoy listening to fictional facts by Chase."

"Perfect." I say.

He checks the time. "We have forty minutes."

I cut across the deck. And wait to take their picture after the couple in front of us finishes a selfie with my reindeer.

The cold cuts through the hoodie and rushes back into the Atrium—tree sparkling, piano tinkling, newlyweds sipping champagne like it's a verb—and line up at Guest Services.

The queue is three couples deep with a man complaining about "cruise Wi-Fi throttling my crypto," a woman requesting extra pillows "for our fort," and an aunt announcing she lost her niece "somewhere near the towel moose." Maggie Jo offers the aunt a map. She looks at him as if he had handed her the moon.

My turn. The agent's name tag says "Priya." Her smile is holiday-customer-service brave. "How can I help?"

"Photo consent," I say, steady, like I'm not vibrating. "I want written confirmation that no photos of me are to be published, printed, circulated, or otherwise used without my written consent. Also, no images to be printed without my written consent." I inhale. "Consent both ways."

Priya's eyebrows go up a millimeter. "Of course. We can note a block on your folio for print and digital. Our photographers will honor it."

"And a copy?" Maggie Jo adds, warm and firm. "For our files."

Priya clicks like an octopus at a keyboard. "I'll print it."

I feel relief emptying my chest.

"We need some shopping therapy," Maggie Jo announces.

The shop is a glitter cave filled with jade pendants under glass, ulu knives engraved with salmon, parkas that cost a semester of textbooks, plush sea otters holding hands. The attendant chirps, "Welcome! I hear we have a mega-credit prize to spend."

"She does," Maggie Jo gushes.

I drift to a display of tiny carved ravens, black and clever. "Raven, in Eyak and Tlingit stories, brings light to the world." I think of the halyard raven, the way it watched me and didn't blink. Did he see my light and want to steal it?

"You can afford the earrings," Maggie Jo says.

"I can afford the truth," I say, and the words arrive before I know I've invited them.

She doesn't look surprised. "Then buy that too, if you afford it, Honey."

I try on the jade. It's cool and heavy, green. I catch my reflection in a sled ornament—distorted and small—and stick my tongue out at it.

I orbit the shop filling my basket with mittens for Dad, a sea-otter plush for Lisa, a mug that says, "I Put the Val in Valdez," and the earrings, because sometimes you must sparkle. I feel almost... normal. Shopper. Daughter. A person who can live in daylight. Now time to see what kind of warm clothes they have in here—

My phone buzzes.

Darius messages, "Chase says that sea otters are just long-haired seals, his facts are hilarious! Lol!"

I grin.

Unknown Number. “You’re shopping without me. New meeting for tonight. You better not run or hide.”

Chapter 17

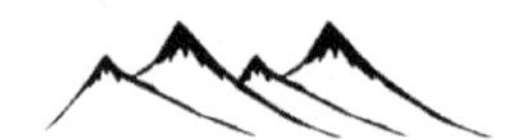

March of the Doomed Newlyweds

Day 5: Skagway, Alaska

"Slow down," I hiss, catching myself on the polished rail as the hallway tilts under my feet like the ship's trying to buck me into the sea. The Holiday Princess hums softly, all warm wood panels, luxury, and faint Christmas music, as the thickly carpeted hallways sway.

Darius glances back, gingerbread-themed sequined blazer flashing under the soft gold sconces. "Wifey-Poo, if we slow down anymore, we'll be moving backwards in time. We have an important meeting—"

"My execution," I correct automatically.

We pass by a big round window, and I'm yanked sideways by the view. Outside, the December night is deep blue and black, the harbor lights of Skagway scattered along the snow-blanketed shore. The ship's wake glows faintly under the deck lights, cutting through the dark water. In the distance, glacier-white mountains loom, their tops ghosted in low clouds.

Darius steps beside me, his reflection a glittery ghost. "Guuurrrl, have you been hitting Captain Cook's lounge without me? You can only blame so much of your drunken stagger on the boat."

"Rude."

"Accurate."

He bumps my shoulder. A sprig of fake spruce wrapped around the window frame scratches my wrist, and I stumble.

"The crew thinks I'm a recovering alcoholic, and I'm too famous–" I shrug in my Bride jacket, "–for them to not recognize me. The only way I'm getting a drink is if I steal it from a buffet-comatose passenger or if I sneak a drink from Maggie Jo.

I reread the text,"2200/10pm. My office. Come alone."

"Not ominous at all," I mutter. "Very super-duper casual. Very normal. Definitely not the opening scene of a Netflix documentary called 'Holiday Princess: The Disappearance of the Newlywed Con artist'."

"You are not disappearing," Darius says. "You are going to go in there, bat your Disney Princess eyes, and tell her, 'No, ma'am, we will not be signing any NDAs or any other contracts, including your secret sex contract!'"

I swallow, ignoring his joke. "What if she actually can ruin us, though? She's the captain. She literally controls the boat, and this is our first assignment for work."

"Okay, Grant didn't assign us this cruise to test us." He rolls his eyes. "Aurora, you're his daughter. He wants you to have fun–to enjoy a vacation because you are working hard for him *and* going to school full time. Your dad is not going to fire us if we can't make any official recommendations on this cruise or if your slutty ways get us kicked off this cruise. *Probably*. I'm like sixty percent sure."

"Wow, so reassuring."

We start walking again. The only sound is the rhythmic slap of my flip flops thumping on the carpet. The air smells like cinnamon, sea salt, and a particular cruise-ship scent that's part disinfectant, part expensive floral mix.

We pass the atrium opening, where fairy lights drip down six decks in a glittering curtain. A fake polar bear in a Santa hat grins up at us from the photo stage. Somewhere below, a band plays a jazzy version of "Jingle Bells," and I catch a glimpse of couples dancing—holiday beanies, sequined dresses, tourists enjoying the cruise vibes, and beautiful Alaskan mountains outside.

My chest squeezes. Happy couples enjoying a vacation. This should have been us. Not us us—me and Darius—but me and...

I picture Alexis in a black suit, her vibrant yellow loafers, glasses glinting, her arm around my waist as we spin under the chandelier. Her hand was secure at the small of my back. Her quiet murmur, *Breathe, Trouble. I've got you.*

"Stop that," Darius says softly.

"Stop what?"

"Doing the sad puppy eyes at every happy couple we pass."

"I am not—" My voice wobbles. "Okay, maybe a little."

He hooks his arm through mine. "Alexis had her chance. She had many, many chances. She made her choices, and it's not like you wouldn't take her back in a second if she popped out of a Christmas cake at the buffet.

I can't help but laugh thinking of my serious girlfriend–ex-girlfriend, popping out of a cake.

He squeezes my elbow. "Tonight is not about her. It's about a different terrible dominant woman with boundary issues."

"Wow, love that for me, dominate hotties."

"Pattern, babe. We need to talk to your therapist."

"Donna already has me on her appointment schedule for next week."

We turn another corner and nearly collide with Chase, the cruise director, who bursts out of a service door like an enthusiastic confetti cannon.

"Winning Newlyweds!" he booms, voice echoing off the metal ceiling. His smile is Florida-bright, tan golden against his too-white teeth. "There you are! I've been hunting you down."

Darius straightens unconsciously, glitter catching the light. "Hey, Sunshine."

Chase's gaze flicks over him shamelessly. "Wow. I love that blazer. It could guide bush planes in for landing."

"Only the worthy can land here," Darius purrs.

I throw my hands up. "Hi, wife over here, literally holding his arm., Remember the ring, very married. That's what makes us newlyweds."

Chase winks. "Oh, totally. My bad, Mrs. D. I respect the union. I just also respect... a fine dressed passenger." He gestures vaguely at Darius's torso.

Despite the panic simmering in my stomach, I snort. "You flirt more than Darius. Ugh. To be bold and gay!"

"Thank you, *I think?* Anyway, I just wanted to remind everyone, tomorrow is Glacier Glam Formal Night. We are anchoring near Columbia Glacier if the ice cooperates, so we're talking big blue walls, calving ice, bald eagles, maybe some harbor seals—otters as I like to call them—if they're feeling photogenic. You two need to be ready for your photo shoot at oh-eight-hundred sharp in the Sky Lounge. That free upgrade honeymoon package doesn't photograph itself. I want some stellar promo shots."

"Can't wait," I say, weakly. "Nothing says romance like being aggressively photographed at eight a.m. with non-alcoholic eggnog and my toes freezing in flipflops."

Darius squeezes my hand. "It will be okay, I bought you those shoes at the atrium shop, you can use a pair of my socks..."

"Sorry," I mumble. "Those shoes are thin canvas deck shoes. I'm getting boots and wool socks at the next stop. I'll be less grumpy with warm toes."

"She must be a delight to sleep with," Chase says, winking at Darius as I roll my eyes and bite my tongue.

"We gotta run. Good seeing you."

"Meeting with the Captain?" he guesses.

My stomach drops. "Why would you say that?"

He pulls a face. "She asked me where you were. Twice. Using her authoritative tone."

"Ah," Darius murmurs. "The Voice of Doom."

"Hey, she's not that bad," Chase says, but it sounds automatic. "She just... likes control. And rules. And starch."

"I kinda like the person steering the ship I'm on to be confident and follow the rules," I say, defending her for some odd reason.

He agrees. "Okay, yeah, you're right. She has the best record of the cruise line and her pick of ships and routes."

That's new. My heart flips, traitorously. Why is she so competent and respected by her staff?

Darius gives me a look that says, *do not soften.*

I straighten. "Well, then she should be a complete professional at our meeting today."

He backs away, thumbs up. "Break a leg, Newlyweds! Not literally, we only have one doctor on the ship and getting around in a cast with the number of stairs onboard would be a nightmare!"

He disappears around the corner, humming "Feliz Navidad."

Darius' gaze follows him, he murmurs. "I kind of hate him and love him."

"You absolutely do not."

"Okay, I hate that I want to climb him like a Christmas tree and lick a candy cane–"

"Stop now! I don't want a nightmare," I say, but my voice comes out thin.

We reach the end of the hallway. A small brass plaque reads Bridge Deck – Authorized Personnel Only. The Captain's Office is next to it. A tiny string of white fairy lights is wrapped around the doorframe, like someone tried to convince the door to be festive.

My heart tries to exit through my throat.

Darius turns to face me, hands on my shoulders. "I'll be right here outside the door."

His eyes are serious now, "remember the plan. No signing. No agreement. No kisses, no closed doors, no 'let's just keep this between us, Cara mia.' You're not someone's secret lover, Aurora. You deserve the best, because you are the best!"

The flash of my mother's voice, sharp as broken glass. "Keep your legs crossed, your mouth shut, and be invisible."

I shove the memory away. "Right. No secrets. I'm the best."

"And if she tries anything, you scream, and I'll come, kick the door down."

"You're not athletic."

"Emotionally, I'm a bull."

I nervously giggle and give him my finger guns for luck. "Okay."

He presses our foreheads together for a second, grounding. "You're strong, babe. Stronger than you think. Stronger than Rossi. Stronger than whatever weird mind game she thinks she's playing."

I take a breath that tastes like cinnamon and fear and far-off snow, then knock on the captain's door.

"Enter," comes the voice, muffled and accented through the door. Even through wood, it makes my knees reconsider their job description.

I open the door just enough to poke my head in. "Hi. It's me. The holiday pri... I mean Aurora. Aurora. Wow, off to a great start."

Captain Rossi sits behind a sleek, dark desk, lamplight painting her in warm gold. The room smells like coffee with a hint of something sharper—sea air sneaking in through a cracked window, or her cologne, or the ghost of every bad decision I've ever made.

She raises one perfect eyebrow. "Buona sera, Cara." Her Italian lilt wraps around my name like velvet around a knife. "Come in. Close the door."

I slip inside, leaving my hand on the knob. "Actually, um... I'm comfortable with it open. Maritime... breeze. Safety. Fire code."

Her gaze drops to my hand, then slides back up slowly. "You are afraid I will eat you, Cara?"

"That phrasing feels... intentional." A hint of waiver in my voice.

"Humor me," she says, voice softening. "There are some matters that should not be overheard by passing guests."

I hesitate, heart pounding. Darius's voice echoes in my head, "No closed doors, Wifey-Poo."

"I'm more comfortable with it open," I repeat, forcing my fingers to unclench. *Boundaries.* My therapist would be so proud. "If that's a problem, we can talk tomorrow with someone else present. Or not at all. That's also an option."

For a heartbeat, her expression flashes—annoyance, surprise, something like respect. Then she rises smoothly, strides past me, and brushes me as she pulls the door, leaving it cracked an inch. I hold my breath but notice the latch does not fully click.

"Compromise," she says.

I exhale. "Okay. Compromise. We love a boundary-respecting—"

"That is not how I have been described," she says drily, moving back to the desk. "Sit."

There's a small seating area with two navy armchairs facing each other with a low table between, a bowl of wrapped chocolates on top. The chocolates are aligned like tiny soldiers. I sit on the edge of one chair, hands folded so tightly my knuckles ache.

Rossi doesn't sit immediately. She moves to a shelf, pulls down a carafe. "Cocoa?" she asks. "Non-alcoholic." Her mouth twists into a smirk.

I flinch. She notices.

"Sure," I mumble.

She pours rich, dark cocoa into a mug and hands it to me. Our fingers brush. My skin sparks like I stuck it in an outlet.

I wrap my hands around the mug, grateful for the comforting warmth even as my stomach churns. Tiny marshmallows float on top like the last survivors of the Titanic.

"You were not at the dessert buffet tonight," she says, returning to her chair. "Your husband was with the promiscuous cruise director."

The word *husband* puckers her lips, sour in her mouth.

"I was tired," I say. "We're fine." Lie. Half-lie. Fractional lie. "I just needed air and space."

Her eyes flick to the window where snow dusts the glass from outside, the ghost of Valdez's harbor lights reflects faintly. "Then you chose to come here... to be with me, Cara."

I wince. "Can we not—"

"Okay, Holiday Princess. I like the nickname," she says. "It suits you. You are all tinsel and chaos, shining very brightly while everything under you is tangled and overworked."

"That is disturbingly accurate."

"I am a captain," she says with a shrug, finally sitting. "I read storms and know how to read people." She winks along with her sly smile.

I look at her over the table. Up close like this, I notice small details of the faint line at the corner of her mouth where she presses her lips when she's irritated. The way one rebellious piece of dark hair escaped her hat under her temple. The gold captain's bars at her shoulders, polished to a mirror sheen.

Objectively, *she is gorgeous.* Subjectively, *she is an ethical hazard.*

I force my gaze to the mug. "So. Why am I here?" I blurt. "Is this about missing our meeting last night? Or you noticed that Darius cheated on the 'who said I love you first' question in the Newlywed Game. He definitely said it first, and it was about my shoes."

Her lips twitch. "No. There are others... matters we must discuss."

She taps the tablet in front of her. The screen lights up with a photo, and my stomach plummets. It's us on the deck yesterday—me and Darius, mid-laugh, snowflakes in my hair, his arm around my shoulders. We look stupid, unfairly happy. A red caption bar across the bottom reads, "WINNING NEWLYWEDS!"

Rossi swipes—another photo shows me alone on the railing, watching the water. My smile is small, private. The angle is slightly lower than eye level. It feels too intimate, like someone spying.

"Did you know," she says, voice mild, "that as part of the Star Newlywed package, the cruise line's photographer team actually requires an NDA from the couple because of the instructions to capture candid images? For promotional use. Social media. Advertisements. Holiday brochures. We need to know that you won't say anything that contradicts the image we are portraying of your vacation."

"Yeah." My voice comes out thin. "We heard them say something. I can't quite recall as I was busy having a meltdown about not being in the Caribbean."

"Si." She swipes again. My heart stutters. This one is in the couple's spa cabana—me, lying on my stomach, face turned toward Darius, laughing so hard my eyes are squeezed shut. The angle captures my bare back, the curve of my waist, the tiny scars near my knees from learning to bike on gravel roads. Darius's hand is resting over mine, both of us slick with massage oil and ridiculousness.

Then another. The mistletoe kiss from the welcome party—the captain herself leaning down, lips grazing mine, my eyes wide, cheeks flushed. The elevator picture and then pictures of my topless white body when I slipped overboard.

My breath stops.

"Interesting," she says quietly. "Interesting."

"I—" My lungs forget they're allowed to function. "Why are you showing me these?"

She turns the tablet around, so the glow faces her again. "Because, Aurora, the company intends to use them. You and your—" her mouth twists slightly "—husband are very... marketable. Young. Attractive. Diverse. Relatable. The marketing department is... how do you say... salivating."

"Oh good," I croak. "My humiliation is on brand."

Her gaze sharpens. "Do you wish these images to be used?"

I think of my father's company and how I'm supposed to be reviewing this cruise, not honeymooning on it.

Most of all, I think of Alexis scrolling casually one night, seeing me with the headline of "Holiday Princess's Favorite Newlyweds! Alaska's Cutest Couple!"

My throat burns. "No," I say. "I don't."

"Because you don't love Darius in that way," Rossi says, not a question.

Blood rushes to my face. "I... It's not just that. I mean, yes, that, but also the privacy thing, and I'm literally exposed in some photos ... It feels... unprofessional. And weird. And—"

"And dishonest," she finishes. "Because you are not married to your soulmate. Because you are not straight."

The words hang between us–a dropped and shattered ornament, glittering and dangerous. My fingers tighten around the mug.

"I didn't say—"

"You didn't have to." She leans forward, forearms resting on her knees. "Cara mia, I am not blind. You look at women starving in a bakery. You look at men like... socks. Sometimes useful. Never thrilling."

"That is an oddly specific analogy."

"I have seen many people, many couples," she continues. "You and Darius aren't a forever match."

"I love him. He's my best friend," I say with complete honesty.

"Yet, you kiss me twice," she says softly. "You wear a ring and play a game. Why?"

Anger flares, protective. "Because everyone is counting on me. Because this cruise... You gave us a prize and labelled us, and I was flattered and too far in to deny it."

Her jaw tightens. "I did not tell you to throw yourself at me and beg for my attention or for a free suite and cruise perks. That was your choice."

I open my mouth, stunned, and shut it again. *She's not wrong.* I *hate* that *she's not wrong.*

She swipes again. A new document fills the screen—dense text, my name at the top. My insides freeze over.

"What is that?" I ask.

"A non-disclosure agreement and all image rights agreement," she says. "Prepared by the corporate office, modified by me. It states that the candid photographs of you and Darius will not be used for any promotional or advertising purposes without your express, written, separate consent. It also states that the events of the last four days—the mistletoe incident, your... personal circumstances—will not be shared with anyone in a way that could negatively affect you."

I stare. "So... you're... protecting me?"

She inclines her head. "It is my ship. I protect what happens on it."

Suspicion creeps in, cold and thin. "What's the catch?"

Her gaze is steady. "You sign this, and I delete any pictures of the two of us together and pictures of your breasts...in return, you agree to certain... considerations."

Yeah, there it is. My heart sinks through the floor.

"What kind of considerations?" I ask, voice brittle.

"You will continue to be happily on your honeymoon until disembarkation," she says. "No mention of me or sudden confessions to guests or staff that you had anything but friendly interactions with me. No dramatic stories about when you kissed me. We avoid scandal and the ship still has its promotional material for our honeymoon cruises."

"So... act like you didn't threaten to blackmail me to go into your room late at night or try to create a sexual relationship between us."

"For three more days," she says. "Then you go home, you play your games with whomever you like. The company remains intact, the guests remain happy, and I do not have to answer questions from corporate about why the winning newlywed bride was spending so much time with the Captain."

The word queer in her mouth lands somewhere between insult and affection. I shift uneasily.

"And?" I ask. "Because I feel like there's an 'and.'"

She is silent for a beat. Then says, "You must stop avoiding me."

I blink. "What?"

"You keep running away," she says calmly. "You duck behind decorations. you schedule spa appointments. you disappear to the lower decks."

I lick my lips, and her lips press into a smirk.

Her eyes glitter. "I just want you to admit the truth, Holiday Princess. I want you to admit what you feel when you look at me."

My pulse stutters. Panic claws at my ribs. "This is wildly inappropriate."

"Is it?" she murmurs. "Or is it only inappropriate because you are playing wife to a man you do not love? Because you are pretending a life that does not fit, while everything in you reaches for something else?"

My throat closes.

She rises, slow and deliberate, and steps around the table. I sit frozen as she comes to stand in front of me.

"Stand up," she says softly.

Every cell in my body yells no, but my legs obey. I stand. She towers over me by a few inches, the captain's bars gleaming at my eye level.

"You need... to say it," she says.

She lifts her hand, and I flinch as her fingers brush my wrist, where it hangs at my side. Her touch is warm, thumb pressing gently over my pulse.

"You like me," she says. "Admit it. I want to hear you say that you want me and you want me to please you, to do anything I want with you."

I jerk back like I've been slapped. "Are you serious?"

Her eyes are dark. "Do you think I am playing, Bella Holiday Princess?"

Rage spikes, hot and bright, cutting through fear. "You would risk my marriage, my happiness, Darius's vacation all because your ego can't handle me not stroking it?"

Her jaw tightens. "Do not reduce this to ego. I saw right through your lies the first day. You should be with a woman."

She steps closer again, backing me toward the wall near the slightly open door. My shoulder blades bump the cool wood. The crack of hallway light is at my left peripheral, tantalizing.

"Tell me you feel nothing," she says, palm sliding up my wrist to my forearm. "Tell me you do not replay that mistletoe kiss when you fall asleep. Tell me you don't imagine what it would be like to be with someone who will take total control of you."

Alexis's voice echoes in my head. *You aren't wife material. I love you, but I'm not in love with you.*

My mother's voice follows with, *Be grateful anyone wants you.*

And beneath them, a quieter truth. *I am tired. I am so, so tired of never being enough.*

"Stop," I whisper. "Please."

Her hand pauses. "Sign the agreement," she says softly. "I'll let you leave after you do one thing for me."

"What thing?" I ask, though I already know.

She lifts her free hand to my cheek, fingertips feather-light. My breath hitches.

"A kiss after you tell me." She says, "A kiss that you choose."

My heart slams. "That's not a choice. That's coercion."

She flinches, barely. "You know disaster when you see it," she says. "You told me that on deck. I am giving you the map out of this one. Sign, kiss, and walk away with your life intact. Or walk out that door and see what happens."

My vision blurs.

My therapist's voice faintly says, *You deserve relationships built on consent, healthy boundaries with no power imbalance.*

I stare up at Rossi. Her gaze is intense, hungry, but there's something else too—a flicker of vulnerability, of loneliness carved into lines at the edges of her eyes from years of being the person in charge, the one everyone fears but no one touches.

"I hate this," I whisper.

"No you don't," she says.

The worst part? Some awful, treacherous part of me *does* want her. Wants her sharp edges and that terrifying confidence, the eyes that see every secret I try to hide. Wants a distraction big enough, dangerous enough, to numb the heartbreak clawing at my ribs.

I close my eyes. "If I do this... you delete everything. Not just the brochure photos. The candids. The topless pictures. The other files. All of it. And you never bring it up again. You never threaten me or Darius."

"Agreed," she says immediately.

"And you stop asking me to come to your room or do anything else," I add, voice cracking.

She goes very still. "All right," she says at last. "I will." She sounds like the word is new in her mouth.

I open my eyes. "Get the tablet," I say hoarsely.

She releases my arm, steps away. I sag against the wall, nausea rolling. She returns with the stylus and hands it to me. My name stares up from the NDA like it's already disappointed.

My fingers tremble as I scroll, skim, and sign where she indicates. The stylus squeaks softly on glass as I scrawl my crooked signature. It feels like signing away a version of myself I haven't even fully met yet.

When it's done, she sets the tablet on the desk and taps a few commands. "The photos are flagged for deletion from marketing's drive," she says. "My personal copies?" She hesitates. "I will erase them."

"Now," I say.

She sighs, opens a folder. Thumbnails of the two of us kissing and my topless pale form wink up at me. With a sharp motion, she selects them and hits delete. They vanish.

The relief is immediate and hollow.

"There," she says.

"Okay," I whisper. My heart thrums in my throat. "Then... the other part."

She looks at me like I'm the last warm thing on a frozen planet.

"Say it," she demands.

I square my shoulders. "I wanted you from the first moment I saw you," I say and take a deep breath, then continue. "I have wanted to feel your hands on me and lips against me, taking control of me."

"You have," she murmurs.

She steps close again, slower this time, giving me space to bolt. I don't. My feet remain rooted, working against me.

Her hand comes up to my cheek, warm and calloused. "Look at me," she says.

I do. Her eyes lock onto mine—amber warmth layered over something sharp, almost dangerous.

I swallow. She leans closer.

The kiss is soft at first, testing. No audience, no mistletoe, no cameras. Just lips and air and the faint taste of cocoa and coffee. It deepens as she presses closer, her hand sliding to firmly hold the back of my neck. My fingers, not listening to reason, grasp and curl in the crisp fabric of her uniform.

Heat flashes through me, confusing and electric. For a brief, terrible second, I forget everything—the lie, Alexis, my mother's voice, my therapist's notebook. There is only the surety of her mouth on mine, the solidity of her body, the way she makes the world go very, very quiet.

Then the guilt slams into me.

I tear myself away, stumbling back. My lips feel swollen. My chest heaves.

"Enough," I gasp. "That's enough."

Rossi's pupils are blown wide. She steps back, jaw working. "All right," she says roughly. "We are... that's enough for now."

I swipe at my mouth like I can remove the memory. "No," I say. "We are done, this is it."

"I gave my word," she says with a sharp tone. "Go, Holiday Princess. Enjoy the rest of your fairy tale honeymoon but I hope you think of me when you are lying with your husband tonight."

I fumble the door open the rest of the way and spill into the hallway. Everything out here is too bright—the carpet too colorful, the Christmas music offensively cheerful. I spot Darius and blow past him.

"Uh—Aurora?" he calls, confused, but he hurries after me as I walk fast, then faster, my steps barely hitting the floor.

I don't stop until we reach our suite. I slam the keycard against the sensor—wrong angle, wrong side, shaking too hard—*wrong. Wrong. Wrong!* Until the light finally flashes green.

Chapter 18

Marriage Blizzards & Broken Promises

Day 5: Skagway, Alaska

Darius's eyes narrow once we have our cabin door closed. "What happened?"

Here it is. The edge of the cliff.

The meeting, my heart pounding, the document, I tell him everything, ending with, "I kissed her," I whisper. "I kissed her."

The ship's hum fills the room. The documentary guy on the TV mouths silently about calving glaciers.

He lets out a strangled squeal. "Wow. Just—wow. Why didn't you leave or get me? We explicitly decided you would stall, Aurora. Stall. Not go in there and kiss the puppet-master Captain like you're auditioning for 'Fifty Shades of Maritime Law.'"

"The door was cracked," I say, then immediately groan. It sounds idiotic even to me.

His eyes go sharp, a hurt wrapped in fury.

"We had a plan. A plan you agreed to. And instead of following it, you sacrifice yourself on the altar of yet another domineering alpha jerk because you think your body is the currency that will rescue us from this mess."

My throat burns. "I didn't have time to call a committee meeting, Darius. It was happening fast. She had the documents. She had the photos. I made the call."

"No." He shakes his head so hard his curls whip his cheeks. "You made the same bad call you always make. You picked to submit to a sexy woman that you secretly are attracted to and holds a position of power instead of picking yourself."

"That's not—"

"Sandra," he says, holding up a finger. "Alexis." Another finger. "Captain Rossi." He fans his whole hand. "Different uniforms, different fonts, but the same damn operating system of controlling, charismatic, competitive, allergic to your boundaries."

"I *have* boundaries," I whisper.

It sounds pathetic even to *me*.

Darius doesn't soften. Not this time.

"Do you?" His voice cracks—not with anger, but with heartbreak. "Because from where I'm standing, your boundaries fold faster than origami whenever someone strong-willed looks at you too long."

I flinch like he slapped me. "Darius... I—"

"I'm not mad," he says quietly, but the edge could cut steel. "I'm disappointed."

The word detonates inside my chest. It lands harder than any argument. Harder than any business accounting lecture. It lands like a glacier calving—violent, cold, irreversible.

Tears spill over before I can stop them. Hot, humiliating.

"I'm sorry," I choke. "I'm so sorry. I keep thinking I've grown past this awful pattern where I bend for people who make me feel like I have to earn every scrap of approval. But put me in a fancy room with someone in a uniform and I turn into a... a steaming pile of bad decisions."

He lets out a hollow laugh. "At least you admit it. That's a step."

"I don't know how to stop," I whisper, shaking. "I don't know how to choose people who don't expect me to shrink. I don't know how to stop chasing people who make me feel small because maybe—maybe I've believed that's what I deserve."

Darius's face crumples. The anger melts into something rawer. Sadder.

"You start choosing yourself," he says. "You stop letting other people write your story just because they have a shinier pen and a scarier voice."

"I signed the NDA," I whisper. "I didn't stall. I didn't get the photos back. I didn't hold the line. I'm sorry."

He closes his eyes briefly, like he's absorbing the hit.

"You signed the NDA," he repeats, voice trembling. "Do you know what that means? Our entire job—our whole chance to prove ourselves? Gone. Just—gone. You didn't just risk you, Aurora. You risked us. Our future. Our work. Everything."

I collapse onto the nearest chair. "I know."

"You promised me," he continues, voice cracking. "You promised you'd set boundaries. You promised you'd tell her no. You promised you'd get those files destroyed, not get tangled deeper in her games. And instead—"

He gestures helplessly toward the door. Toward the whole ship.

"—you gave her more power."

My throat burns like I swallowed fire. "I know," I whisper. "And I hate myself for it."

"No," he says gently. "Don't hate yourself. Just... stop being your own worst enemy, choose yourself, choose your happiness."

The room shrinks. The swan, heart-shaped towel leers. The untouched champagne looks accusatory. Even the glacier glinting outside the window feels like it's judging me.

Then—

Bzzt. BZZT.

My phone lights up on the coffee table.

For one brief, hopeful second, my heart leaps.

Alexis?

Anyone to pull me out of this mess, even if it's just for a breath.

Darius and I look at the phone.

Bzzt. Bzzt. BZZT.

Lisa messages, "Babe, Alexis just texted me. CALL ME."

My heart trips over itself.

"Of course she did," Darius mutters. "The universe is invested in your chaos arc."

BZZT.

"Aurora, I'm serious. Call now."

Darius turns to me, eyes wide, equal parts fear and frustration.

"Aurora. Are you serious right now? Are you actually about to jump into the emotional woodchipper that is Alexis?"

I swallow hard.

"Aurora," he says, softer but infinitely more stern, "you cannot keep choosing people who dim your shine just because you're used to the dark."

"I'm not— I don't know—"

He cuts me off. "I'm sleeping on the couch tonight."

The sentence knocks the breath from my lungs.

I stand there—between the honeymoon-suite towel swans and the glittering glacier outside, between the half-finished cookies and the empty champagne flutes, between Darius wrapped in a blanket like armor and my phone buzzing like a live grenade—and I realize something.

This is the lowest point.

Not kissing Rossi.

Not the NDA.

Not Alexis's name haunting me on my screen.

It's Darius looking at me not with love or exasperation or the usual soft indulgence.

But with disappointment.

It hits me painfully, a physical blow. Because I didn't just mess up a plan. I didn't just put our assignment—or our futures—at risk.

I let down the one person who has always chosen me and loved me.

The one who believes in me without conditions. Who never asks me to shrink, earn, perform, or pass some ridiculous test to be loved.

And somehow that hurts more than anything Rossi threatened. More than Alexis's cold perfection. More than any NDA, kiss, blackmail, or mistakes that I keep stumbling into.

This pain? This quiet, honest *Darius-is-disappointed-in-me* pain?

Cracks something inside of me. It splinters the small, sharp breaks I didn't realize I was barely holding together.

Chapter 19

Port-Day Panic & Holiday Charm

Day 5: Skagway, Alaska

Cold slaps my face the second we step into Skagway's air—sharp, clean, glacier-chilled.

"What the hell," I gasp as frost knifes up my nostrils. I yank my hoodie tighter, layering a tank top over a T-shirt, then over a long sleeve. I'm dressing for a survival class that I'm failing.

The dock is dusted in that specific Alaskan snow texture—half powder, half crunchy ice, all malicious.

"Careful," Darius says without looking at me. "I do not have the emotional strength to drag your corpse back up the gangway. Or explain it to your dad."

"So caring," I shoot back. My breath ghosts into the air like little white gossip clouds.

"Should we go back for your lover's jacket?" he says, giving my outfit a slow, judgmental sweep. "You'd be warmer in the Captain's coat than in that cotton billboard for our faux relationship."

"I returned it," I say, quickly. "I mean, I asked the room attendant to return it. Close enough."

"That's growth," he says. "You are severing that emotional tie. Good job."

His tone is flat. He still won't meet my eyes.

We haven't really talked since he exiled himself to the couch after our fight last night.

We did the Winning Newlywed Glacier Glam photoshoot this morning like two professionally miserable mannequins—him in a velvet blazer, me in a borrowed lost-and-found parka that smelled like pine and despair. We smiled on cue. We held hands like people who vaguely tolerated each other.

We are basically an old married couple... except ours is built on lies and disappointment.

But today—finally—no schedules.

No Captain.

No curated Winning Newlywed Activities.

No threats.

Just Skagway.

The Holiday Princess towers behind us, a floating winter palace, all twinkling lights and white steel. Her name glows in blue across the hull, shimmering on the dark green water.

"Wow," Darius breathes, finally sounding like a person again. Darius's breath fogs in front of him, and he murmurs. "Okay... okay, this little village is *adorable* as hell."

I grin despite myself.

Ahead, Skagway huddles at the base of enormous mountains—tiny, colorful storefronts smashed together. Old-timey signs. Gold Rush fonts. The whole Klondike cosplay.

"Oh my god," I whisper. "It looks like someone took a Wild West set from Disneyland and dropped it in the middle of nowhere."

Darius snorts. "Honestly? I'm into it, girl." He smiles for a selfie.

We step forward, and my hood twists in the wind, the cold bites, but something warm unfurls inside my chest.

"Was it really like this during the Gold Rush?" I ask. "Or did tourism decide Skagway should dress up like the Old West from movies?"

"Definitely a small village playing dress up," he says. "But she's serving frontier fierceness and is perfect for pictures."

Behind the themed shops, I spot the real Skagway—tiny houses tucked into frosted trees, smoke curling from chimneys, quiet streets.

And something in my chest... loosens.

I swallow. "I could live here."

Darius side-eyes me. "Aurora, you said that about Seward, and that one weird gas station town with the giant salmon statue."

"That statue had charm."

"It had teeth."

We walk down the dock, pace steady, breath pluming in unison.

"Still," I say softly, "this place feels... peaceful. I can breathe."

Darius's voice softens. "Maybe because we are finally relaxing and not pretending to be the perfect newlyweds. Being married to you isn't easy, Wifey poo."

"Ouch," I mutter.

He shrugs, utterly unapologetic. "Accurate."

We pass souvenir stalls—tiny carved ravens, totem pole magnets, hoodies that say, *Alaska. Where the Men Are Men, and the Women Win the Iditarod.*

Darius stops reading it. "Iconic. My favorite new favorite Alaskan phrase. I want one."

"You'd never take it off."

"Correct."

We continue toward the small terminal building—a squat brown box advertising every excursion imaginable from Klondike walking tours, whale watching, dog sledding on a glacier, to helicopter flights offering, "A View You'll Tell Your Grandkids About!"

"Yeah, we're not doing the helicopter," I say.

"We are absolutely not doing the helicopter, you have terrible luck, so I can't even imagine what would happen to us on a helicopter," he echoes. "Even if we 'won' a tour, I'd be too worried the Captain would have the pilot drop you into a volcano, and I'd be dropped in too, as collateral damage."

"Too soon," I mutter.

Inside the terminal, warmth hits us like a welcome hug. The place smells like wet wool, halibut and chips, and over-brewed coffee. Passengers queue at a makeshift post office table, mailing postcards home with little Alaskan stamps.

Darius leans closer, bumping my shoulder. "Okay, let's find the mailing station, buy some postcards, take in some local culture, and then, later, confront the rest of your emotional issues."

I laugh under my breath. "You're still mad at me."

"Mad?" he scoffs. "Oh, sweetie, no. I'm just... annoyed and selectively speaking to you in short, clipped sentences so I don't scream in frustration of watching you make the same bad choices over and over."

"Valid."

He sighs. "Let's enjoy Skagway. At least until the next crisis. Which, knowing you, will be... in about—" He glances at his watch. "Twelve minutes."

"That's generous."

"I know."

The bells on the door jingle as we step into the post office. Darius beelines to a counter where a woman in a fleece vest stands behind a stack of packages.

"Hi!" he chirps with a fake brightness. "We're from the Holiday Princess. Someone said there was a delivery from... a Lisa?"

The woman brightens. "You must be Aurora and Darius. Your friend is upbeat and was excited to send you a special gift."

"That's our girl," he sighs.

She notices my hoodie, "I'll get that for you. Congratulations on the new marriage."

She ducks down and comes up with a medium-sized shipping box decorated in Lisa's glitter-pen handwriting with stickers, sparkly snowflakes, hearts.

YOU'RE DOING GREAT BABE!□

My throat tightens. "Oh no," I whisper. "She care-packaged me on vacation."

The woman scans something and hands the box over. It's surprisingly heavy, with edges dented and tape reinforced with washi in a candy cane pattern.

"Happy holidays," she says. "You folks enjoy Skagway. The whale-watching's good today—they say a humpback was bubble-net feeding right off the channel this morning."

"Cool," I say faintly. "Love those whales."

We step aside. Darius plops the box on a bench and pulls out a keychain pocket knife because, of course, he has one–he's Alaskan. But because he is also Darius, it's in the shape of a tiny sequined boot.

"This is either going to be life-changing or hilarious," he says, slicing the tape.

"Knowing Lisa, *both*."

The cardboard gives, and a puff of cold air and dryer-sheet smell hits my nose. I peer inside.

On top, there's a letter in a neon-pink envelope.

AURORA OPEN FIRST or I'll tell your therapist.

"Seems sus," Darius says.

"It's like she knows me," I mutter, tearing it open.

Lisa's looping handwriting explodes across the page.

> BESTIE
> 1. YOU ARE NOT ALLOWED TO FREEZE TO DEATH ON A CRUISE.
> 2. YOU ARE ALSO NOT ALLOWED TO HAVE AN IDENTITY CRISIS IN ONLY SUMMER DRESSES.
> 3. I love you.
> I talked to Darius and confirmed that you're in actual freezing-cold Alaska, not the Caribbean. I did a Target run for you.
> You're welcome.
> Also... don't freak out... but Alexis helped.
> <u>I KNOW. BREATHE</u>. I actually enjoy hanging out with her.
> Read her card next.
> Love,
> Lisa

My heart does a weird lurch-twist. "Alexis helped?"

Darius makes a face. "Oooh. Plot twist!"

He parts the tissue paper before I can. Inside the package is folded denim, thick wool socks, and a deep-green winter jacket that looks way too nice to be from Target. There are also boots—actual winter boots, waterproof with good tread, not the fashion-suicide flipflops I've been recently skating in.

"Holy... wow," I whisper, running my fingers over the jacket. The fabric is smooth, lined with faux fur at the hood. Embroidered in small gold thread on the inside is Aurora Thompson. Beneath it, a tiny stitched compass.

My chest squeezes. "Alexis had this custom made."

"That is Alexis' signature move, isn't it? Unless she mugged someone with your name who wears very stylish REI clothing," Darius says. But his voice is soft now.

I spot a small navy envelope tucked into one of the jacket's pockets. The paper is thick, expensive, and familiar.

My fingers shake as I pull it out. Only a simple, recognizable "A" is on the f written across it.

Alexis's precise, compact handwriting.

Read it, a stupid hopeful part of me whispers. *Don't,* the self-preservation part of me argues.

I open it.

Her scent hits me faintly even here—clean, like cedar and citrus, or maybe that's just my brain filling in blanks.

> **Aurora** – Lisa told me where you are.
>
> Alaska in winter?
>
> On a ship?
>
> Wearing summer dresses?!
>
> It made me smile. It made me worry. It made me miss you more than I expected.
>
> This isn't me asking for anything. It's not a ploy. It's an apology I should have given you long before now.
>
> You deserved someone who made you feel seen and safe. I made you feel small.
>
> You deserved someone who asked what you needed. I asked you to fit into what I needed.
>
> And still... You brought this brightness into my life. A warm presence that improves the office systems and the people around you.
>
> You're good, Aurora. Kind. Smart. Capable. And so much more powerful than you give yourself credit for.
>
> The jacket is to keep you from freezing.

> The boots are because you always lean too far over the railing to get a better look.
> The charm is a reminder of you I carry, and of being better in relationships.
> If someday you want to talk—not to fix anything, just to be heard—I'd like that.
>
> Stay warm,
> And stay safe.
> **Alexis**

Something heavy that I didn't know I was holding inside me just... cracks and falls away.

Darius is watching my face like it's a courtroom drama. "Well?" he asks. "Is she still a workaholic robot, or did she catch feelings?"

"Both," I croak. "She apologized in her businesslike way."

"That's pretty much the closure you needed, right?"

I sniff, laugh wetly. "I guess."

I reach back into the pocket like she instructed. My fingers close around something cool and metallic. I pull it out.

It's the tiny holiday charm—a miniature enamel aurora borealis, streaks of green and pink over a line of black mountains. We saw it in a shop window in Anchorage, and she bought it, clipped it to her keys, and said, "*Now I'm always carrying a piece of you... or at least your name.*"

My vision blurs.

"I forgot about this," I whisper. "I thought she'd... thrown it out."

"Maybe she cares more than you think," Darius says with a shrug, adding, "Competent women who apologize and buy expensive gifts. This is progress and it should be your new kink."

I laugh, the sound cracking in the middle. "She says I'm good at this. At... this," I wave vaguely at the ship outside, at the tide, at everything.

"You are," he says. No hesitation.

The words settle somewhere deep, like warm sand in winter.

For the first time since boarding, I feel a flicker of something that isn't panic or shame.

I feel... proud.

I'm reviewing this cruise and helping my dad's business. I'm seeing Alaska with tourist eyes and home eyes at the same time, listening to Alaskan stories and Alaskan tourists. I'm good at connecting it all, translating chaos into something useful.

I'm not just a walking disaster. I'm a person with skills that people love.

"Maybe..." I say softly, trailing off without finishing my swirling thoughts about Alexis.

He nudges my shoulder. "What do you want? Not from her. For you."

I stare at the charm in my palm. "I want... to be with someone who sees me like this," I say slowly. "Not as a prop or a fling."

"Dream big, Aurora," Darius murmurs.

I snort. "Thanks."

"It's what you deserve."

I tuck the charm carefully into the inner pocket of the new jacket. It's like sliding a little piece of my past into a safer place.

"Are we... okay?" I ask, voice small.

He looks at me for a long second, then sighs. "No," he says honestly. "But also yes. I love you and I want the best for you."

Outside, the raven on the pole calls, loud and rough, like it's laughing. The mountains loom quiet and old, their glacier valleys carved by time and pressure, not speed.

For the first time, I let myself imagine a future where I'm not constantly bending myself into shapes to fit someone's plan. Where maybe, just maybe, Alexis could be part of that future... if she keeps bending too.

Darius bumps my shoulder. "C'mon, wifey."

I slide into the jacket. It fits like it was made for me. Which, *apparently,* it was.

Somewhere between the snow and the salt air and the weight of the charm over my heart, a new thought slips in.

Maybe I'm allowed to want more than survival.

Maybe I'm allowed to want a love that is like this jacket—warm, chosen for me, respectful of where I'm going, not just how I look or an easy date, and keeps me safe.

In the afternoon, the sky fades from pale blue to silver-gray, as if someone had dimmed the giant overhead light. Snow flurries swirl intermittently, dusting the docks and the stacked crab pots.

Outside, the Holiday Princess's horn sounds low and long across the harbor, breaking my thoughts to beckon us back to the ship.

Curious about that Alaskan phrase:
'Alaska... where the Men Are Men, and the Women Win the Iditarod.'

Check out the bestselling opposites-attract romance of Brynn and Morgan during the Iditarod sled dog race in

Wilderness Rescue: Iditarod Love.

CHECK IT OUT HERE or HarmonyNoble.com

Chapter 20

Farewell, Skagway. Hello, Boundaries

Day 5: Skagway, Alaska

We trudge back up the Massive ship's gangway, boots thunking. For the first time on the cruise, my toes are not icicles. The new jacket warmly hugs my torso, hood down, fur tickling my neck.

"This is heaven," I say, flexing my toes. "My feet have never known this feeling."

"It's called insulation," Darius says. "Some of us discovered it before turning nineteen."

"You're just jealous that Alexis bought me stylish boots and didn't get anything for you."

"True," he agrees. "But not having to watch you rush inside to warm up and thaw your toes is a gift for me too."

We step back onto Deck 5, the promenade. It's lined with faux-gas lamps wrapped in white lights and red bows. The air smells like the sea mixed with cinnamon from the nearby cocoa station for the "Farewell to Skagway Deck Party." Couples pose by the railings, breath puffing, cheeks red.

Ahead, near the midship doors, Maggie Jo and Baron lean against the rail like two spectators at a drama they paid top dollar to see.

"Well, if it isn't my favorite little scandal muffins," Maggie Jo drawls. She's in a fur-trimmed white coat and sparkly earmuffs, lipstick a defiant candy-apple red. "Turn around, lemme see this coat."

I twirl automatically. The hem swishes around my thighs, boots squeaking on the wet deck.

"Land sakes," Maggie Jo whistles. "You look downright functional, honey."

"Warmth looks good on me," I declare. "I'm rebranding from 'Frostbite Princess' to 'Competent Queen' in outerwear."

"About time, dear," Baron murmurs. His practical parka is zipped to his chin, and his glasses are delicately fogged at the edges. "We were placing bets on when you'd lose a toe."

"Rude," I say, crossing my arms, then shoot him a smile.

Maggie Jo waves a mittened hand. "Honey, I have *never* seen a woman with feet your size, or I'd have lent you my spare boots days ago!"

She eyes the embroidered name inside the collar like she has X-ray vision. "That jacket custom?" she asks. "That's quality stitching, not gift shop nonsense. Who's spoiling you, sugar?"

I hesitate. Darius jumps in. "Her ex," he sings. "The hot one I told you about with the jawline and the control issues."

Maggie Jo claps her gloved hands so hard her earrings jingle.

"Oooh, *that* one. The fancy CEO who let you slip through her fingers?" She sees my face and gasps.

"Oh honey, bless her cold corporate heart. You're too darling to put up with that foolishness. Makes me wanna march right up to her and whack her with my church-lady handbag—the heavy one."

"She sent an apology package," I say. "Jacket, boots, some good vibes."

Baron raises a brow. "Handwritten?"

"Yeah."

He nods once. "Promising."

Maggie Jo slants her head at me. "And how does that make your little heart feel?"

"Confused but happy," I blurt and blush.

"Speaking of whales and admirers," Baron says dryly, "Darius, your personal sunshine dispenser and source of questionable Alaskan trivia is approaching."

We all look up.

Chase is striding down the deck like it's his runway. Clipboard in hand, branded beanie tugged down over that perfectly sculpted golden hair. The second he spots us, his whole face lights up—like someone cranked his brightness to *blinding*.

"My favorite newlyweds!" he booms.

He stops in front of us, giving Darius a slow once-over that should—by all laws of physics—melt at least three inches of snow. Then his eyes shift to my boots.

"WOW," he says reverently. "New boots. Cozy vibe. Big fan."

I blink. "Uh... thanks?"

He grins wider. "You'll need them, because we're about to pass a whole *pod* of humpbacks bubble-net feeding, and guess who pulled strings so his favorite honeymooners and their entourage could get the best view?"

Maggie Jo gasps and claps. "Shut your sweet mouth, Sunshine. We get whales?"

"We get whales," Chase confirms, practically vibrating. "We picked the *perfect* day to sail out of Skagway! The locals told me the whales are working this channel today—filling up on krill and seaweed before migrating to Mexico. Like full National Geographic. Phones *out!*"

"Whales don't eat plants," I say automatically.

Baron pats my arm in sympathy—the "don't waste your breath correcting him" pat.

Chase checks his watch with unnecessary flair. "Anyway—move your married buns. The Captain wants as many guests outside as possible. Something about 'enhancing the Alaskan immersion experience' blah blah brochure talk. Also, if we're lucky, some of them will *sing*."

He cups a hand to his ear.

"The whales, not the guests. Though if inspiration hits and you two feel like a duet? You KNOW I support dreamers."

He winks and jogs off, immediately pivoting to yell helpful-but-wrong advice at a family about glove etiquette.

"Should we—" I start.

"Yes," Baron says firmly. "You do not skip whales."

Maggie Jo loops her arm through mine. "C'mon, honey. Let's go see the magic."

We follow the stream of people toward the bow. Snowflakes kiss my cheeks. The air tastes briny, electric. The ship pushes through slate-gray water, the wake foaming white behind us. Dark tree-lined hills rise on either side of the channel, their tops lost in low clouds.

My heart beats faster. Whales. Alexis's letter.

"Earth to Aurora," Darius murmurs at my other side. "You're doing that thing where you stare off all sad and quiet."

"I'm thinking," I say.

We reach the forward observation area. Staff have shoveled most of the snow, but a thin layer remains, crunching under boots. Guests line the railings three deep, cameras ready, voices buzzed with anticipation.

And there, of course, near the center, is Captain Rossi.

She stands a step above everyone else on the wing, gloved hands clasped behind her back, eyes scanning the water. Her white-topped cap is tucked under her arm.

My stomach plummets, then winds back up, rollercoaster-style.

Her eyes flick to me, and for half a second, her face softens. Then the captain's mask slides back into place.

"New coat," Darius mutters. "New boundaries. You got this."

"Do I?" I whisper.

"That jacket is waterproof," he says. "We can bounce bad decisions right off."

There's a crackle from the overhead speakers. "Ladies and gentlemen, this is your captain," Rossi's voice rolls out, smooth and low. "We are approaching a group of humpback whales bubble-net feeding off our port side. This is a special behavior where the whales work together to herd herring with bubbles."

A ripple of excitement moves through the crowd.

"As we watch, please remember these are wild animals," she continues. "We do not throw food, we do not make loud noises, and we do not... fall overboard." A tiny beat.

"She made a joke," I whisper. "Is she teasing me?"

Darius shrugs, looking for the whales.

The ship slows. People hush, breath hanging in the air.

I lean forward, hands curling around the cold rail, metal biting through my gloves. The water, slate moments ago, suddenly comes alive with movement—ripples, bursts of white foam, geysers of breath as dark backs break the surface.

"There," someone murmurs.

A ring of bubbles appears, a circle in the water. Then, in the center, the sea explodes.

Humpbacks surge upward, mouths open, pleats on their throats expanding, water cascading off their backs. Gulls scream overhead, diving for scraps. The whales' bodies are mottled black and white, huge and impossibly graceful.

I suck in a breath that feels too big for my chest.

"Oh my God," I whisper. "They're... they're right there."

"Holy sh— sugar," Maggie Jo breathes.

Baron's eyes are bright behind his camera, taking video. "Magnificent."

Another burst of bubbles. Another coordinated surge. The whales move together like they're dancing, or singing, or both. The sound of their exhale carries across the water, heavy and alive.

The ship rocks gently as we angle closer, just enough that I shift my footing.

And then the sea to our port side explodes in a totally different way.

A single humpback breaches—launching its entire massive body out of the water in a slow, impossible arc. Its white flippers flash. Its dark back gleams with spray. Time slows. Everyone gasps at once. The whale crashes back down with a thunderous slap that sends waves radiating out, rocking the Holiday Princess with a surprising punch.

The deck jolts. I lose my footing.

"Oh—!" My boots skid on a patch of ice I absolutely should have seen. My center of gravity tilts, the rail rushing toward me in awful slow motion.

A hand clamps around my arm.

Another braces the small of my back.

I'm yanked upright with calm, controlled strength.

The world steadies. *My heart does not.*

"Easy, Holiday Princess," Rossi murmurs, her warm breath brushing my ear.

Of course it's her.

Her hands are firm even through my jacket, anchoring me. She smells like cold wind, coffee, and something woodsy—cedar, maybe—from the Tlingit-carved charms sold in the atrium earlier.

"May I?" she asks quietly—so quietly I almost think I imagined it.

My brain short-circuits. "What?"

"May I steady you?" she clarifies. "Is this touch acceptable?"

It takes me a full second to understand that she's asking. Rossi. Asking for permission. After everything.

"Yes," I manage. "For not dying, yes."

"Good." Her fingers ease a little, transforming from restraining to supportive. "I would hate to explain to your husband—or the cruise line—that I let the star newlywed plunge into the drink after a whale sighting."

"That would be... awkward," I say, trying desperately not to lean into her.

She steps just close enough that our sleeves nearly brush, her hand still a warm point on my arm.

The crowd gasps as two whales surface together, sleek backs arcing, tails slapping in perfect unison. I force my eyes to stay on them and not on the thumb stroke she is absolutely, definitely not making against my sleeve.

"Beautiful, no?" she says softly.

"They're everything," I breathe.

I feel her gaze lingering on me, not the whales.

"Yes," she murmurs. "They are."

Flustered, I blurt, "Thank you. For catching me."

"Prego." Her eyes flick over my face, thoughtful. "I'll see you around."

Darius squeezes into the space beside me, breathless. "Did you see the baby? The tiny one? I swear it waved at me."

He glances between Rossi and me, taking in the careful distance, my intact personal bubble. His shoulders drop a fraction—relief.

Rossi shifts away to answer a question from another passenger, drifting off like she was never there.

The whales sound again, their tails slipping beneath the gray water. The ship begins a slow, gentle turn, engines humming beneath our feet.

My phone buzzes in my pocket.

I step back from the rail, heart still echoing with whale songs and weird, almost-apologies. My fingers are stiff from the cold when I tug my glove off to check my phone.

One new text from Lisa. "Babe u get the package?? Also, Alexis is currently showing emotion we are having dinner together–weird?! She's starting to grow on me. Call me when you have wifi or signal again."

I smile despite myself. Darius peeks over my shoulder.

We wander back toward midship as the crowd disperses, people buzzing with whale energy and cocoa cravings. Snowflakes drift down, landing on my lashes, my jacket, Darius's hair like glitter dandruff.

"Can we talk tonight?" I ask him quietly as we walk. "Like... really talk?"

He sighs. "Yeah," he says.

"Okay." Relief loosens my chest a little.

"And maybe," he adds, "you should call Lisa. Get the Alexis update."

We duck inside, the warm air kissing our frozen faces. The polished atrium floors gleam, reflecting the twenty-foot Christmas tree studded with faux-glass icicles and tiny carved ravens like something out of a very Alaskan Hallmark movie. A trio in aggressively festive sweaters fiddles out carols. Kids run around waving candy-cane sticks like battle flags while parents shuffle behind them with the haunted joy of people briefly off duty.

By the time evening falls for real, the ship is already pulling away from Skagway, the little string of village lights shrinking into the dark. Inside, the crew dims everything for "Aurora Hour"—the nightly ritual where guests gather outside just in case the sky decides to get magical.

Tonight, the sky is mostly clouds—no green ribbons, no cosmic ballet—but everyone still shuffles out wrapped in blankets with cocoa and toddies. The deck is lit with soft string lights, a low, slow-jazz "Silent Night" humming from hidden speakers, as if the ship itself were exhaling.

I stand near the aft rail, hands wrapped around a too-hot cup of cocoa. It smells like cinnamon and chocolate and safety. The ship's wake churns white behind us, fading into ink-black water.

My thumb brushes the charm in my pocket—Alexis's charm—and her words loop in my head like a whisper, *Stay warm. Stay safe.*

Weirdly... thinking of her doesn't feel heavy this time. My stomach flutters, soft and confusing.

"Penny for your thoughts, Wifey-Poo," Darius says, appearing at my elbow.

"I'm sorry," I blurt.

He sighs dramatically. "We are really overachieving on the apology quota this cruise."

"I mean it," I insist. "Not just for last night. For... all the times I made you feel like you had to guard me. That's not your job. You're my friend, not my emotional babysitter."

He studies me, jaw working, then nods. "Thank you," he says softly. "And I'm sorry, too."

"For what?"

"For using your past and patterns against you when I was hurt. I meant every word, but I could've said it with fewer knives."

"You used all the knives," I say.

He breaks into a laugh. "Terrible metaphor. That's one of the many reasons I love you."

We smile—tentative, tired, but real.

Around us, passengers tilt their heads toward the sky. A small ripple of excitement moves through the crowd as the clouds shift, revealing a faint pale streak—maybe the aurora, maybe just moonlight masquerading as the aurora. Hard to tell. People oogle anyway.

My phone buzzes again. Annoyingly insistent.

I pull it out.

This time... not Lisa.

It's Alexis.

My breath catches.

"I know you're at sea. No need to reply. I just wanted you to know... I'm proud of you. Not for forgiving me. For being there. Learning. Working. You look happy in the photos online—though the Bride jacket is a quirky choice."

Another message arrives immediately, "When you're back on land, can I take you out for a coffee?"

She continues, "If the answer is no. I'll respect it. I had to ask."

I stare at the screen.

Darius leans closer. "That look on your face better not be the same look you give the Captain."

"It's not," I whisper. "It's... something else."

He bumps my shoulder gently. "Well. Whatever this is... don't decide anything tonight."

I swallow hard, pocketing the phone.

He's right.

But my heart—the traitorous thing—beats a little faster anyway.

Chapter 21

Holiday Bingo Hijinks

Day 6: Juneau, Alaska

The ice cave breathes.

That's the only way my brain can describe it. Under Mendenhall Glacier, the air moves in cold drafts that smell like ancient snow and lake water. We are standing inside the lungs of an Alaskan ice dragon.

My boots crunch on packed snow as we shuffle single-file, helmets bumping, crampons scraping. Blue light glows from everywhere and nowhere, turning Darius's face into an alien mood lamp as he keeps half an eye on our guide. And half an eye on the gorgeous butt of the cruise naturalist in front of him.

Aren't the crew supposed to stay on the ship?

I tug my new jacket tighter. The inside is a safe hug. The outside is waterproof and windproof, making me a cozy, very fancy, green marshmallow.

"This is the most alien place I've ever been," I whisper, breath frosting in front of my face. "I can't believe this is Alaska."

Darius snorts, his breath puffing white through his balaclava. "We need to get out more, like further than a karaoke bar."

The guide—a local woman with a smooth braid- turns back to us.

"We're under the lower edge of Mendenhall," she says. "Please remember this is sacred land to the Tlingit people, and the glacier is changing every year. Respect the ice, respect each other, and don't lick anything."

She looks pointedly at Darius and Chase, and I wonder if she's actually referring to the glacier.

Behind her, Chase leans close to us.

"You know," Chase drawls, "this whole glacier actually floated here from Antarctica."

The guide closes her eyes briefly, as if communing with a higher power. "That's not true," she says. "The glacier formed from snowfall over thousands of years."

Darius's eyes glitter. "I'm sure both can be true."

He's openly flirting, which feels... ill-advised, considering he is *technically* my fake husband for the next forty-eight hours.

"I'm just saying," Chase goes on, oblivious, "ice is like the planet's memory. You can read ice bubbles like... tree rings."

"I think you mean ice layers," I murmur.

"Thank you, Aurora," the guide says. "Just... maybe listen to her, the Alaskan, instead of him."

"Love that for me," I whisper. "Unpaid naturalist consultant. Maybe I can get a new position in my dad's company—Accountant/Naturalist."

Darius shakes his head as we shuffle deeper into the cave. The ceiling curves above us like frozen waves, ridges and ripples in translucent blue. The glacier light makes everything unreal, as if we're walking through the inside of a sapphire.

I reach out, fingers hovering an inch from the ice.

"Don't touch it with bare skin," the guide warns gently. "It can burn–the ice is so cold it'll kill cells and damage bare skin."

I drop my hand. I knew this, and now I'm being a dumb tourist.

"Don't do that," Darius murmurs.

"Do what?"

"Feel dumb. We all want to touch it."

"And lick it," Chase adds.

The guide leads us to a vast chamber where the ice arches high overhead, the blue deepening to indigo. The surface is ridged and pocked, shot through with tiny white bubbles. Meltwater drips steadily from somewhere, echoing softly.

People gasp. Phones come out. There's the faint click of cameras, the shuffle of boots.

"This is..." I trail off, overwhelmed.

"Yeah," Darius says, uncharacteristically quiet. "Okay. Alaska wins."

"In Tlingit stories," our guide says, voice low, "ice is alive. It moves, it listens. The glacier is always coming and going, like a relative visiting. It remembers what we do."

I shiver. Not from the cold.

Ice as memory. Oceans as relatives. Whales are cousins. It all knots together with my emotions and the yearning for family and belonging.

"What are you thinking?" Darius asks.

"That I don't want to be cold and alone," I say quietly. "I mean I want family and history, like this cave."

"Bold," he says. "You already have that girl. With Lisa and me. Your dad and family. And Alaska."

Our guide moves us along, warning us about overhead ice.

The guide is calling us to move. The group starts shuffling toward the exit tunnel, breath fogging. Outside, I can see a sliver of gray sky and distant, snow-dusted spruce trees—the Tongass National Forest, stretching for miles.

"Aurora, are you okay to go with the main group?" Darius asks. "Chase wants to show me... 'subalpine lichens' Russian ice worms or something. I'll meet you back at the bus, promise."

We just promised each other to stick together until the cruise is over and to attempt to look like newlyweds as much as we can. And he wants to go on a glacier quasi-date with a man who thinks glaciers drifted from Antarctica?

"No," I say automatically. Then, softer, "I mean... yes?"

"Thanks," he mutters. "You're still the best Wifey-Poo."

No. "Yes. I'll be fine. The ice has me."

He grins and follows Chase toward a side tunnel, helmets bobbing. I watch them go, a knot forming in my chest that feels suspiciously like jealousy and fear and abandonment issues all braided together.

"Okay," I tell the ice. "It's just you and me, babe."

A droplet falls from the ceiling, splattering my cheek, freezing instantly.

"Cool," I say. "Love that you're giving ice kisses that can freeze me to death."

By the time we are back on board the Holiday Princess, my fingers have thawed, but my emotions have not. It's weird how deeply spiritual and emotional being in the center of a glacier is.

The ship's atrium daily announcements say in big print, "Holiday Bingo Bash! Featuring Your Star Honeymooners!"

"Of course," I mutter. "*Of course*, there's another event we *have* to attend just when I start enjoying myself."

Passengers are already gathering in the lounge area, snagging seats around little round tables. Snow falls gently outside the tall windows, flakes glowing in the ship's lights.

"Aurora!" Maggie Jo beams at me from the front table, waving like she's trying to land a plane. She's in a sequined reindeer sweater and a Santa hat that says, "Naughty-Ish." Baron sits beside her with a bingo dauber like it's a serious financial instrument.

I weave through the crowd toward them, my boots squeaking on the polished floor.

"Where's your handsome holiday husband?" Maggie Jo demands as I flop into the empty chair beside her.

"Appreciating bad Alaskan historical facts," I say, glumly.

Baron adjusts his glasses. "Speaking of Chase. Did you hear Chase telling everyone the northern lights are caused by polar bears having a rave?"

I shake my head. Chase is more of a hapless comedian than an Alaskan expert. I wonder if he does the same thing on Mexican cruises, calling the Aztec buildings leftover signs of alien invasions.

Maggie Jo pats my arm. "Bless your heart, letting Darius pursue him."

I sip the cocoa Maggie Jo shoves at me. It's sweet and hot and burns my tongue. *Perfect.*

Up on the small stage, Chase should be bouncing across the boards, hyping up the bingo crowd. Instead, a junior staffer fiddles nervously with a mic, whispering to someone offstage.

My stomach flips. "Well, who's running bingo?"

As if summoned by my dread, the lights shift slightly. A spotlight snaps to the side of the stage.

Captain Rossi steps into it.

She's in her crisp white uniform jacket, gold bars gleaming at her shoulders. The contrast of her stiff uniform under the twinkle lights is unfair to my heart rate. She takes the mic with the easy authority of someone used to talking over during storms.

"Buona sera, signore e signore," she says, her voice amplified through the lounge. "I am, of course, Captain Ophelia Rossi. Our cruise director is... unavailable. So tonight, you have me."

The crowd cheers, whistles. I realize then that there is hot, rummy eggnog in everyone's hands. Maybe this won't be so bad, drunken bingo with friends.

Rossi smiles, small but pointed at me. "We will be playing Holiday Honeymoon Bingo," she announces. "There will be prizes, and nonstop eggnog."

Maggie Jo squeals. "Oh, sweet girl, she's about to flirt with you."

"What?" I choke.

On cue, Rossi's gaze slides across the crowd and locks onto mine. It's like being pinned by a lighthouse. Or a searchlight. Or a particularly intense cat.

"Of course," she continues, "a honeymoon bingo needs a honeymoon couple." Her lips curve. "Our Star Newlywed bride. Will you join me onstage? Where's your husband?"

The lounge erupts in applause and shouts of "YES!" "KISS!" "WOOO!"

I want to be back at the glacier, hidden safe under several tons of moving ice.

I raise my hands. "He's not here!" I call, shouting over the noise. "My... husband. He's, uh, resting, um, meditating. On... nature."

Rossi taps her mic lightly. "Then perhaps we simply need... the better half of the honeymooning couple," she says. "Aurora, Cara mia, will you help me pull the numbers?"

"DO IT!" someone yells.

A chant starts up disturbingly fast. "AU-RO-RA! AU-RO-RA!"

I sink lower in my chair. "Can't they chant for more eggnog instead?"

Baron sips his coffee. "You'll be fine. We're watching and she can't try to make out with you on stage."

"When Darius shows up, send him to rescue me," I hissed.

Rossi waits, patient, one hand extended toward me. "Holiday Princess, our favorite bride," she says into the mic, but her eyes are just on me. "Come. Please."

Something in the *please*—soft, careful—gets me.

Plus, if I refuse, she'll probably come down here and physically drag me up there, which will be a much bigger scene.

I stand on shaking legs. "Wish me luck," I whisper to Maggie Jo.

"Good luck. Pull my numbers!"

I clomp up the side steps in my boots, aware of every eye. The stage lights are warm on my face. The room beyond is sea-dark with scattered islands of lamp light. I can smell coffee, sugar, faint whiffs of wet wool, cologne, and Rossi's subtle woodsy scent.

Up close, she smiles at me, not quite smug. "Grazie," she murmurs, covering the mic. "You look lovely."

"I'm sweating in three layers of fleece," I whisper back. "I look like a baked potato."

"A very adorable baked potato," she says. "Ready?"

She moves aside, gesturing toward the clear plastic bingo drum full of numbered balls. The drum's handle glints.

"We will be playing standard straight-line bingo," she tells the crowd. "Horizontal, vertical, diagonal. If you win, scream like it's your wedding night."

The crowd laughs.

She turns to me. "Our lovely Aurora will assist with pulling the numbers," she announces.

I want to sink into the floor. Instead, I grip the edge of the drum.

Rossi leans in, voice low for just me. "If you wish to stop at any time, say so," she says. "You are not trapped."

That shouldn't make my eyes sting, but it does. And suddenly I feel challenged. She can't do anything to me with everyone watching, after all.

"Let's bingo."

We start.

Rossi spins the drum with practiced ease. The balls clatter like hail on a tin roof. She reaches in, plucks one out, and hands it to me with a little bow.

My fingers brush hers. Zing. Stupid body.

I squint at the tiny stamp. "Uh... B-seven," I say into my mic. My voice echoes. I cringe. "B-seven, like... the number of layers I'm wearing to not get hypothermia."

Laughter bubbles up from the crowd. Someone yells, "Work it, snow princess!"

A few cheers as people daub their cards.

Rossi smirks. "Already a natural," she murmurs.

We fall into a rhythm. She spins and plucks. I read.

"I-23," I say. "I-23, like the number of times I've almost fallen on deck this week."

"O-69," I blurt, immediately turning red and wanting to sink into the floor. The room roars, waiting for my commentary.

"Ah," Rossi says, eyes glittering. "A classic."

"Grow up," I hiss at her. Into the mic, I add quickly, "O-69, which is the... *year*... Alaska Airlines started flying jumbo jets from Alaska. Aviation history, people. Get your minds out of the gutter."

More laughter. My cheeks burn, but in a... weirdly good way? They're laughing *with* me, not at me. I'm not faking being married or anything. I'm just Aurora, awkward microphone gremlin.

Rossi's lips twitch. "Very good, Cara."

"Stop encouraging me," I say, but I'm grinning.

The tension I've been carrying—about the kiss, the NDA, Alexis's text, Darius's glacier dalliance—doesn't vanish, but it... shifts. It's still there, a knot in my chest, but now there's something else bubbling inside me. The fizz of performing, of being seen and the spreading energy from the crowd.

The crew member running the prize table gives me a thumbs-up. Somewhere off to the side, a couple of teen girls are recording on their phones, whispering to each other. I catch "...she's so funny, oh my God," and my heart does a weird little pirouette.

Rossi stands beside me, a steady presence. She's close, but not quite touching. Every so often, she gives me a tiny nod or a soft "bene" under her breath. It's weirdly supportive.

Down, girl. I tell myself for the sake of my absent husband.

Another spin. Another ball.

"N-33," I say. "N-33, like the number of times I've returned to the dessert buffet."

A few chuckles.

My phone buzzes in my jacket pocket like it heard its name. I ignore it. I'm in the zone now, high on cocoa and validation.

"Who knew bingo could be this entertaining?" Baron murmurs to Maggie Jo.

Halfway through the second game, during a brief lull while the crew hands out little candy cane pens, Rossi leans toward me, mic lowered.

"You are very good at this," she says quietly. "The guests adore you."

"Yeah, well, I contain multitudes," I reply, heart racing. "Glacier panic, bingo chaos, crippling abandonment issues."

Her mouth quirks. "I could use someone like you," she says. "On my staff."

My pulse stutters. "What?"

She straightens, speaking low and fast, the way she does when giving orders. "When this cruise is over, you could stay. We have guest engagement roles. Activities hosts. Cultural liaison positions. I could ensure you receive training. A salary. Your own cabin. Travel the Inside Passage, learn every port. You are good with people, with stories. You could be... very successful here."

My thoughts explode like flashbangs. What? Stay. On the ship. No tuition stress, no student loan panic, no awkward family issues. If this were a year ago, I'd jump at the offer.

But I'm happy and comfortable with my life. I don't need to run away on a cruise ship with a captain who has questionable intentions.

She hesitates. "And... perhaps... you could be with someone that wants to show you love and worship our body... that you can really care about."

There it is. The emotional blackmail. And it doesn't make me crack, but it strengthens my resolve to finish this cruise and talk to Alexis.

Somewhere, a person shouts, "Eggnog me!" The lounge lights flicker as someone adjusts the dimmer for an atmospheric effect. Outside the windows, the harbor snow falls in soft sheets.

Inside me, a different kind of snowstorm starts.

The part of me that might've once been flattered by the offer is silent. Completely still. I don't see a future with the Captain—not in any universe.

Instead, I picture Alexis's neat handwriting. *You're good at this, Aurora.*

I picture my therapist's office, her calm voice saying, *You deserve spaces where your "yes" is never confused with survival.* I picture *Darius's face when he told me, Stop being your own worst enemy. Choose yourself. Choose your happiness.*

Captain Rossi waits, eyes flickering with something sharp and expectant.

"I appreciate the offer," I say softly. "I really do. And it feels like a... grand gesture. A shiny solution to fix my life and make your life a little easier."

"Aurora—"

"And I don't want to be fixed or saved," I say, louder this time. "I want to build something real for myself. With people who see me as a partner..."

She flinches like I slapped her.

My phone buzzes in my pocket again, insistent.

I grip the drum handle, mind spinning faster than the plastic barrel.

"Okay," I say, forcing a grin. "Let's do this. Do you feel lucky?"

The crowd laughs. I spin, pull, and read.

"I-19," I say. "I-19... which is how old I am and definitely old enough to make good choices and not, say, fake-marry my best friend for a free cruise. Hypothetically."

Maggie Jo howls. Baron shakes his head slowly, but he's smiling.

As the room fills with laughter, daubing, and the faint cling-clang of ice in glasses, my phone vibrates a third time.

I yank it out between spins, holding it below the podium where no one can see.

One new text.

Not from Lisa. Not from Alexis.

The message is from Darius. "Aurora, I messed up. Emergency! Get to our cabin. NOW!"

Upbeat holiday jazz plays over the speakers. People cheer as someone yells, "*Bingo!*"

"Uh, we have a winner!" I say, brightly into the mic, voice only a little shaky. "I'm gonna hand things over to our very capable Captain, while I go... Refill my eggnog."

The crowd laughs.

Rossi arches a brow.

I shove the mic into her palm and bolt.

Chapter 22

"Baby, It's Bold Outside" — Aurora Finds Her Voice

Day 6: Juneau, Alaska

Sprinting down the corridor, boots squeaking in frantic little shrieks, I barrel past wreaths, garlands, and aggressively cheerful nutcrackers. "Jingle Bell Rock" blares over the speakers like the ship is mocking me—each jingle falling completely out of sync with my pounding heartbeat.

I pass a porthole, and the whole world outside feels wrong. Juneau's harbor is glowing gold, snow piling on rooftops like frosting gone wild, the mountains black and jagged under a cloud-choked sky. It feels distant, unreal, like a painting I'm running past instead of a place that exists.

My boot catches on the cursed floral-scroll carpet—a pattern clearly designed by someone who hates joy. My body *lurches* forward.

I *hit my knees hard.* Pain shoots up my shins.

I hiss, scramble up, and shove the humiliation aside. No time.

My phone buzzes again—a relentless wasp of urgency.

Darius texts me, "Seriously. PLEASE hurry!"

"I'm hurrying!" I yell at the phone like it can hear me. "Stop texting me, you absolute drama tornado!"

My pulse is too loud. My lungs are burning. My breath comes out in visible puffs because the damn air conditioning is set to *Arctic funeral.*

I whip around the final corner, hand skimming the wall because my legs feel like noodles dipped in adrenaline. I nearly wiped out again on a rogue patch of melted snow someone tracked in. My brain is frantically chanting.

Please be okay—please be okay—please be okay—

I slam the keycard against the reader, trembling.

Red light.

I smack it again. "Come on. Come on. *Come on—*"

Green.

The lock clicks. The door swings open.

"Darius? What—"

I stop.

Dead.

Darius is sitting on the edge of the ridiculous heart-swan honeymoon bed, still in his glacier-tour clothes—beanie crooked, parka half-zipped, crampons abandoned in a defeated heap by the door. His eyes are red.

Next to him is...

Chase.

Also red-eyed.

"Oh," I breathe. "Okay. This is... very interesting."

Chase wipes his cheeks with a sleeve. "I am *so* sorry," he blurts.

"For what?" I say. "Being from Florida."

Darius lets out a strangled sound that is thirty percent laugh, seventy percent emotional collapse. "We had a situation," he says. "Tell her, Chase."

"*I didn't know!*" Chase babbles, hands flapping. "I swear, I didn't know anything was going to happen. And then it *did,* and now everything's exploding. I mean. Emotionally. Metaphorically. Spiritually. Like the Alaskan People of the Wolves say—"

"Okay," I cut in, panting from the sprint and already trying to peel off my sweaty layers. "Let's start with the truth. I'm glad you're sitting down. Darius and I, are *fake* married."

They stare.

Then burst into laughter.

"He *knows* that," Darius says, wiping his face. "He's not blind. I mean—my god, Aurora—" He spreads his hands. "I wanted to ask if it's okay if *Chase and I take the bed?* You can take the couch tonight, okay?"

"What? That's the emergency?" I drop onto the couch and start yanking off my boots. "We need to establish rules. Basic rules. Rule one is no making out when I'm in the room. Rule two is do *not* tell anyone we aren't married. I can't afford this suite. You can't afford to pay back this suite. And I'm assuming *you*," I point dramatically at Chase, "cannot afford this suite."

Chase groans. "No. Obviously not. I'm working here, not vacationing."

"See?" I say, throwing my hands up. "We *all* need to continue this newlywed scam."

"It's not a scam," Chase insists. "It's marketing continuity. The cruise line wants to show happy newlyweds. You guys have that sparkly 'rom-com on a boat' energy."

"Oh, we have *something*," I mutter.

"That's just our karaoke chemistry," Darius says, patting the bed beside him.

"And also—" Chase lifts a finger. "He kissed me in the hallway."

Darius flops backwards with a groan. "In a very respectful, mutually enthusiastic way," he clarifies. "Consent was *achieved*."

"Fabulous," I deadpan. "Consenting passion on *my* honeymoon cruise. With my husband."

"*Fake* husband," Darius corrects.

"Hot daddy," Chase adds, entirely unhelpful.

"Oh, my biscuits. Rules!" I shout, throwing a pillow at them.

Chase catches it like it's a bridal bouquet. "I support rules."

Darius rubs his face. "Anyway. That's not the issue."

"There's *more*?" I demand.

"Yeah," he says miserably. "A staff member walked by right after the kiss and went, 'OMG! The Star Honeymooner is cheating on his wife!' And now the crew gossip is that I'm a homewrecker."

Chase nods vigorously. "It's spreading *so* fast. Faster than when word got out that someone saw you walking into the AA meeting and got you the special mocktail status."

"I was hiding from the captain," I yell. "Not getting sober."

"Alcoholism is a real disease," Chase tells me solemnly. "Don't let him minimize your journey."

"My. What?" I pinch the bridge of my nose. "Okay. Continue."

Chase rolls onto his stomach like he's at a slumber party. "Captain Rossi is *obsessed* with you, by the way. On the plus side, she's in a great mood. Like weirdly great."

"That is *not* a plus side," I say.

Darius raises one trembling finger. "And *that* is not the worst part."

My stomach tightens. "There's a *worse* part?"

"Apparently," Darius says, flinging his arm toward the ceiling, "Someone tried to catch a photo of us. And instead, they took a video of Chase and me on the *balcony*. I was flirting with Chase. Trying to convince him it was alright to kiss me. Then he kissed me."

"A video," I repeat. "A. Video."

"Yes." Darius groans. "Because this ship has cameras everywhere."

Chase grimaces. "Security sent *me* a still photo from the video like, 'Hey, is this a problem?' because they recognized me. And I—uh—*panicked.*"

"That's why we texted," Darius finishes, softly. "We didn't know what to do."

My brain screeches.

"You're already a WE?!"

Chase leans forward. "I didn't mean to blow up your... arrangement," he says. "I thought we were having fun and being flirty but the love feels hit us hard. I heard you guys were open, too."

He trails off with a shrug, and I want to be mad, but their vibes and perfect opposition create a kind of perfect couple, I mean, if I wasn't married to Darius.

"Assumptions are the leading cause of ice worm heart break disease," I say. "*Fun Alaska Fact.*"

Darius bursts out laughing, and Chase cocks his head, trying to understand what's so funny, not noticing I was imitating *him.*

"At least we have one more allies on our fake marriage team. Let's drink to that," Darius says and jumps up to pour a round of champagne.

"Super idea! And look, I can talk to security," he says. "Or the captain. Or both. I'll say it was my fault, that I misread things. We can nip the rumor in the bud before it gets you guys thrown out of the honeymoon suite or embarrassed in front of the entire ship."

I choke. "Do not talk to the captain."

Darius groans. "Never talk to the captain."

Chase blinks. "I mean... she already knows."

Ice slides down my spine. "What do you mean she *knows*?"

"She's the captain," he says helplessly, palms up. "You think those cameras around the ship are just for photographers? Honey, no. There are, like, three times more cameras than you've noticed. She sees *everything.*"

My stomach twists. "Chase—"

"She already flagged it," he rushes on. "Sent a note through the crew channel telling everyone not to 'interfere with *her* honeymooners.'" He swallows. "It was... a lot. Honestly? Threat-adjacent. I low-key wondered if there was, like, a threesome situation brewing."

"Not my thing," Darius cuts in immediately, tossing us drinks like a bartender in crisis. "I mean the Captain part. *Obviously* I'm open to a ménage à trois."

I start pacing the length of the suite, boots thumping on the carpet, because if I stop moving, I might scream into the honeymoon swan towels. The room smells like roses from the romance package—and faintly like cologne, which is just Chase. Snowflakes streak past the balcony glass like tiny white comets disappearing into the harbor.

"So, the Captain knows," I say. "Okay. Fine. GREAT. That totally changes things." I whirl around to face them. "We need a late-night dessert committee meeting."

Chase wrinkles his nose. "A... committee?"

"Yes," I say. "A gathering of our emotional support adults. Maggie Jo and Baron. Because clearly, *we* should not be trusted to make decisions when we collectively share three brain cells and unlimited champagne."

Darius lifts his glass again, instantly soothed by structure. "To the Board."

As they drink, I grab my phone and message, "Emergency board mtg. Captain Cook's Bar in 10. Bring your best 'how not to get sued' advice."

I don't even set the phone down before it pings with Maggie Jo saying, "On my way, honey."

Baron messages, "I'll bring a notebook."

I exhale, tension loosening a single millimeter. "Okay," I say. "We've got this."

Chase raises one tentative hand. "Am I invited to the Board? Or Committee? Or do you want to gossip about me behind my back?"

"Keep a low profile," I ordered him. "No public fondling, no balcony dramatics, nothing that makes people wonder if we're polyamorous, super-newlyweds until we have a plan."

He nods solemnly. "Understood."

Darius plucks the glass from my hand. "Now get out so we can have some *private* fondling, and I'll meet you there in fifteen min—"

"*Nope.*" I grab his jacket from the chair and fling it at him. "Absolutely not. I know your 'fifteen minutes.' You're coming with me. Chase, *Bye*."

Chase salutes dramatically as I shove Darius out the door with me.

Maggie Jo and Baron have claimed a corner table at the Captain Cook bar next to an ice sculpture of a reindeer that actually looks like a reindeer. Maggie has three eggnogs in front of her and a plate of mixed Christmas cookies. Baron has a black coffee, a legal pad, and a calculator, because of course he does.

"There they are," Maggie Jo says, standing up and flinging her arms wide. "My favorite newlywed couple, heading to the rocky shores of relationship disaster...again."

"That's fair," I say.

She hugs me so hard, my ribs creak, eggnog sloshing dangerously.

"Sit," she orders. "Tell Auntie Maggie everything."

Darius munches a cookie and says, "Chase's in our suite."

Baron raises an eyebrow. "I see we're opening with the hookup, not the fraud."

"Hey! I thought this was a safe space," Darius mutters.

"It is," Maggie says sweetly. "Safe spaces can still have shade."

We all settle. I clutch my eggnog like it's my sweet, cinnamon-sprinkled flotation device.

"Okay," I say. "Bullet points."

I give them the condensed version of Chase, the balcony almost-scandal, the Captain watching us through her personal surveillance network, the NDA I signed, the creepy kiss, how she *claimed* to delete the photos... the Captain's behavior at bingo, the unnerving job offer, and the fact that I'm ready to end the entire charade even though there are only two days left of this cruise.

Maggie Jo whistles low. "It's gettin' messier than homemade taffy on a humid day, sugar." Her drawl softens into concern. "Deliciously messy... but also dangerous."

"So now the Captain knows," Baron summarizes, pen already moving across a notepad, "and she may have more photos."

"Correct," I say, miserable.

"And only *you* signed any agreement—not Darius?" he asks without looking up.

I nod. "Also correct."

Baron's pen freezes mid-stroke. "Then Darius remains free to write any reviews, send any reports to your employer, and post anything online. His employment isn't impacted. Only yours is."

Maggie Jo leans forward, eyes twinkling like she's about to reveal the twist ending of a soap opera. "We can all agree something right now." She points at me with a mittened hand. "Aurora is incredible. She has every person on this boat—Captain included—wrapped around her finger. She shines. She deserves joy."

I blink. "Wait—what?"

"Seconded," Baron says immediately.

"All in favor of Aurora bein' her whole authentic, shiny self?" Maggie asks.

Darius raises his hand without hesitation.

Baron raises his.

Maggie's is already up.

After a beat, I raise mine too.

"Motion passes," Maggie declares with a proud smile. "Aurora honey, you deserve good things. From friends, from partners, from jobs... and absolutely from captains with too many cameras. Regardless of how many times you've tripped over nothin' at all, we adore you. And frankly, I think the whole ship does."

The lump in my throat gets sharp. I look down, deflecting. "They only care because I'm the winning Newlywed Bride—"

"No, honey," Maggie says gently. "You're a delight. A firecracker. A sparkler on the Fourth of July. People see that. That's the *truth.*"

"Oh my God," I groan, hiding my face in my sleeves. "I wasn't prepared to be aggressively love-bombed."

Baron pushes his glasses up. "You two deserve supportive, long-term partners," he says, surprisingly earnest. "You already have that in friendship—finding it romantically is harder, but it will happen for both of you."

He squeezes Maggie Jo's hand. They share a look that's warm enough to melt permafrost.

My eyes sting. "But my mom—"

"Is not invited to this table," Maggie interrupts sharply. "She can sit outside in the snow with a lukewarm spoiled eggnog. We are not usin' her as the blueprint for love."

I choke on a half-sob, half-laugh. "Okay."

"Motion two," Baron says, tapping his pen. "We prioritize safety. Emotional *and* professional. That means clear boundaries." He meets my eyes. "The Captain cannot force favors, or secrecy, or use your feelings against you."

I flinch.

Darius's gaze darts to me, gentle and firm. "Seconded."

"Opposed?" Baron asks.

Silence.

"Motion passes," he says. "Now—strategy."

He laces his fingers. "You tell her politely, but firmly, that she does *not* have your consent to share images or stories about you beyond what you've authorized. You remind her you're a guest—and that retaliation or coercion is a legal matter, not a romantic one."

Legal.

My stomach flips. "I don't want to cause drama—"

"You're not causing drama by asking not to be exploited," Baron says calmly.

Maggie Jo nods, squeezing my hand. "Honey, existing with boundaries isn't drama. It just *feels* like drama because your mama raised you to believe you only deserved love when you were useful."

I inhale sharply. "Wow. Okay. Direct hit."

"Truth hurts, sugar," she says, "but it'll also set you free."

Darius reaches under the table and squeezes my knee. "You're not Sandra's daughter on this ship," he says quietly. "You're Grant's daughter. And Grant? I already know he's the kind of dad who'd choose truth over perfection."

I close my eyes—my dad's kind face flashing in my mind, the way he'd said *I'm proud of you, kiddo.*

Then Alexis's words—*You're good at what you do, Aurora.*

Two very different people telling me the same thing—My worth isn't measured in obedience. It's measured in being myself.

"Well, you go talk to your captain," Maggie says. "You try to use your words. Maybe you nail it, maybe you don't. But you try. And then you try again. And we will be right here, drinking eggnog and refusing to allow a grown woman to use coercion as romance."

The knot in my chest loosens another percent. "Okay," I say. "I can... try."

I drain my eggnog, set the mug down with more confidence than I feel, and stand.

"I'm going," I announce. "Before I lose my nerve."

Darius stands too. "Do you want backup?"

"I love you," I say. "But I think this part has to be just me."

Outside the lounge windows, the ocean is white-capped and stormy, heading to Juneau. The ship lights reflect off the harbor, glittering on the dark water. Somewhere up on the bridge, Rossi is steering this floating hotel through someone else's map.

For the first time, I'm determined to draw my own.

I find Captain Rossi on Deck 10, outside. She stands near the bow, hands clasped behind her back, staring at the channel where the Holiday

Princess will dock as soon as daylight hits us. The mountains loom dark to either side, their peaks disappearing into low clouds. Ship lights paint the snow along the shore a soft gold. A bald eagle sits on a navigation marker, judging.

Her coat flaps slightly in the wind, white against the night. Her hat is tucked under one arm.

For a second, she looks... lonely.

I clear my throat. "Captain?"

She turns. Her eyes soften a fraction when she sees me. "Aurora," she says. "Come. It is cold tonight."

We stand side by side, leaving a respectable two-foot gap like I'm in some kind of emotional etiquette manual. My breath fogs. Hers does too. The ship hums under our feet.

"I wanted to talk about boundaries," I say, before I can chicken out.

She wrinkles her nose. "All right," she says. "I'm listening."

"I know you are aware of Darius and Chase," I start.

Her jaw tightens, barely.

"I..." I inhale. The air is sharp, cutting. "I need you to very clearly hear that you do not have my consent to use any photos of me, or stories about me, in any way that could harm my reputation. Or Darius's."

She regards me for a moment, expression unreadable. "You think I would... punish you," she says softly.

"You already did," I say, heart hammering. "With the NDA. With the kiss-for-safety deal. With the job offer that is a cage more than an opportunity."

She flinches, just slightly.

"Maybe you didn't see it that way," I say. "But it's how it felt. And I grew up with a mother who made everything a transaction. Love for compliance. Safety for silence. I'm... done with that. I need you to know I won't play that game anymore. Not with you. Not with anyone."

The words leave my mouth and hang in the freezing air between us like little ghosts.

Silence. The wind whistles around the bow.

"You are still hiding something," she says quietly. "About your 'marriage.' About yourself."

"I don't owe you anything," I say.

Her gaze sharpens. "You owe the truth to yourself, at least," she says. She's quiet for a long beat.

Then she laughs softly, but there's no humor in it. "You are very bold tonight," she says. "The bingo crowd has made you brave."

"Turns out being loved for being loud and weird and honest is... addictive," I say. "I'd like more of that. Less of lying and people pleasing to keep from making waves."

She winces. "Aurora—"

She doesn't finish, and we lapse into silence.

I exhale slowly. "So," I say. "About the new photos and videos. Will you... delete all copies? Not use it as gossip or keep them for leverage?"

She is very still.

We stand there, two stubborn women on a frozen deck, neither willing to move.

Finally, she says, very softly, "I will see what I can do. About the image. About the rumors. I cannot promise everything. But I will try to... minimize harm."

"Thank you," I say.

"But," she adds, and there's the steel again, "you must understand, Aurora—this situation exists because you chose a lie. You and your friend. I did not put the ring on your finger and parade around in a *Bride* jacket."

The words slap me. I flinch. I hate that she's right. I hate how much I hate that she's right.

"You're not wrong," I say. "But there's a difference between being complicit in a lie and being coerced into kisses."

Her eyes flare. "I know," she says. "And I will regret that... for a very long time."

We stare at each other. It feels like we're standing on shifting ice—cracks spidering under our feet, water dark and cold below.

"I should go," I say finally. I turn and leave.

My phone buzzes in my pocket as I walk back to the suite, my emotions conflicted, and I wonder if I did the right thing. It would have been easier to just ignore the situation and hide for the rest of the trip.

I look down, intending to ignore it until I'm someplace warm. But the notification preview makes my blood run colder than the wind.

Lisa's name flashes on my screen.

"Hello Chaos! Why is there a pic of you + the captain practically kissing in an elevator on the cruise?? It's tagged for the cruise line AND your personal socials?? ALSO there's a picture of Darius kissing a hottie on your balcony???"

My stomach plummets through my boots.

I tap the notification, shaking my fingers.

The screenshot loads at the speed of heartbreak—ship Wi-Fi buffering like it wants to prolong my suffering.

Then it appears.

Grainy security footage.

Fisheye distortion.

Me—pressed against the elevator wall, eyes wide, lips parted in that horrible, almost-kiss moment.

Rossi—braced over me, hand on the wall beside my head, her face inches from mine, every pixel screaming *scandal*.

I whisper, "No. No, no, no—"

Another screenshot.

Darius and Chase.

On *our balcony*.

Full face-eating make-out mode. Hands everywhere. Passion-level... soap opera season finale.

Below them, the caption says, "Spotted on the Holiday Princess. Is it just me or do the "star honeymooners" have an EXTRA guest in their marriage?" #elevatortea #balconybumping

My pulse blasts like a fire alarm in my ears.

Every muscle locks.

Another notification dings.

Alexis. "I saw the photo."

My heart stops. Then slams back to life in a panic.

My lungs forget how to function.

Another message pops in from Lisa. "Do NOT panic. OK. Panic a little. Alexis is here. We are going to try to report and block this pic."

My phone vibrates again, and this time it's a long message from Alexis.

I click it with numb fingers.

"I'm so sorry you're going through this. And none of this is your fault. If you want help, legal or otherwise, say the word." Alexis typed, then adds, "If you don't, I'll still be here, on the other end of this screen, believing you.

My eyes blur. The charm inside my jacket burns against my skin.

I look from the photo on my phone—me, trapped in that elevator frame—to the dark sea beyond the ship's bow, endless and cold. To the faint reflection of my own face in the glass. To the woman beside me who wants to control the narrative. And to the message on my screen from the woman on land who's finally offering support without strings.

Snowflakes drift down, catching in my hair, melting fast.

For the first time, the urge to run doesn't win.

The urge to step up to the mic and tell the story myself. Out here, I realize—I can't keep failing at honesty forever.

At some point, I have to pick a truth, say it out loud.

Chapter 23

The Holiday Ball & the Truth Bomb

Day 6: Ketchikan, Alaska

The window behind Darius shows Ketchikan's harbor dusted in powdered-sugar snow, the docks glowing blue in the early dusk, beyond, a glacier-fed inlet glimmers like crushed diamonds. The Holiday Princess ship is all warm yellows and glittering icicles and red velvet bows. The whole thing is a floating, layered Christmas cake.

I look down at my black sequin dress with the red bow at my waist. *I'm the ornament,* thanks to the last of my cruise store credits and Darius's fabulous styling.

The suite smells like peppermint body spray because Chase "accidentally" sprayed it directly in Darius's face ten minutes ago. Chase is now pacing, hands on his hips, his candy cane holiday cologne making my eyes water.

"Okay," Chase blurts, "I swear, Aurora, I didn't leak that photo. Nobody on staff would leak that photo. Guests are furious. Crew is furious. Even the penguin cruise mascot is furious—I promise. He's giving the finger to whoever posted it."

I stare at him. Slowly. "Does the penguin mascot... *have* fingers?"

"Yes," Chase says confidently, then hesitates. "Well, Alaskan feather fingers."

Darius pats his arm. "Sweetie pie, no. You look prettier when you don't talk."

"I look pretty and smell pretty!"

I fall dramatically onto the couch, face down. "I'm going to die at the Holiday Ball. The band is going to play 'Deck the Halls' while everyone publicly stones me with day-old gingerbread cookies."

"Aurora." Darius pulls me upright and straightens my dress. "This is good."

"Good?!"

"Yes," he says, tilting his head. "A cruise employee leaked the photo. That means you finally have leverage, babe. They can't make us pay back the difference in the honeymooners' perks. They can't fire us. They can't even revoke our unlimited dessert and champagne package."

Chase brightens. "Yeah! And Maggie Jo is already rallying the passengers. She told everyone you're besties and an Alaskan cruise couple, LGBT-style. And honestly? They love you and don't care about the picture."

My chest tightens in that yearning way, the way that always comes right before I break my own heart. "Being in the spotlight and everyone knowing who I am and thinking that I'm this winning newlywed... I just... I don't want to hide anymore. Any of it. Not who I am. Not that I kissed the Captain and liked it. Not that she was trying to manipulate me."

Darius squeezes my cheeks and then pats them to make them pink. "Then don't hide, sweet-pea. Use tonight. Use the stage. Chase is literally the Cruise Director—he can hand you a microphone like Oprah."

Chase chimes in. "Absolutely. I can also provide glitter confetti... wait, I have a glitter gun somewhere."

"*No confetti*," Darius and I say simultaneously. Then we side-eye each other.

He whispers, "Maybe confetti."

"If it matches my dress colors," I say with a laugh.

Outside, through the window, the foghorn bellows—deep, cold, mournful—like some ancient Tlingit sea spirit calling from the harbor. I shiver and almost hear it whisper–The truth will set you free.

The yearning aches in my ribs.

Alexis's words echo in my head, "I'm here if you need me. No strings. No judgment. Just me."

My throat closes.

God, I miss her. And I want to see her.

"Okay," I whisper. "Let's go blow up my life... or at least this Farewell Formal Cruise Ball."

The ballroom is a snow-globe-come-to-life.

Shimmering icicle chandeliers. Garlands of cedar and cranberries. Live band in matching reindeer bow ties. Crew members in sparkly Santa hats. The giant windows show Ketchikan's late-evening lights twinkling through falling snow.

Chase beams from the stage, mic in hand. "Ladies, gents, and festive beings of all kinds! Please make joyous noise for our Winning Newlyweds, Aurora and Darius!"

The room cheers. People clink champagne flutes. Maggie Jo shrieks in a pitch that could summon beluga whales or halibut from the bottom of the ocean.

Darius nudges me as we walk toward the stage, his hand squeezing my waist. "Last chance to bail, Wifey-Poo."

"Nope." My stomach flips like a salmon escaping a net. "I'm done running."

We get onstage. Chase is sweaty with excitement. "Wanna give a little Newlywed Thank-You Speech?"

Darius whispers to me, "Do it."

I take the mic.

The ballroom hushes, and my sequin gown sparkles on stage under the spotlights.

Captain Rossi stands in the back—uniform crisp, jaw tight, arms behind her. Her gaze is burning into me. *Possessive. Angry*—then gone.

My heart hammers.

Okay, Aurora. Time to be real.

"Hi," I start. "I'm Aurora. *Obviously.* You've probably seen me fall, crash, spill cocoa, or scream on at least three decks this week."

The crowd laughs. Someone says, "the epic bingo!"

I swallow.

"Tonight, I have... a few truths to share."

My voice wobbles.

Darius squeezes my hand behind my back.

"Truth #1," I say, lifting a champagne flute. "I am not an alcoholic. I like champagne. I also like people who are fighting to stay sober. If you're in recovery and you're here tonight—" I raise the glass. "I see you. I support you. And I'm proud of you."

A wave of applause ripples across the room.

I take a drink, then laugh. "I guess it's odd to celebrate with a drink, but I have been unwillingly alcohol-free most of this cruise, thanks to all your support."

My breath steadies.

"Truth #2 is Darius and I are not married."

Gasps.

Maggie Jo gives me the thumbs up.

Baron calmly nods.

Darius blows kisses theatrically.

"You probably saw the pictures and maybe heard some rumors. Which leads me to Truth #3. I am a lesbian."

The room erupts—cheers, claps, whoops. And some cat calls from the women that make me blush.

I laugh too loudly. "Uh-huh, big reveal! Except... come on. One glance at me in flannel and boots and most straight guys assume I'm here to chop wood and steal their girlfriends."

I continue.

"Truth #4 is that I'm intersex. I found out a few months ago. Let's drink to a spectrum of sex characteristics because it's super-common–one in sixty people–and not talked about. *Honestly?* Being different is okay. I'm done hiding it. I deserve to exist without shame."

People stand. The applause is loud, soft, warm—like being wrapped in a holiday blanket.

"And Truth #5." My voice sharpens.

"I liked the Captain's kiss. *I did.* But it wasn't romance. It felt *forced.* Something I didn't really get to choose. No one should be or feel uncomfortable, guilty, or forced when it's love."

Gasps. Crew members freeze. Rossi's jaw flexes.

"I'm done with manipulation, even by super-hot powerful women."

"So hot," someone whispers from a table.

"And Truth #6—"

My hands shake.

My heart cracks wide open.

"I am still in love with someone else. Someone who supports me without conditions. Someone who doesn't use rank or fear or pressure. Someone who showed up the moment everything went wrong. Love is being there for another, with no conditions and fully accepting a person for their flaws and differences."

Darius takes my hand and hugs me.

A collective *"Oooooh!!!,"* sweeps the room.

"Alexis accepts and supports me," I whisper to Darius.

Rossi's face crumples.

Just a flash.

A wound.

Then she turns sharply and walks out—stiff, furious, humiliated, hurt.

The doors slam behind her.

I exhale shakily.

The room explodes in cheers, applause, clinking glasses, Maggie Jo screaming, "You tell 'em, Honey!"

I step off the stage.

Baron nods approvingly. "Strong delivery. Excellent pacing."

Darius hugs me, again, whispering, "You did it, Girl. You freed us."

Ding. DING!

A text from Dad.

"I saw the live stream. Proud of you, kiddo. I'm sorry for the added pressure about this cruise. I meant for it to be a relaxing trip and a fun introduction to the family tours and cruise business. You never have to pretend for me or be anyone but YOU."

I tear up.

Then my phone rings. Unknown number.

Alexis?

I answer cautiously.

"Hi! Aurora? This is Brad from Royal Caribbean marketing!" a chipper voice says. "We *loved* your speech. Viral already! Also—we're not mad about the honeymoon mix-up. Actually, we are totally rebranding this cruise as 'The Alaska Found-Family Holiday Experience.' Would you let us use your photos?!"

My phone pings with pics being sent to me, tagged with me. The images flood in. Images I hadn't seen since my pictures were quarantined by Rossi.

They're beautiful. Laughing. Hugging. Us being exactly who we really are, friends, finding joy.

"Only," I say carefully, "if you add LGBTQIA+ visibility to your promotions. And you have to offer exclusive deals to my employer—Alaska Cruise & Travel."

"DONE! Immediately! And you and Darius can have another free cruise wherever you choose. You're amazing!"

I hang up, dazed.

Everything is... *working out?*

Is this even my chaotic, messy life?

And then—

The last photo loads.

Darius and I at the ball, glittering, smiling, free–hugging on stage after my truths.

I smile—

But a shadow creeps into my happy haze, one that taints it and makes me swallow hard, Captain Rossi.

She looked angry and left early. Her eyes were dark, hurt, stormy—as if I just capsized her entire world. She won't be winning Captain of the Year after my speech, but the truth is more important than her feelings.

The music increases, and the ball around me spins into a blur—lights, music, people hugging me, Maggie Jo crying with the fake snow sticking onto my shoulder.

Eventually, Darius gets pulled away by Chase, leaving me standing alone by the midnight-blue Christmas tree. Ready for the next part of my plan.

I pull out my phone.

Alexis.

She deserves to know what I said.

What I chose.

I press call.

It rings once.

Twice.

Three times—

"Hello?"

A woman's voice.

Not Alexis.

Soft. Sleepy.

Intimate.

My stomach drops.

"Who is this?" I whisper.

"Oh—sorry, are you looking for Lexi?"

I can't even put myself together to respond. Who is this?

"She's in the shower," the woman says, casually. "Can I take a message?"

My chest caves.

I hang up instantly.

The new confidence I just built—every sparkly brave piece of it—crumbles like thin ice beneath a sturdy Alaskan boot.

The band keeps playing. Guests keep cheering. People smile and pat my shoulder in support as they walk by.

The snow keeps falling outside.

But inside me?

Everything has gone horrifyingly, terrifyingly still.

Chapter 24

A Snowy Showdown

Day 7: Ketchikan, Alaska

“Why are we awake at dawn *again*?” Darius grumbles behind me. “I thought VIP stood for Very Into Pillows.”

Ketchikan smells of fresh snow as we are led to the special departure area, travel mugs of cocoa in hand.

“It’s the last winning honeymoon perk, a ‘pre-disembarkation experience’,” I say, mimicking the perky Guest Services voice from the voicemail. “Also, I want to see and review our last port, Ketchikan. That is the reason we’re here.”

He grumbles and yawns hugely, rubbing his eyes with the back of his hand. “Honestly? At this point, we’ve done all the experiences already. I think we deserve the ‘sleep-in and relax’ experience for our last day, before we head home.”

“We can sleep all day tomorrow as we cruise back to Anchorage. And btw, you need to pack up your bag, because I’m not organizing the crazy amount of accessories back into your little travel bag.”

We round the corner toward the gangway area. The air gets colder, tinged with wind and salt. Out of the enormous picture window, Ketchikan’s dark harbor spreads wide—wooden docks dusted in soft white, fishing boats gently bobbing, strings of yellow lights rippling across the dark ocean. Snow falls in steady, powdered flakes, frosting the red roofs and the spruce-covered hills behind the town.

Chase told us last night that Ketchikan rarely gets much snow—it's the Rain Capital, not the Winter Wonderland. But today, the whole place looks like someone dumped a powdered-sugar shaker over a fresh donut.

"There she is," I whisper, pressing my forehead briefly to the glass.

"Who?" Darius asks. "Your next disastrous girlfriend?"

"No!" I elbow him. "The Tongass." I nod toward the dark, endless forest beyond the town. "Do you even listen to the port briefing on the TV? It's the biggest temperate rainforest in the world. *A rainforest. In Alaska.* It sounds more made-up than sasquatch."

He pats my shoulder. "Maybe we'll get to see both."

"Aurora? Darius?" The Guest Services Clipboard Lady asks. "Perfect timing! We're getting you onto the tender early for your special Honeymooners' Shoreside Breakfast Package."

"Nothing says romance like reindeer-sausage biscuits and gravy before my workout," Darius mutters.

I lean into him. "At least if you *eat after* the boat ride, you won't puke."

He gives the staff a long, suspicious look. "You're too chipper and your wit is too sharp for this hour. How much coffee did you have?"

"No coffee," I say, lifting my travel mug. "Just cocoa. But being honest, last night worked. I actually slept. Dreamed about taking a honeymoon cruise on my *real* honeymoon."

"With Alexis," he says, pointedly.

I bite my lip. I didn't tell him about Alexis having a new partner.

I guess I'm still hiding a few things.

He raises an eyebrow at my silence but doesn't push me. Instead, he looks out at the town again, the falling snow reflected in his eyes.

I shift my mug between my hands and force myself to breathe in the view, the moment, the peace instead of my standard panic.

Ketchikan looks magical. I straighten my jacket and resolve—silently, fiercely—to enjoy our day here.

Before everything blows up again.

"It'll just be a few minutes," a crew member says as we wait for nearly twenty minutes. We're the only guests waiting. No other honeymooners. No staff with cameras.

"Where is everybody?" I ask.

"This is just for you two," Clipboard says. "Very exclusive."

We step out onto the tender platform. The little orange boat bobs at the side of the ship, its engine chugging quietly. Snow swirls around us. The big hull of the Holiday Princess looms, white and gigantic, lit up with holiday lights that twinkle in the gray morning like stubborn cheer.

A single crew member bundled up in a puffy navy work jacket, hood up, beanie pulled low, head tilted down, is ready at the boat's controls. I can't see his face from here, but the way his gloved hands grip the wheel, I'd guess he'll be happy to have a hot cup of coffee after dropping us at the dock.

Guest Services help us on to the tender. The plastic seats are cold through my leggings. The little boat rocks as we settle. The crew member unhooks the tether, steps lightly in, and shuts the door with a thump. The sound feels final.

My heartbeat picks up. There's an unease settling in my chest, despite the quiet morning. I squint at the dock, not too far away, then at the crew member, who ignores us, gunning the engine to get us to the pier.

Ketchikan grows closer as the tender pulls away. I watch the docks coming in—the carved poles near the waterfront, ravens perched on light posts, snow clinging to cedar branches behind the houses.

Darius is unusually quiet, too, and he scans the area with his hand tense around the mug. "Look on the bright side," he says, bumping my knee with his. "If we get murdered, at least we die in Alaska."

"That is the *opposite* of bright," I say. "Where's your holiday adventurous spirit? We are going to find sasquatch and get a free breakfast."

He shrugs. "I'm a realist. There's something off about this, *right*?"

I stare at the approaching dock, at the snow, at the string lights. Somewhere in my pocket, my phone buzzes. I don't look because I don't want to re-read Alexis's text from late last night. It simply stated, "Sleep well. I'll see you soon."

The tender bumps softly against the dock.

The crew member kills the engine. The sudden quiet makes the world feel too loud—gulls crying overhead, the slap of water against pilings, the far-off hum of the dock lights is the only other sound. Everyone else is asleep, and I wonder if there's even a restaurant open at this hour. Snowflakes cling to the boat's orange hull and melt in the faint warmth of the exhaust.

He ties us off with quick, efficient loops.

"Okay," he says, with an odd accent. *"Off you go!"*

A chill pricks at the back of my neck and goosebumps crawl up my arms with a sense of foreboding.

He turns and reaches for the latch. As he does, the edge of his hood slips back just enough for the light to catch his jawline.

Sharp. Clean. Unfairly handsome.

My insides clench with sudden dread.

He opens the side door and steps onto the dock to help us out. Up close, I see the curve of her lip, the glint of gold on her shoulder where the jacket gap reveals a flash of rank.

"Careful," he murmurs, offering a gloved hand.

Darius takes it and hops down. "Thanks, man."

The crew member's mouth twitches.

I step to the edge, heart pounding. As she offers her hand to me, our eyes meet under the shadow of the beanie.

Dark. A storm is burning in them. *A familiar storm.*

"Buongiorno, Holiday Princess," Captain Rossi says.

Every hair on my body stands up.

I stumble on the final step and almost go down. Her hand tightens on mine, hauling me upright with zero effort or care.

"Easy," she says, voice too smooth. "We would not want you to fall."

Darius whips around. "Oh my God," he whispers. "What weird honeymoon twilight zone is this?"

Captain Rossi releases my hand and reaches up, pulling the beanie off in one fluid motion. Her dark hair spills out from the hood. She looks rougher. Less polished. More dangerous.

"Surprise," she says, spreading her hands. "It's me driving. I drive ships, tenders, and people crazy." She smiles thinly. "Today, I drive a point home."

Behind her, the tender door remains open. The Holiday Princess looms far away. It's then that I notice the suitcases behind her. *Our suitcases!*

"Where's the rest of the crew?" I ask, throat tight. "The shuttle to take us to breakfast? The camera guys… Anyone?"

She shrugs one shoulder. "They will not be coming. I will be sailing the Holiday Princess and back to Juneau for the last port before the trip back. It looks like there's a docking problem here that requires a last-minute itinerary change."

Darius snorts. "Funny." He fails to take note of our luggage that somehow appeared in the tender. It must have been placed in the small boat when we were waiting to board.

My heart races with a certainty that Captain Rossi is planning something sinister.

Her eyes flick to him, cold. "This is between me and Aurora," she says.

"Incorrect," he says. "Everything that involves her involves me. We're a two-for-one package."

I take a shaky breath, snow landing on my lashes. "All right," I say. "You want to talk. Let's talk without cameras or an audience. Say what you need to say." I lift my chin in defiance. I'm no longer the quiet people pleaser she met at the start of the cruise.

Rossi studies me for a long moment. The wind picks up, tugging at her hood, making her hair become unfastened to whip behind her.

"Your speech last night," she says finally. "It was a mistake. You are a liar and I am not letting you take down my career and reputation."

I blink. "That's… I'm… I just wanted to tell my truth."

Her mouth twists. "You spoke of lies. Of coercion by *me.*"

"She didn't lie," Darius says, stepping between us. "You were wrong, and you should be apologizing to her, *not be asking her for an apology.*"

"You humiliated me," she says, very softly.

There it is.

A knot tightens in my chest. "I told the truth about my experience," I say.

"Online. In front of my guests," she snaps. "In front of my staff. In a room where I could not respond. You framed me as a villain, as a predator, to an entire cruise."

Snowflakes cling to her dark lashes. Her cheeks are flushed—anger or cold, I can't tell.

The heat rising under my jacket makes me start sweating. I hiss, "You made your own choices. The kiss. The threats. The job offer with strings. I didn't invent those."

Her jaw clenches. "You forgot to mention that you kissed me back. You liked it. You wanted it."

"I did kiss you," I say quietly.

Darius mutters, "A kiss isn't a contract, and you are the Captain. Don't you have some ethical code to not take advantage of your passengers."

"Not helpful," I murmur to him, as her jaw clenches.

He mimes zipping his mouth shut but doesn't move away.

Rossi steps closer. The dock is narrow. The water laps dark and cold a few feet away.

"You made me look harsh and you risk me losing my job. I hope your happy with yourself."

"She is!" Darius says.

A part of me wants to apologize. Another part remembers, I am brave.

Her eyes flash. "You are responsible for this," she says. "You could have come to me first. Give me the chance to address this privately. Instead, you chose the public stage."

"I tried. Privately has not gone great with you," I say.

"Privately is where the manipulation happens. The power imbalance. The deals. Publicly was the only place I could." I shout.

Snow falls harder, dusting our shoulders, the dock, the tender's orange hull. The sky darkens as grey clouds roll in, rather than brightening with the morning.

Silence. The gulls cry overhead, circling.

I will not apologize to her. I will not beg her to take us back to the boat. I will not break.

"Why do it?" she demands. "Why not stay quiet until the end of the cruise? Why not enjoy having the attention you were getting?"

"Because I was done with lies," I say. "I didn't want the attention or your attention."

My voice cracks. I push on.

"I have spent my entire life being someone else's problem–the outcast," I say. "My mom's burden, a workplace disaster that needed a mentor, a 'weirdo lezzy' in school. Even dating... I didn't fit. I am just the weird, tall girl that has to be extra charming, a people pleaser, to fit in."

Darius takes my hand, and even Rossi slows her roll to consider my words.

I continue on, the truth easily spilling as if I could no longer hide myself for anyone. "I'm not your Holiday Princess, a person for you to toy with, and maybe keep, if I behaved. That speech was the first time I got to be the one holding the mic. I wasn't going to give that up because someone... *You* were uncomfortable."

Her face goes pale. Her voice drops. "I am not like those other people in your past."

"Aren't you?" I ask, gentle and deadly. "The first time I told you no, you tried to trap me with paperwork. Last night, when I told the truth in a way you couldn't control, your first thought wasn't 'Good on her for being honest.' It was, 'How dare she do this to me."

She takes a step closer, rage and hurt warring in her eyes. "I am very important. You do not understand what I risked for you," she hisses. "I deleted the footage. I watched you and would make you happy. I would have made you very happy. I offered you a job, a place with me on this ship, and a place where you could be yourself."

"I wasn't myself. This wasn't for me," I say. "Those things were for you."

Her breath fogs between us, quick. Mine matches, a small blizzard of emotion.

Her gaze hardens as ominously as the changing weather. "You want to be an adult, Aurora? Fine," she says, voice icy. "Here are the adult, honest consequences. Unless you take back everything you said about me, I'm leaving you here. The ship is leaving you here."

My breath catches, and even Darius is silent, finally understanding the depth of her anger towards me.

I feel his strength beside me and remember the cheers of all the passengers who have become my friends and family over the last few days.

"No," I say.

The word is small, but the tone is final and confident.

Rossi's eyes narrow. "Think carefully," she says. Her nostrils flare. "You are being childish," she says. "You are throwing away a golden opportunity."

She pauses, the silent tension hangs in the snow between us.

We stare at each other, two stubborn silhouettes on a white-dusted dock, Ketchikan still sleepy behind us, the tender swaying as our silent witness.

Something inside Rossi shifts. I see it happen—her expression smoothing, warmth draining, posture going even more rigid.

"Very well," she says stiffly. "If that is your choice. Here are your bags. Enjoy Ketchikan." She steps back into the boat and easily tosses out the heavy luggage onto the dock.

Darius rushes to grab it as she yanks the boat's rope in one swift motion as she steps on, untying the quick knot. Pushing away to leaves us before I can react.

"Wait!" Darius tries to get our bags, which are haphazardly on the edge of the dock, with one balancing against the tender that's departing.

My heart slams against my ribs. "Wait." Cold floods me. "You can't leave us!"

She pauses, hand on the boat's door. "You have made it clear you no longer feel safe under my command," she says. "I am respecting your wishes. You will not have to step foot on my ship again."

"That is not what she meant, and you know it," Darius explodes. "You can't just dump us on a dock with our luggage because you're mad she didn't choose you."

Her jaw tightens. "It's routine that disruptive passengers disembark early for their own comfort and the comfort of others," she says. "Guest Services has already processed your check-out."

The words sting.

Her eyes flash, then go flat. "Goodbye, Aurora," she says.

My heart thrashes. "Don't," I say. "Please. Don't do this."

She hesitates. For a fraction of a second, something flickers in her gaze—regret. Then it's gone.

The tender's engine growls to life.

"Captain!" I shout. "Rossi!"

Her hand tightens on the wheel. She stares straight ahead, down the stretch of choppy water that leads back to the Holiday Princess. Back to her ship. Away from us.

Darius grips my arm. "Aurora—"

The tender begins pulling away from the dock. The engine hums, then roars. Snow swirls in the large wake.

I lunge forward to stop her, but the boat is already accelerating.

Five feet. Ten. Twenty.

I can see her profile. Her face is a rigid mask, jaw clenched, and eyes locked onto the boat. She doesn't look back.

At the end of the dock, our haphazard luggage pile wobbles. My bag falls.

I watch it tumble off the dock, hit the choppy grey water, and bobbing on the surface too far to reach.

My passport.

My keys.

Credit cards.

Clothes.

Makeup.

My life.

"Holy *shit*," Darius whispers. "She's actually doing it. She's leaving us."

My knees give out. I drop onto the wet dock hard enough that the breath punches out of me.

"I did this," I whisper. "I should've just apologized—I should've— I'm so, so, *so* sorry—"

"Hey."

Darius kneels down in front of me, grabs my face gently but firmly between his hands. His fingers are freezing, but his voice is not.

"No. She did this. You did good. This is not on you."

"I could've stayed quiet," I manage, tears sliding hot against the freezing air. "I could've avoided all of this—"

He shakes his head, eyes fierce. "Aurora. Stop. This is her behavior, not yours."

Behind him, the tender reaches the Holiday Princess. Only a breath later, the ship's engines growl deeper. The enormous vessel begins moving—slow at first, then steady—turning away from the bay, away from us. Churning water froths white behind her.

I stare, numb, as the ship grows smaller. All those twinkling holiday lights shrink into faint dots against a wall of stormy grey.

Snow thickens, settling on my hair, on Darius's glittery lapels, on the empty space where my bag should be.

He leans his forehead against mine. "Hey. Look at me, Aurora."

I do, barely.

"We're going to be fine. We're Alaskan. Getting abandoned on a frozen dock is basically a rite of passage."

A tiny hysterical sound escapes me—half laugh, half sob.

"You're right," I say brokenly. "I'm sorry I'm a chaos magnet."

"Babe," he says with a soft snort, "I love that you're a chaos magnet." He finger-guns me. The absurdity almost helps as I snort.

But then my chest collapses again. "My dad is going to kill me. I got stranded because of the scene I caused—"

"He literally texted you last night saying he's proud of you. Didn't you just secure a business win for him? If anything, he's going to kill Rossi." Darius squeezes my shoulders. "We're okay. Worst case, we call your dad, grab the next flight home, and spend the layover hunting Sasquatch."

Another laugh slips out as I shake my head—wet, miserable.

I glance back at the sea.

The Holiday Princess is a distant shape now, slipping into the channel. Her lights shimmer faintly through the morning darkness and falling snow.

And then I see it—my bag, the last piece of it—bobbing once at the edge of the dock, sinking into the grey-black water.

A soft, strangled sound rises in my throat as my life sinks.

Stranded on a snowy Ketchikan dock, with nothing but my best friend, my phone, a jacket, and the ruins of our vacation trailing behind me like smoke.

I watch everything slip beneath the surface.

Curious who finds Aurora's passport?
The answer unfolds alongside Serena and Bree's forced-proximity romance in *Wilderness Rescue: Tides of Love.*

CHECK IT OUT HERE or HarmonyNoble.com

Chapter 25

Aurora's Last Christmas Surprise

Day 7: Ketchikan, Alaska

A raven watches from a piling nearby, head tilted like it's judging my life choices and finding them lacking.

"Same, buddy," I gasp.

"I can't believe she actually did it," I whisper. "She's really gone." Snowflakes settle in my hair, melting as fast as my dignity.

Darius huffs beside me, hands on his knees. "Yeah, girl," he says. "She is a liability lawsuit waiting to happen for Royal Caribbean. She is definitely losing her job. I mean you were the face of this new cruise and she kicked you off the boat without warning."

I swallow, feeling guilty.

Darius senses my overactive empathy. "She did this to herself."

The Holiday Princess's lights have long disappeared, but I hope somewhere there is a crew-wide mutiny, if they've even noticed the change of plans and that we are missing. Maggie Jo will be leading the revolt, Baron calmly drafting emails, Chase swearing at corporate, all the while giving them widely inaccurate facts about the ways we might die if we are stranded in Ketchikan.

I wrap my arms around myself, jacket crinkling, the aurora charm inside pressing warm against my sternum. The yearning for Alexis cracks through my chest, sharp and real, as if opening my emotional gate let even my secret desires escape.

"Well," Darius says dryly, opening his phone to see no bars, no coverage out here on the deserted dock, "unless you suddenly develop the ability to teleport to a cafe, we better start walking."

I laugh, watery. "I lost my purse. *Everything.* I hope you don't mind buying."

"I got you, girl."

The dock shudders faintly as a low, distant thumping starts up. At first, I think it's my pulse in my ears, but the rhythm is too steady, too mechanical.

WHUMP. WHUMP. WHUMP.

The air vibrates.

Darius's eyes go huge. "Wait—was that thunder? Here?"

I stare up at the gray, heavy sky.

"In Alaska? At dawn? Why not. It would be my luck if we get struck by lightening. Add it to the list of disasters."

But then the sound intensifies. The air pressure changes. Wind picks up in chaotic gusts, whipping my hair into my face.

"Not thunder," I say. "That's—"

WHUMPWHUMPWHUMP.

A helicopter appears over the town, emerging from behind the snowy hill. The aggressive metal invader dips lower, skimming over the waterfront, rotors churning the falling snow into a frenzy.

"Oh my God," Darius croaks. "Is this a Christmas miracle?"

"Pretty sure it is not for us. I bet they are dropping a VIP to their yacht," I shout back as the helicopter swings toward the harbor.

Snow blasts into our faces in stinging, horizontal sheets as it descends toward an open patch of dock a few yards away. My hair slaps me. My jacket flaps. My brain short-circuits.

"CROUCH!" Darius yells, yanking me down behind a stack of huge rope coils.

We huddle there, laughing hysterically and screaming at the same time as the rotor wash pounds us. We only thought it was cold before the sudden onslaught of mist, ice, and rotor wind hit us. The world is all noise and wind and white chaos.

Somewhere under the panic, something weird flares up in my chest.

"Is this the Coast Guard?" I shout over the roar.

"Maybe it's Grant," Darius yells back. "Chase noticed us gone and called him."

"Grant would not send a helicopter," I say.

"Grant might," he says. "He is very supportive. Plus we can't drive home from here. Helicopter or plane is our only option."

Maybe he did listen to the Ketchikan briefing—there are no roads or trains out of here.

We risk peeking over the ropes blocking the worst of the frozen wind to watch the helicopter settle onto the open dock. The skids touching down with a snowy crunch. The rotors keep spinning, slower now, still sending snow swirling around creating a small blizzard.

Darius grabs my arm so hard he might bruise me. "Holy shit," he whispers.

My eyes are too dry to see anything.

My heart stops. Then slams back into motion.

The helicopter door slides open.

A figure steps out.

Tall. Dark leather bomber coat. Red boots that I recognize. Hair pulled back, shining dark under a fur hat. Aviator sunglasses, despite the lack of actual sun.

We watch, our mouths open as Alexis climbs down onto the dock like she owns the whole harbor.

Which, knowing her, she might.

For a second, I just stare.

The wind whips her coat, sending it flaring around her like a cape. Snowflakes swirl around her hair, her lashes. She pushes the aviators up onto her head. She scans the dock, eyes sharp, assessing, looking for her target.

Then her gaze lands on me.

Time does that weird stretchy thing it always does with her. Everything slows. The helicopter noise fades to a dull thud in my ears. The snow hangs suspended between us.

Her face, which is usually composed enough to be carved, cracks open. Relief floods it. And something else—fear, maybe. Or the residue of it.

"Aurora," she breathes.

My knees go mushy.

Darius is whispering something that the wind steals away.

Alexis starts walking toward us, boots sure on the slick dock, coat flapping. The pilot turns off the motor and stays by the helicopter, clearly giving us space and quiet.

"Aurora," Alexis says again, stopping a few feet away. "I saw the ship leaving and thought I might have missed you."

Her voice is deeper than I remember, maybe because it's vibrating through my soul.

"You... came," I say, brilliantly.

She huffs out a laugh that sounds half wild. "You seemed like you might need a rescue after that speech. I didn't know you'd get stranded, though," she says.

I blink. "You know me. *Trouble*, right? I could get lost and need a rescue in an elevator."

"Or a bathroom," she teases with her eyes dancing at the joke.

Darius pops up at my elbow, my fashionable friend at the ready. "Hi," he says, sticking out a gloved hand. "Thanks for the rescue. We also need a latte."

Only Darius can turn a rescue into a coffee order.

One corner of her mouth lifts, but her eyes never leave my face.

His phone buzzes, and I see Chase calling him.

He leans in, murmurs in my ear, "Excuse me for just a sec, Wifey-Poo." Then he retreats, putting his phone to his ear.

Now it's just me, Alexis, the helicopter, the snow, and the heavy weight of unsaid things hovering in the cold air.

I stuff my cold hands in my pockets to stop them from shaking. The aurora charm presses into my palm.

"You flew here," I say, because my brain is stuck on logistics. "In a helicopter."

"Yes," she says, simply.

"What about your girlfriend?"

"Girlfriend? I'm hoping to find one of those here. Have you seen any good options?" She jokes, stepping closer, as her eyes shine fiercely.

I gape, swallow, and gain some confidence to confront her.

"When I tried to talk to you last night, *your girlfriend* answered your phone."

Her gaze softens, and her lips quirk in an unfamiliar way that looks good on her serious CEO face.

"That was my new Executive Assistant and cousin, Trixie," Alexis says, and the quirk on her lip turns into a full, heartbreakingly handsome smirk.

Trixie? I blink. "Your... cousin?"

"She answered while I was packing and getting ready for this dramatic entrance to impress you," Alexis explains.

The snow keeps drifting down around us, soft and glittery, like we are in a shaken-up snow globe someone forgot to put back on the shelf.

"I'm impressed," I say. "So, she's *not* your girlfriend." My voice comes out small, compressed by the weight of the last few minutes.

Alexis steps closer, boots crunching in the snow. We're only a foot apart now, *maybe less.* I can see the tiny snowflakes dancing around her eyelashes.

"No," she says, very clearly. "She is my cousin. I don't date cousins. Even if I am from Alaska."

I snort, half laugh, half sob.

How did Alexis become the funny one and me the serious one?

The laugh cracks something open in my chest. All the hurt from last night, the humiliation on the ship, the way my heart fell through the floor when I heard a voice answer her phone—it all rushed out of the emotional gate that wasn't closed.

"Aurora," she says, quietly, "I have been thinking about you nonstop since you left."

My lungs forget how air works. "Oh."

My chest's compressed spring is released, sending a dizzying rush of relief straight to my head. I sway slightly.

"I thought," I whisper, the words thick, "I thought I'd made an utter fool of myself for nothing. I gave an entire dramatic speech, Alexis. I was kicked off the boat and lost my luggage. I thought I ruined everything."

Her eyes, those fierce, dark eyes, are suddenly startlingly gentle and soft. She lifts a gloved hand—black leather, naturally—and gently brushes a snowflake off my cheekbone. The contact is electric, short-circuiting every remaining logical thought in my brain.

She pulls off a leather glove, fingers pale in the cold, the edge of her familiar tattoo snaking up her arm. Reaching very carefully for my hand still buried in my pocket, she takes it in hers.

"Are you okay?" she asks.

The question alone makes my throat close.

I nod too fast.

"Yeah. Yes. Totally, fine. *I mean*, I can't feel my fingers. If they fall off, at least they died touching something they loved. That's what people say... about fingers..."

The corner of her mouth lifts more. She curls her bare fingers around mine, warm and firm and very, very real. Her touch bumps the aurora charm, pressing it between our hands.

"What's this?" she asks quietly.

"Your charm from the pocket," I say. "Oh, I guess I should thank you for the jacket and boots. Thanks."

I'm nervous rambling, but at least my hand is hot, and I won't be losing any fingers.

Her eyes don't leave mine. "I like taking care of you, *Trouble*."

Snowflakes catch in her hair. The helicopter sits behind her like some ridiculous fairy-tale carriage with propellers. The ship is gone, taking my fake marriage, my lies, and Captain Rossi with it.

"I came," she says, "to tell you that I heard every word you said. I see you. I was wrong to push away by using my career as an excuse. And if you're still interested in me, I would very much like the chance to figure out how to be a girlfriend. Preferably somewhere warm," she adds. "I'll leave the plan up to you."

I shake my head. It is a lot to take in. "Don't you have to rush back to work? I'm sure you have meetings and conferences you can't miss."

"I stepped back from my CEO role to focus on more important things."

My breath catches, and my chest swells. "I don't have anything. I mean clothes, money... even my passport..." I wave my arm to the ocean.

"It's all gone." I sob.

"You don't need anything. I'll get you whatever you want."

"What do you want? Where do you want to go?"

"Palm Springs." It comes out of nowhere. I've never been there, and it is the most glamorous and warmest place I can imagine.

Behind us, Darius lets out a muffled shriek into his phone. "WHAT? She's FIRED? Put me on speaker—no, never mind, tell me later, I'm...yes, I'll be there. Right now, there's a helicopter and a romantic kiss about to happen—"

My head snaps around. "Fired who?"

Darius hangs up. "Captain Rossi is fired. She leaked the elevator/balcony photos and completely broke her employment contract, 'demonstrating an abuse of power' according to the corporate email everyone received."

"Wow. That was fast."

Alexis nods and adds, "I'm sure legally she gave them no choice but to terminate her."

Darius says, "*Karma!* And Chase said I can join him in Juneau for a free cruise. They are sailing down the coast to California after dropping off the passengers and picking up their new captain in Anchorage."

"I think I can help you get to Juneau," Alexis says. She turns to me, "Now about that romantic kiss?"

The warmth that floods me has nothing to do with how good she looks in a leather jacket, the helicopter rescue, or the fact that I compare every kiss to hers.

"Juneau then Palm Springs?" I say, filling the silence.

Her eyes shine now, not just from the wind. "Of course. But what I want," she says slowly, "is to kiss you. And then put you on that helicopter before your friend faints from second-hand anticipation."

"Do it!" Darius hollers.

My heart slams against my ribs. The dock, the harbor, the whole cold world tilts.

"You can," I manage. "Kiss me, I mean. If you still want to, you know."

She steps that last tiny distance closer. Her free hand comes up to cup my cheek, thumb brushing away a half-frozen tear. Her glove smells like leather, and her familiar scent I have missed.

My heart moves to my throat, and I gasp at the sudden desire that doesn't care that I have not seen her in months. She says yes with her sparkling eyes.

The world narrows to the warmth of her mouth on mine. Her lips are firm but careful at first, testing, like she's waiting for me to pull back. I don't. I lean in, fingers fisting in the front of her coat, pulling her closer like I can anchor myself to her and not the swaying dock.

Heat rolls through me, all the pent-up anticipation and longing now unravels. This is... soft. Grounded. Swoony? Yes, but not dizzying. It feels like an answer to a question I was too scared to ask.

Heat blooms through me, chasing the cold out of my bones. The snow keeps falling, melting on our cheeks, our noses. Her lips are warm and soft, tasting faintly of coffee and winter air.

She smiles against my mouth, just a little, and the curve of it sends a soft shiver straight down my spine.

She pulls back slowly with our foreheads resting together, and breath mingling in little clouds. Her eyes hold a certainty and warmth that was missing before.

"I have been wanting to do that since you announced your truths into a microphone. Since you demanded to be seen," she murmurs.

I let out a watery laugh. "*Demanding.* Not very romantic," I say.

"It was an extremely romantic speech," she counters. "You were choosing yourself. That is brave... and sexy."

I snort. "You have issues."

"Probably," she says. "We'll unpack them in Palm Springs."

Behind us, there's a strangled squeal. We turn to the sound of Darius clapping and smiling.

"Don't mind me," he calls, voice cracking. "Just having a happy little stroke over here."

"Finally," he stage-whispers. "Ketchikan was getting super boring."

We break apart, but only barely, foreheads touching. Our breath mingles in little clouds between us.

"So," I say, voice shaky and stupidly happy. "Does this mean we are dating, again?"

"Exclusively," she says.

"Palm Springs as our first date," I say, the words tasting like sunshine and possibility.

"Palm Springs for Christmas," she echoes. "And anywhere else you want to see."

"Okay," I say, grinning so hard my face hurts.

Behind us, the pilot clears his throat politely.

"How about we load your bags," Alexis pulls back, but her hand stays wrapped around mine.

"They are all Darius's bags," I explained at the pile of embellished, purple-flowered luggage cases.

Darius opens a bag and pulls out something black. "Not to worry, you still have your sequin Christmas dress."

"It's another Christmas miracle!" I giggle.

"Come on," Alexis says. "Let's get that latte and help Darius find his holiday romance."

I smile and follow her.

"We can call your dad on the way. I'd like to personally reassure him that his daughter is safe."

The heat in her hand is nice. I squeeze Alexis's hand back, feeling the aurora charm pressed between our palms, a small warm promise.

Above us, the sky dawn is trying to break over the horizon, clearing in a soft, low-hanging cloud cover. But for just a second, I swear I see a faint green shimmer of a morning aurora borealis above, an omen that everything is right in the world.

"Hey," I say as she boosts me up into the helicopter. "Thanks for the rescue."

She smiles up at me, eyes bright and fierce in the snow. "Trouble, I'm ready to rescue you for the rest of my life."

Darius clears his throat loudly behind me.

Alexis turns to the helicopter pilot. "Can you help him load these and make a flight plan to Juneau then to Palm Springs?"

She takes the final step, and we are close enough now that I can feel the radiating warmth from her coat, a welcome heat against the Alaskan chill.

The rotors start to spin, the world blurs, and with my best friend at my back and the girl I chose at my side, I finally, finally feel like I'm heading in the right direction.

A slow smile spreads across her face, dissolving the last traces of the CEO's composure. It's a genuine, dazzling, girlish smile.

"The truth is," she says, moving her hand from my cheek down to cup my jaw, her thumb resting on my bottom lip, "I flew here for a girl I couldn't stop thinking about... her smile and her terrible life choices, and her authenticity. But I needed her to rescue me more than she needed me to rescue her. Will you rescue me?"

She leans in.

My voice is gone, so I just nod and smile. Before I can shape another witty comeback—before I can even breathe—her lips are on my smile.

It isn't the soft, testing kiss from earlier. It's desperate and winter-warm all at once—a cold-air-and-holiday-spice kiss, firm and certain, charged with every ounce of tension and yearning that's been simmering between us since day one. Her gloved hand curves around my jaw, tilting my head so she can deepen the kiss, and suddenly the whole world—the snow, the dock, the ship, the helicopter—falls away into a single, blazing moment.

I fist my hands in her coat, pulling her closer, forgetting that my fingers are numb and that we are, in fact, standing in the middle of a literal emergency landing zone in Alaska. My heart pounds a frantic, joyful rhythm against my ribs.

When she finally draws back, just an inch, her breath ghosts across my lips—warm, sweet, intoxicating. Her eyes are dark and bright with happiness, and the look she gives me could melt the whole glacier behind us.

"Now," she whispers, a final, playful note of command in her voice. "Get in the helicopter, Trouble. I'm buying the lattes."

I grin, unable to stop the relieved, giddy laughter bubbling up.

"Yes, ma'am." I look over at Darius, who is smiling with tears in his eyes.

The helicopter hums behind us. Snow swirls around us. The raven hops a little closer on the piling, for a front row seat.

My heart is pounding. My brain, for once, is... quiet.

"I'm done being afraid of being myself," I hear myself say.

Alexis's eyes deepen. "Yes?" she whispers.

"I want to be loved for all of it," I say, voice trembling but steady. "Not in spite of it. I want to be honest and be me."

Her thumb brushes away a tear that's escaped. "You deserve that," she says. "You've always deserved that."

"Perfect!" Darius exclaims. We turn and see him snapping pictures. "These are fire. This one belongs in the family album."

Then Alexis's arm curves around me—sure and protective. She presses a soft kiss into my hair. "Family," she whispers, the word curling through the cold like a vow.

I look at her, and something inside me settles. "Yeah. *Family.* You're stuck with me."

Behind her, the helicopter lights paint the snow gold. The dawn light is filtering in, softening our surroundings. Time seems to tilt.

I used to think family meant cold nights and acting like everything was okay, that love came with rules I could never quite get right.

But this love—my love—is different.

It's the first chapter where I'm the hero.

It's the beginning where I truly belong.

Wilderness Rescue Series

Welcome to the breathtaking wilderness of Alaska, where love blooms as wild and beautiful as the northern lights.

Prepare for an exhilarating journey through diverse, LGBTQ+ inclusive romances set against the backdrop of charming small towns and untamed frontier.

Immerse yourself in a series that celebrates Alaskan culture and heartfelt relationships featuring trans, lesbian, bisexual, and two-spirit characters. From gripping rescues to soul-stirring connections, these standalone sapphic tales celebrate strong women navigating love and life with grit and determination in Alaska's rugged beauty.

Explore the standalone sapphic romance stories in the Wilderness Rescue Series.

CHECK IT OUT HERE or HarmonyNoble.com

"I loved learning more about Alaska... I also loved when they finally got their happy ending, it was super satisfying."—**Reviewer on Crashing Into Love**

She took the job in Alaska's wilderness to prove herself. Instead her journey to love is the adventure.

City nurse Riley Thompson has her future perfectly mapped out—until she's stranded in a remote village. The only bright spot? The village elder who saved her life and sees right through her polished outer image.

Mary's wisdom as a Yu'pik elder has guided her people through countless storms, but talking a drunk pilot into landing safety—and saving a beautiful city nurse in the process—might be her greatest test yet.

With Riley's career pulling her back to city life and Mary's deep commitment to her people's traditions anchoring her to the village, they face the ultimate question...

Can love bridge the gap between their worlds, or will tradition and personal ambition pull their hearts in opposite directions?

Join us at www.HarmonyNoble.com **to read this love story and more when you** Embrace True Love!

"Unthaw My Heart" is a thrilling standalone novella to warm your heart and prove love reigns even in deadly conditions."

—Reviewer on Unthaw My Heart

In the harshest of winters, can a Christmas Eve storm turn two broken hearts into something beautiful?

Caught in a Christmas Eve blizzard, Dr. Makayla (Mak) and Army mechanic Pauline (Paul) are trapped together in a remote Alaskan cabin—facing more than just the freezing cold. As the storm rages outside, the two women must fight for survival while grappling with the emotional storms brewing inside.

In the unforgiving wilderness of Alaska's Caribou Hills, survival isn't just about staying warm. It's about opening your heart, facing your fears, and finding the strength to trust someone new.

As they navigate icy car crashes, broken promises, and the harsh realities of coming out in a town that feels too small, Paul and Mak discover that second chances are real—and sometimes, love is the one thing that can unthaw even the coldest hearts.

Join us at www.HarmonyNoble.com **to read this love story and more when you** Embrace True Love!

"This is my first Female/female romance I believed and I thought it was very cute and entertaining. The plot line was fresh and unique and I loved the characters."—**Revi ewer on Winning Love**

Lights, camera, complication: Two coworkers team up to face off in Alaska's ultimate reality dating show, but when the game is love, who's really keeping score?

In the Last Frontier's hottest reality show, get ready to be swept away by a sizzling romance with coworkers.

Poppy and Baby are stranded in isolated Seldovia, Alaska, with no work, shelter, or money when their cruise jobs sink. They upon an absurd reality show: "The Smoking-Hot, Arctic Bachelor." They hatch a plan to win the hefty cash prize and the heart of the hunky Bachelor.

As Poppy and Baby navigate the reality show's challenges, their alliance blossoms into something more. When faced with the choice between love and the prize, they deviate from the script, turning the romantic game show into an unforgettable spectacle of true love.

Join us at www.HarmonyNoble.com **to read this love story and more when you** Embrace True Love!

"A Riveting Rollercoaster of Love and Life in Alaska!" —**Reviewer on Stormy Hearts**

I steer my ship into the vast sea to lose my past. Instead, I found her. Now I chart a course to search for her lost love... A course that ends in my heartbreak.

In the chilling Arctic waters, Maria's world shatters when her husband vanishes overboard, lost to the icy depths of Kachemak Bay. But in a twist of fate, fearless Alaskan boat captain, Jackie, swoops in to save her from the storm's clutches.

Despite Maria's grief and the town's judgment, their bond deepens, weaving a tale of love against the odds.

As they navigate through the stormy seas of prejudice and their own hidden pasts, they must choose—risk everything for love or let fear tear them apart?

Join us at www.HarmonyNoble.com **to read this love story and more when you** Embrace True Love!

"This novel is an absolute gem! The author skillfully weaves a romance that feels genuine and inclusive. Sterling and Chloe's love story is not just about love but also self-discovery and embracing life's unexpected twists... Wilderness Rescue: Scoring Love is a triumph in the sports genre!"—**Reviewer on Scoring Love**

Hockey was her game plan until love changed the rules.

In the heart of Fairbanks, where temperatures drop to -66°F, a hockey star's perfectly planned life is about to get checked by love.

When hockey hotshot Sterling saves local artist Chloe from falling through the ice into the freezing waters of Chena Lake, neither expects the heat that ignites between them.

Can Sterling trade in her player status to win Chloe's heart?

Can Chloe open up to love and reveal her age and that the hockey coach is her ex-husband?

Join us at www.HarmonyNoble.com **to read this love story and more when you** Embrace True Love!

"I enjoyed the story a lot. . . some angst, and plenty of comic fun. I enjoy the insights into Alaskan life."—**Reviewer on Flooded Hearts**

In Alaska's wildest kitchen, a chef discovers that the best recipes can't be found in any cookbook—especially when love is on the menu.

When uptight chef Lucy Zhang flees her toxic ex (think Gordon Ramsay with worse anger issues) to Cooper Landing, Alaska, she has one goal: turn her small-town restaurant into a Michelin-starred sensation.

Deb Walker—beloved local farmer, walking ray of sunshine, and keeper of indigenous traditions—believes any disaster can be fixed with Native wisdom and a community feast.

When a flash flood threatens their tiny town, these opposites are thrown together in a rescue that proves even the most carefully crafted plans can go sideways. Suddenly, Lucy—who doesn't do chaos, nature, or feelings—finds herself knee-deep in all three.

Between Deb's persistent optimism and a town full of locals who think "personal space" is just a suggestion, Lucy's perfectly organized life is getting messier by the minute.

"A captivating journey of love and self-discovery that will stay with you long after you've turned the last page."

Sometimes the steepest mountains lead to the sweetest collisions–a story of skiing, healing, and love.

Get ready to race down the ski slopes where two paths cross on a wild ride of love and self-discovery to navigate physical and emotional obstacles to find heartwarming love in this couple-swap, small town romance.

Caitlyn, affectionately known as Cat, must overcome her inner turmoil and grumpiness to reclaim her belief in herself and find love.

Peekaboo has an infectious zest for life and shines as a dedicated ski instructor, she inspires others with disabilities to embrace joy and adventure. Yet, behind her vibrant facade lies a heart yearning for something more...

On the pristine slopes of Alyeska, Cat and Peekaboo's paths converge, sparking an unlikely connection that defies the odds.
Torn between loyalty to her devoted partner and a longing for fiery passion, will Peekaboo choose love?

"If you love opposites-attract romances that make your heart race, this is your next favorite book." —**Reviewer on Tides of Love**

Some days change your life forever. This is one of them.

Serena lives for adventure, but when a once-in-a-lifetime storm sweeps her into a dangerous rip tide off the Alaskan coast, she ends up stranded on a rocky outcropping, face-to-face with a cute, but unimpressed local.

Bree, a self-proclaimed Alaskan loner, wants nothing to do with the thrill-seeking surfer. But when the rising tide traps them, they'll have to rely on each other to survive.

What starts as a fight for survival turns into something much more—one storm, one day, and an undeniable connection that neither of them saw coming.

The excitement of the rescue takes a backseat to the spark between them in this opposites-attract sapphic romance.

"...If you are a fan of insta-love, this novella will be right up your alley. It is a cozy, sweet romance, with an exciting backdrop of the Alaskan Iditarod." **—Reviewer on Iditarod Love**

Love, survival, and the untamed Alaskan wilderness collide in the race of a lifetime.

Brace yourself for a thrilling journey through snow-swept trails, where fierce competition meets an unexpected spark between a determined musher and an annoyingly cheery veterinary tech.

Brynn Dawson has ice in her veins and one goal—winning the Iditarod with her legendary dogsled team. She's conquered brutal winds, frozen rivers, and the Yukon Quest, but nothing prepares her for Morgan, an upbeat race volunteer with a knack for getting under her skin.

When disaster strikes during the start of the race on the crowded streets of Anchorage, their worlds collide in a daring rescue that ignites something neither of them saw coming.

Other Titles by MELODY BEST & HARMONY NOBLE
For the most up-to-date list visit Harmony's website at
www.HarmonyNoble.com

Aurora's Wilderness Love:

Hot Girl Summer Love
Just a Little Fall Crush
Christmas Cruise Mistake

Wilderness Rescue Sapphic Romance Series:

Crashing Into Love
Unthaw My Heart
Winning Love
Stormy Hearts
Scoring Love
Flooded Hearts
Healing Hearts
Tides of Love
Iditarod Love
Tangled Love

Coffeehouse Romance Series:

Love, Joy & Lattes (Joy's Story)
Test Driving a Millionaire (Tara's Story)
Shattering Crystal a Bully Romance (Crystal's Story)
Choosing Love, Namaste (Meaghan's Story)
The Wrong Bride for Christmas (Monica's Story)

Coffeehouse Romance Short Stories:

Joy's 4th of July Holidate
Tara's Valentine Holidate
Crystal's Easter Holidate
Meaghan's New Year Holidate
Monica's Halloween Holidate
My Accidental Christmas Fiancé
Joy's Coffeehouse Romance

Snag the latest swoon-worthy reads and stay tuned for upcoming stories at www.HarmonyNoble.com.

About Author –
Melody Best & Harmony Noble

Meet the unstoppable twins from the rugged wilds of Alaska, the writing duo, Harmony & Melody. Fueled by endless lattes, their character-driven stories brim with authenticity, humor, and heart—featuring Alaskan grit, journeys of self-discovery, and swoon-worthy happily-ever-afters.

When they're not crafting adventure romances, these twins can be found hiking trails with breathtaking views, enjoying charming coffee shops, or exploring new worldwide destinations together.

Join the e-newsletter for exclusive content and giveaways at website:
https://harmonynoble.com

Email: TrueLoveWriters@gmail.com
Instagram/Facebook/TikTok: @truelovewriters

www.ingramcontent.com/pod-product-compliance
Lightning Source LLC
LaVergne TN
LVHW010646110826
845149LV00014B/2967

* 9 7 8 1 9 6 3 0 7 4 5 1 2 *